LANDED

LANDED

Tim Pears

WINDSOR
PARAGON

First published 2010
by William Heinemann
This Large Print edition published 2010
by BBC Audiobooks Ltd
by arrangement with
The Random House Group Ltd

Hardcover ISBN: 978 1 408 48655 9
Softcover   ISBN: 978 1 408 48656 6

British Library Cataloguing in Publication Data available

Printed and bound in Great Britain by
CPI Antony Rowe, Chippenham and Eastbourne

For Gabriel and Zosia

Part One

Hold

COLLISION INVESTIGATOR'S REPORT

On Friday 18 June 1996 I attended the scene of this incident on Fielding Avenue, Selly Oak, Birmingham, as part of my overall analysis. During my attendance I took various measurements and a series of digital photographs using a Kodak DC40 camera.

1. THE CASE
1.1 The collision occurred at 8.03 p.m. on Saturday 4 April 1996, between a 1989 green Peugeot 205 Look, 4 cylinder, 1124 cc, petrol driven, manual 3-door hatchback car, driven by the Defendant, and a 1995 white Volvo FL7 Hook loader, multi-axle, rigid body, 32-ton skip lorry, driven by the Claimant.

1.2 The Claimant in this civil action is the Defendant in the criminal case concerning the same incident brought by the Crown Prosecution Service.

2. THE LOCATION
2.1 The location of the incident is a dual carriageway urban road. When travelling west on the immediate approach to the collision scene the westbound carriageway is straight and flat, and consists of two lanes initially separated from the opposing carriageway by broken white lines leading to a central reservation which forms part of a pelican crossing.

2.2 The road is subject to a 40 mph speed limit on the approaches and throughout the scene, as clearly indicated by speed restriction signs.

2.3 Street lighting is present at the collision scene and consists of intermittent pole-mounted overhead sodium lamps on both sides of the road.

2.4 The pelican crossing consists of three pole-mounted traffic signals for each direction of travel: one directly facing traffic on the near side of the road and two facing traffic from the central reservation.

2.5 Pole-mounted green and red man signals are also provided on each side of the crossing, indicating for pedestrian use. All the traffic lights work in a standard sequence.

2.6 At the crossing the road bears an overall width of 10.2 m. Each crossing point on both sides of the road consists of a dropped kerb and tactile pavers. Pedestrian-operated demand buttons are present on the four signal poles at each corner of the crossing.

2.7 The crossing is preceded by a 17.3 m zigzag zone leading up to a solid white 'Stop' line, a gap of 2.7 m, and then a line of studs delineating the crossing zone.

3. THE INCIDENT

3.1 It is agreed by those involved and by witnesses that the two vehicles involved in the collision were the only vehicles on the westbound carriageway in the immediate vicinity. Both were in the nearside lane, the car in front of the lorry.

3.2   At the time of the incident it was dark. The weather is described as fine and clear, although there is conflicting witness evidence regarding whether the road surface was wet or dry. According to the witness evidence, both front headlights of both the Peugeot 205 car and the Volvo lorry were displayed at the time of the incident.

3.3   The Claimant asserts that as the car, driven by the Defendant, approached the crossing, the traffic signals changed from red to green in its favour. He asserts that the car then began to accelerate towards the crossing, acting upon the reasonable assumption that the traffic signal would remain green until well after it had crossed. The Claimant also began to accelerate the lorry.

3.4   The Claimant asserts that as the car approached the pelican crossing it suddenly and without warning braked violently, and its wheels spun. The car slewed 90 degrees and came to an abrupt halt facing south across both lanes of the westbound carriageway in the middle of the pelican crossing.

3.5   The Claimant applied the brakes to his lorry but there was insufficient time or distance for the lorry to stop before colliding with the car. The front of the lorry collided with the passenger side of the car. The car was shunted for a distance of some twenty metres along the carriageway before both vehicles came to a stop.

3.6 This version of events is corroborated by the witness evidence of Mrs H, a cyclist who was positioned on the central reservation. She had crossed the eastbound dual carriageway of the crossing and was waiting to cross the westbound dual carriageway at the time of the incident.

3.7 This version of events is corroborated also by the witness evidence of Mr R, a pedestrian who had just crossed the westbound road at the pelican crossing from north to south. He had begun walking east along the pavement away from the crossing. His attention was drawn by the sound of the Peugeot's tyres squealing upon braking and he turned in time to see the collision. It was Mr R who telephoned for the Accident & Emergency services on his mobile telephone.

4. PHOTOS
Views westbound along Fielding Avenue towards the scene of the accident.

Image 1

Image 2

Image 3

Image 4

5. THE CLAIM

5.1 It is the Claimant's contention that in braking so hard without reason or warning the Defendant invited the collision and was wholly responsible for it. The Claimant has never denied accelerating as he approached the pelican crossing, a course of action wholly reasonable given the traffic signal had just changed from red to green.

5.2 The Defendant has said that he braked to avoid hitting a brown mongrel dog that was crossing the road at the pelican crossing from north to south. He says that he was unable to avoid impact, catching the dog with the nearside of his front bumper, which impact he believes was responsible for his vehicle spinning round.

Witness Mr R has said that he thinks he might have heard the sound of an impact before the car came to a halt, and before the lorry hit it, which could have been the sound of a dog being struck. Neither witness saw a dog. Nor did the Claimant.

5.3 Traces of brown canine hair and blood were found on the Peugeot front bumper. They have not been definitively dated to the time of the accident.

5.4 The fatality occurred to the passenger of the Peugeot. The driver of the Peugeot—the Defendant in this case—was taken by ambulance to hospital having suffered serious though not life-threatening injury.

5.5 The Claimant was hospitalised for one month after the accident. He has been unable to work since and although his appeal is pending he has no prospect of resuming driving work in the foreseeable future. He is seeking compensation for damage to health and loss of earnings.

6. ANALYSIS & OPINION

6.1 Accepting the location has remained unaltered, there is no other physical evidence at the location from which to determine the exact series of events as they unfolded.

6.2 Having analysed police records and attended the scene of the accident it is this investigator's assessment that at the moment of impact the Peugeot was indeed stationary and skewed across the carriageway, and the lorry was travelling at approximately thirty-eight miles per hour.

6.3 Regardless of the question of its admissibility as justification for the accident, the Defendant's claim that he braked to avoid a dog crossing the road is not, in this investigator's assessment, proven. No blood was found on the road or pavement. More pertinently, in particular regard to Mrs H, who was perfectly positioned to have seen such, no witness saw this dog.

6.4 In my opinion a collision between a car and a dog would not account for the car slewing upon such forceful braking. More likely reasons would be an involuntary touch on the steering wheel by the driver

9

or an error in the steering mechanism or wheel balance of the vehicle.

6.5 It is my belief that in all probability there was no dog, and that the canine hair and blood found on the Peugeot bumper resulted from an earlier incident.

THE HILL

They walked across the fields up high above the farm, Owen half-trotting to keep up with his grandfather. The old man would periodically stop in his tracks. Owen learned not to walk behind him, for he'd ram straight into his hard back, but to keep off his left shoulder and then his grandfather would put out his left arm to stay the boy, and they'd stand on the hill. Owen would glance up to gauge the direction in which his grandfather was looking, or perhaps listening, ear or eye cocked that way. He might nod for the boy, and Owen peer with his eleven-year-old eyes.

'Fox,' Grandpa would say. 'Buzzard.' Never more. Owen then had to find it for himself. 'Woodcock.' A shadow flitting amongst the trees; a russet blur in the grass, melting into cover.

They walked up towards Lan Fawr then cut right and down the bank behind the ruin. In the pocket of his jacket Owen could feel the animal, entrusted to him for the first time, bumping softly against his hip. Three days earlier he had borrowed needle and thread off his grandmother and sewn two buttons on the pocket, cut eyes in the flap and stitched their edges to stop the fabric tearing further open. The animal, he believed, was excited as he himself was. This morning he thought when he was fussing her that she knew what day of the week it was: Saturday. When Grandpa came in from work Grandma stood out of his way, watched him gobble his lunch. In the shed he found Owen had laid out equipment: lines, wires, nets, pegs.

11

Grandpa discarded snares and mesh, took up a shovel.

Now he stopped and thrust the shovel into the earth, as if to send tremors underground, fair warning, we're here to have you. Said nothing to the boy, it was clear enough. Grandpa clambered across the bank, taking a small purse net from his pocket, spreading it loose across a hole of the burrow. Satisfied he'd found them all when he'd covered five, he came to Owen, who lifted the ferret from his pocket and held it fast around the neck and chest while his grandfather attached its string muzzle. Then, this time, instead of taking the animal himself, Grandpa stood back.

One hole he'd left uncovered. Owen set the ferret there. She sniffed, then turned away lifting her nose, testing the air as if some distant scent, the rumour of some unheard of exotic prey might see her dash away. Her white albino fur trembled with bloodlust and nerves, she turned back to the hole, then after a moment's further ponder and a shiver of momentary distaste, she slithered into the black earth. Grandpa set a new net across the hole, stood back, then changed his mind, stepped forward, took a handful of loose soil from below the entry and rubbed it into the net, darkening the new string. As he did so the ferret reappeared at the mouth of the hole. While she hesitated, peering around with her bright blind red eyes, confused by the brevity of the game or by her own stupidity, Owen came up and took her and set her back to the hole, into which she once more disappeared.

The old man stood back from the bank; Owen beside him felt his grandfather's big rough hand on his chest, over his heart, as if not just to keep him from moving forward but to calm him too. Owen cast down his eyes. A labourer's hand, fingers flattened, skin thickened and knotted, hands half as large again as unworked ones. Yellowed nails. Calluses. The knuckles were bony misshapen arthritic protrusions. His grandfather's hands were no longer delicate flesh and blood like Owen's own, they were heavy tools on the end of his arms, they'd accrued inorganic matter like barnacles, or like the horns of a ram. The dark soil with which he'd just dirtied the string on the new net marked his fingers, but even when he'd wash his hands before a meal the lines still showed up, ingrained with oil and mud and creosote, with tar and paint and the shit of the five hundred ewes scattered across these hills.

When he judged the boy was still enough, steady, Grandpa let his hand fall to his own side. They waited. Owen stared at the bank, the focus of his attention shifting from one to another of the half-dozen purse nets, his ears pricked. He became aware of the tiniest movement of grains of soil subsiding, of a blade of grass, flattened by his grandfather's footstep, springing back to an upright position. He became aware of how blue the sky above them was. A crow flew overhead and he could have sworn it was not black but purple. Closer by, a bevy of starlings veered across the sky, metallic plumage flashing in the sun. He heard a liquid sibilant *seep, seep,* and though he looked and saw nothing he recognised a yellowhammer by its flight-note song. He turned to tell his grandfather, but was baulked from doing so: the old man— some way yet from sixty, in truth, but ancient to the

13

boy—stood just as he had many minutes before, focused as a dog on point.

Owen was certain his grandfather had neither seen nor heard any of the things to which his own attention had strayed. Ashamed, he once again stared at the nets strewn across the bank. Presently his grandfather stirred, stepping quietly, daintily almost, despite his bulk, and reaching the bank he lay with his ear to one of the holes. Owen copied him, tiptoeing forward, bending down and listening at another. He could hear nothing. Perhaps this rabbit warren connected to fissures in the rock, to hidden potholes, deep subterranean tunnels along which the ferret was slithering like an eel in pitch darkness, down, down, after the scent of whatever creatures inhabited the centre of the earth. No. It was his mind, not the animal, that was wandering beneath the ground.

The old man stood up, stepped back. Owen assumed his position beside him. Grandpa had not said a word since before they left the house. Owen wondered what he was thinking as he stood there, patient, alert. The boy understood that his grandfather thought about nothing, that his mind was placid like water, still as the pool in the plantation up by The Bog, dark and oddly ominous, but Owen wondered how he could sustain or even stand it. Had he trained himself, or was this trance a natural state? Did his grandfather not experience tedium? Did his mind not wish to stray, to fill itself with thoughts of other things? Speculation such as this?

Owen was jolted by sounds. Bumps. Coming from the bank, dull thuds, as if furniture were being clumsily shifted inside the burrows, and then

14

a rush and flurry and one of the nets came alive, bursting away from the bank. It rolled over and over, showing brown and white fur inside as it slowed. But even before the rabbit broke Owen had seen his grandfather move towards that particular hole. Owen remembered that between his own splayed hands he held a fresh net at the ready, and he advanced to cover the hole while his grandfather fell upon the full net: he broke the doe's neck with a chop of the side of his hand.

Now the rabbits came tumbling out of their burrows and the man and boy had to move fast, killing or replacing a net as it fell to either of them to do so. Owen at eleven was not yet sufficiently strong or more likely decisive enough to use his grandfather's method: he had to hold a rabbit's hindquarters and neck and break its spine like a stick over his bent knee. The noise was all human: their footsteps, and rustling clothes, and gasping breath. When he found a big old buck in a net close by he called, 'Grandpa!' and the old man was over in three strides and took care of it himself.

And then they found themselves standing by, breathing hard in a silence and stillness that had returned more acute than before. Eleven carcasses lay strewn around their feet: the dogs' meat for a week. Owen gathered them up, tied them by their hind legs in two clutches. His grandfather checked the nets for the ferret's emergence then sat on a tussock away from the bank and rolled a thick cigarette.

'Rarely hear a rabbit squeal,' he said. He lit the cigarette. 'Hare will always squeal when it's caught, see. Horrible sound.' Owen caught whiffs of the smoke, which wafted in lazy drifts in the still

15

afternoon. 'Anyhow, be needing a lurcher you want to catch hares, and I've enough to think of with the collies.' He frowned. 'Not that I've seen a hare hereabouts in a year or two.'

The old man was never as loquacious as after a kill, something about it freed his penned-in personality.

'Need a gun, too, like,' he said, spitting a strand of loose tobacco onto the grass. A freedom about him, a disdain. There was a gun in a cupboard in the cottage, a twelve-bore shotgun that was never used but which Owen gazed at and sometimes touched when his grandparents were busy, drawn to an occult power he sensed it had. He didn't know why his grandfather despised guns. It might have been their intrusion upon the silence he preferred.

'Once had a ferret running the burrows,' he said. 'Out flies this creature. Rabbit? No. Brown owl. Must have laid its eggs in there. Nicely tangled up in the net. Let it go and up it went.' Tilting his flat palm, he raised his arm. 'Whoosh.' He stubbed out the cigarette. 'Come on, boy. Better us do something.'

'Is it blocked?' Owen asked.

'Maybe. Might have cornered one down a blind alley, see, and can't bear to leave it. If she's slipped her muzzle and killed one, she'll suck its blood dry, gorge herself. Settle down for a good long sleep.' He shook his head. 'Not minded to dig her out.'

They gathered stones, blocked the entrances to the warren. 'You can get her tomorrow. She'll come out when she's hungry.' As Owen began to brick up the last hole, his grandfather said, 'Wait. Got that wailing damn thing on you?'

16

Owen had been given a Jew's harp by his favourite teacher when he left primary school at the end of that summer term. He took care to play it out of earshot of his grandfather, who claimed to despise all forms of music, but sound carried on the wind. Owen found it now in one of his pockets, beside a penknife and some rubber bands, and produced it.

'Play it there,' his grandfather said. 'Nosy beggars, ferrets, like. Might bring her out.'

Owen lay kneeling on the bank, the harp between his teeth, and plucked the harp's tongue. He felt foolish, suspected that his grandfather was having a joke at his expense. As he played, however, he overcame his scepticism, began to believe in the ploy, that as the notes twanged down into the dark tunnels, reverberating through the burrows, even if his grandfather was laughing behind his back—perhaps ferrets were famously tone-deaf?—that actually this would work. Like a snake charmer, Owen would seduce this ferret to the surface. And thus, for the first time in unrecorded history, as he would tell his grandmother a short while later, on this day in the summer of nineteen seventy two on the side of a hill on the Anglo-Welsh border, a boy lured a ferret out of the earth with the music of his Jew's harp.

*   *   *

Before the beginning of these summer holidays Owen had rarely been brought out here, though it was less than ten miles from Welshpool. His father and grandfather, it was understood, did not get on.

17

Some slight or argument had occurred that could not be overlooked by either side. Owen was never told exactly what this had been. It was, he imagined, so fundamental a moral breach that to find out more would provide him with a vital clue to the unblossoming mystery of human relations.

No detail was given, even to his direct questions. 'What happened?'

'Old sod's an obstinate bastard,' his father told him.

'What happened?' Owen asked his mother.

'Dislike each other, simple as that,' she said. 'Never could stand to be in the same room.' Not liking your own father had not offered itself, till that moment, as an option, though now Owen saw how it could. Not that he knew his father well enough to love or hate him, his father was invariably just off, just gone, on his way. If they'd had a tent, Owen thought, rather than a house, they could have moved as a little family with his father's moods.

It was his mother who telephoned, and rode with him on the bus. They climbed on, sat down, one of the other passengers came and collected their fare for the driver. His mother told him she needed time alone with his father. 'To bring him round. Better for us all in the long run. Believe me.'

His grandmother stood at the bus stop in the middle of the village in the valley. 'Get in the van,' his mother told him, while she spoke with her mother-in-law, before crossing the road to wait for a bus going back the other way. Owen opened the door on the passenger side of the filthy white van. His grandfather sat gazing out of the windscreen,

18

hemmed in, his rough hands resting on the steering wheel. He was too big for this vehicle. Without looking directly at Owen he nodded his head, indicating the area behind the two seats; with his left hand he tilted the passenger seat, it knelt forward to the dashboard. There were two collies in the back. Owen climbed slowly towards them, expecting them to snarl at this invasion of their territory. To his relief they ignored him. His grandfather kept the engine idling, impatient to return home, get back out in the open.

Shortly Owen's grandmother got into the van. They climbed slowly up out of the valley. The vehicle stank of dogs and sheep, tobacco smoke and human sweat, of petrol and empty canvas sacks and the feed they'd once contained.

*   *   *

His first days in the country Owen spent fearful. Of the isolation of this hilltop farm, the empty space around it, the silence. Of darkness at night. Of his taciturn grandfather, who mumbled unintelligible messages to his grandmother but said not a word to him. He was afraid of the animals: dogs, cats, the two young pigs that ran at him, ears flapping, squealing with pure aggression, probably, and the geese that pecked at his wellingtons, and the sheep that ran away, and the ferrets.

'Handle him often as you like,' his grandfather said, his first words to the boy, his third day on the hill. 'Nervy beggars. Need petting.' The male was fat and lazy, the good-natured son of the rabbit hunter and a polecat father. Its eyes were dark red stones, almost black. Inside its yellow and brown

19

fur the animal wriggled in perpetual motion, consisting not of flesh and bone but liquid pouring itself over Owen's hands. It made a hiccuping noise when it was happy, performed little jumps of excitement. An overpoweringly pungent musky odour that would leave Owen's skin and clothes reeking.

They were kept in a rabbit hutch, and fed on bread and milk. The female—the mother—was starved from Friday morning. She was far more aggressive than the male, especially when coming into season. It took Owen a fortnight to summon up the courage to pet her too. 'Keep your hands steady, like,' his grandfather said, reaching out, making to pass the animal to Owen. Its teeth were beautifully made for destruction, like miniature versions of a sabre-toothed tiger he'd seen in an encyclopedia. 'Twitch and you'll find her teeth in your fingers. Hanging off; won't want to let go.'

*　　　*　　　*

It wasn't his grandparents' farm. Mean as it was, they rented it from some estate. The latest of many, Owen learned, across a wide arc of the Marches, either side of the border, his grandfather falling out with a landlord, proudly moving on. He had five hundred sheep here, split into smaller flocks ranging across a few hundred acres of these uninhabited hills.

At first, when Owen woke up in the morning his grandfather would be gone from the house. The old man issued no invitation, but after a while Owen rose earlier and went with him, trotting in his wake up onto the tops. He feared he was

20

intruding upon a chosen solitude, or privacy, but he didn't know what else he was supposed to do. He waited for his grandfather to take notice of him. The two dogs sniffed the hard ground around them as they climbed, tracing the invisible criss-crossing tracks of nocturnal animals, like they were reading some haywire manuscript written in scent. They looked bewitched by the aromas, but a portion of their attention remained always on their master, who ignored them until they were needed.

Grandpa checked his flocks each day, counting their numbers in groups of twenty, for each score transferring a pebble from left to right pocket in case he lost count. In summer he wore a grey suit, must once have been his best; from a distance he looked smart, it was only up close you saw how worn and frayed it was. Swallows swooped low over the pastures, picking off flies that swarmed around the sheep. After an hour or two the pair would go back down for breakfast. As if Grandma had been standing outside, scanning the green hills with a telescope for the dark specks of their figures descending, she'd have a plate of egg and bacon and a thick wedge of buttered bread on the table as they reached it, mugs of well-brewed tea pouring from a brown-stained, once-white teapot.

After a cigarette, back to check the rest. It was the easiest time of the year. Grandpa had finished shearing shortly before Owen arrived—the spindly naked ewes were barely larger than their robust lambs—but the bucolic calm of a shepherd's life, which Owen had imagined for his grandfather from Bible stories, did not exist on these Welsh hills. There was no time for contemplation. His grandfather was always on the move. He issued

21

commands to the dogs, whistling through his fingers and with guttural yelps. He appraised each ewe as he counted them, Owen realised, and if one caught his eye the collies, following his grunts and array of shrill whistles, set to isolating it. The dogs worked as a team, each with her own role: one went out left around the flock, the other right; one would stop, the other come on, halving the size of the flock with a mad dash, then pausing while the other dog quartered it. Owen had no idea how they knew which particular ewe Grandpa wanted: he was a magician making them choose the right card from a pack.

His grandfather's growls were the monosyllables of a primitive language from which humans had evolved a million years ago the words with which to speak to each other. Owen wondered whether they'd been passed down from one generation to another of farmer and dog from primeval times, or whether his grandfather, and every other shepherd, invented his own. It wasn't so much the syllables of instruction themselves—one sounded like 'Hip, hip; hip, hip,' another like 'Goop, goop, goop'—it was the way in which they were expressed. They weren't formed in the mouth, shaped with the tongue and lips and issued on easy exhalations of breath, but hiccuped and burped out of his grandfather's throat, growled like he was a dog himself, repeated as if he had retched a word he couldn't quite get right out.

The dogs, Meg and Pip, cornered the ewe and Grandpa hooked her round the neck with his crook and yanked her to him. He inspected her just long enough for Owen to see the skin on her flanks red and raw. Back at the cottage Owen heard his grandfather speak words barely more intelligible than those he used for the dogs. 'Scab. On Rock Hill.'

'Fly-strike's caused by blowflies,' Grandma explained. 'Crawl into a ewe's wool and lay eggs. Their larvae hatch and burrow into the host, Owen—maggots eat a sheep alive. The mites that cause scab do the same, and make the sheep rub against tree or stone. Even bite its own skin raw.'

They were like a comic routine in this regard, his grandparents, like a sketch from *The Benny Hill Show* Owen liked to watch with his mother for the way she laughed, sometimes, without constraint: Grandpa uttered a few terse monosyllables and then Grandma translated for the boy, but her explanations were ridiculously long, as she took it upon herself to elaborate. It was funny but Owen bit his lip. Laughter, he sensed, was uncommon in this cottage.

'Dip,' Grandpa muttered, and his wife turned to the boy. 'Your grandfather reckons he'll have to dip the whole flock now. A big gather. Day after tomorrow. Mites can live without food for three or four weeks, see, Owen, on a piece of machinery, a gatepost. Pick it up on your jacket going by, pass it on to the sheep.'

Grandpa added nothing, uncomfortable with words, shy, almost, with his own kin, his wife, his grandson, but it wasn't that. Words came out of his mouth like solid hostile objects he wanted to be rid of. He didn't trust them. Then he would get up and go as if Owen wasn't there, and the boy would rise and follow, apostle of a silent shepherd.

*   *   *

23

Behind the cottage a disarray of sheds, rusted metal, manure and mud, but in front was Grandma's garden. A visitor, if one ever came, would walk from the wooden gate in the stone wall to the front door, through a colourful jumble of flowers. Marigolds and roses, poppies and hollyhocks. Butterflies and bees drifted from one blossom to another. In amongst the flowers Grandma had planted vegetables. Beetroots, cabbages, onions. While Owen helped her digging up or tidying, she enumerated the array of illness and disease to which sheep were susceptible.

'Pasteurella's caused by a bug that's always there in the flock, Owen. It gets dangerous when the sheep's immunity's low, when they're stressed by the freezing sleet drives in from the north at the end of winter.'

He learned that the ewes developed pneumonia, and Grandpa would find a carcass attacked by crows, belly bloated, blood-stained froth bubbling from the nose.

Many sheep limped—like wounded soldiers, Owen thought. It was foot rot. He listened with growing wonder: it seemed that a sheep farmer's life was a manky, maggotty battle against disease. Mange, Grandma said, sheep could catch from a fox. Ewes grew old, lost their teeth, suffered from mastitis, an inflammation of mammary glands in their udder.

*　　　*　　　*

There were times Owen went exploring on his own. At the foot of Roundton he found the cave.

With earth built up in front of it, the entrance was invisible unless you stumbled upon it. He crawled in. Where there was still light he could see the bones of animals taken in by their killers and eaten. Tiny skeletons, of birds, mice, rabbits. The skull and ribs of a sheep. How that came to be in there unsettled him. He crawled further, on all fours, into darkness, turning to see the light behind him. His hands touched stone. Twig. Bone. The air smelled gamey. The temperature grew cooler the further down he went. He began to sense that something lay ahead of him, some kind of wild archaic cat, still here somehow from long ago, undetected by human society. Waiting for him in the dark ahead. He forced himself on into the dank, rotten, inky chamber, his heart thumping so wildly that he became disorientated, it seemed that the tunnel was actually inside him, he was in a winding chamber of his own heart beating. He pressed on, determined, eleven years old, driven by obstinacy as much as courage, until he turned and—the tunnel having curved or perhaps descended—saw no light behind him. In panic Owen twisted around, scraping an elbow, a knee, and scrabbled back, sweating, desperate, back out into the light of a bright summer day.

*   *   *

Owen's mother came out to visit one day towards the end of August. 'This is for you, my darling,' she said. He unwrapped a tiny sword, a Moorish scimitar sheathed in a curved scabbard. A paperknife. 'Your father got it for you.' Even as she said it, Owen understood this to be a lie. His mother had bought it, and pretending she hadn't was the attempt at another gift. She stayed for lunch, telling them of the week's holiday in Spain from which she and the boy's father had just returned. Red Spanish wine, chips, outdoor discos, hungover on the beach and a glass-calm sea, siestas, a swim, then again the drinking. It was almost good again, she'd almost brought him round. She asked if Owen could stay a little longer. Grandpa pushed his plate away, went outside to smoke, but Grandma nodded. Owen followed his grandfather out, crouched nearby as the old man took another drag, spat tobacco off his lips.

'Couldn't be bothered to come himself,' he said, presently. Although, as Owen knew, he'd told his only son he was not welcome here. Owen stole a glance at his grandfather: the old man's grey eyes had darkened. 'A bad 'un,' he said.

His mother came outside. 'Give me a big hug goodbye, my lovely,' she said, drawing Owen tight to her. She smelled of the Polo mints she sucked after every cigarette. She said she would walk down to the valley, there was no need for a lift. She wore tight blue jeans, a hippyish pink cotton top and espadrilles, and carried the posey of flowers Owen had earlier picked for her from Grandma's garden. Owen watched her walk down the track. After twenty yards she half turned and blew him a final kiss. Thirty yards further on her gait changed slightly, slowing to a stroll, and it occurred to Owen that at that moment she stopped thinking about him, her son, behind her, and began thinking of what lay ahead.

*   *   *

That evening Grandpa grasped the neck of the bottle of Tia Maria his daughter-in-law had left as a gift and carried it to the shed. He didn't ask whether Grandma might like a tipple. 'Seen a pheasant down by the gate,' he said. 'Never seen one this high up.' He dipped a tin bowl into a sack of grain, poured in half the bottle of sweet liqueur, left it overnight to steep. In the morning Owen laid a trail of grain up the track. By noon the bird had eaten its way into the barn. They closed the doors and watched it totter in the gloom, lurch like a stupid hooligan towards the dogs, who seemed to understand and played along, teasing the drunk aggressive bird. It was the first time Owen saw his grandfather smile uninhibitedly, a cruel grin of pleasure that lit up the barn.

* * *

Owen would wonder whether anger had burrowed like sheep's lice under his grandfather's skin.

'If I go first,' Grandma said, 'make sure you bury Grandpa with a piece of wool in his coffin.'

'Why?' Owen asked.

'St Peter, on Judgement Day, can see what work he did, why he wasn't at church every Sunday.'

In his chair by the stove Grandpa snorted: he may well have feared God, but had no wish to appease Him. Owen craved his grandfather's approval. The old man's one hobby was making shepherds' crooks in the shed, from rams' horns and hazel cut from the dark, damp wood in the narrow gulley beneath the Graig that received so little sun the switches grew straight up towards the

27

light. Owen watched his grandfather soften a horn in boiling water then squeeze it in a vice to iron out its natural spiral. If the process required more precision, persuading a bend or kink out of the bone and skin, he held it over the chimney of a paraffin lamp, eased it a little further.

Nothing was explained. Owen was obliged to observe for himself how too much heat made the horn brittle. His grandfather offered no tuition. As far as Owen knew, aged eleven, this was the nature of apprenticeship: knowledge had to be stolen from a reluctant master, a slow, forensic theft. Grandpa married the hazel to the horn's heel, drilled a hole through them both and glued in a steel rod. Finally, he'd hold the stick in a variety of ways—across his palm, between two fingers—then cut off a fraction of the bottom of the stick. Hold it again, assessing the balance between the size and weight of the stick and of the horn. Shave off a little more wood. If he judged he'd taken off too much he'd spit in the dust and break the stick across his knee, disgusted with it, and start again with another one.

Owen whittled Y-shaped sticks himself, burned designs into the wood the way the old man did, with a heated nail held in a pair of pliers. One afternoon his grandfather, rooting about at the back of the workbench, found a small, spiralled ram's horn he must have once rejected. 'Here,' he said, tossing it to his grandson. Owen caught it— rough, ancient, almost fossil-like in his hands—his heart weak with gratitude.

*   *   *

On the first day of the autumn term Grandpa drove Owen down to the valley road, from where he caught the school bus, and picked him up the same afternoon. After that he had to walk, three miles down, three miles back uphill. He sat on his own on the bus, but others in his class got on at stops along the way and he found himself forced to explain his presence. 'My Dad's sick,' he said. 'I'm staying with family out of town.' Owen felt himself some kind of changeling, the texture of his self altering, transforming, from urban urchin to rural youth. Acquiring knowledge of the truth of life and death up on the hills, but becoming uncomfortable down in the valley, among men.

Walking uphill, Owen scrutinised the world around him: identified sounds deep in the rural silence, wildflowers in the bank at the side of the lane. Sometimes his attention zoned out, his mind seemed to empty and he walked in a trance— unaware of the direction he took, an unconscious compass guiding him home—a dopiness, a kind of rapture.

Grandma was happy he was up there with them—whether compensating for the failings of her son or glad of a child's presence once again, Owen wasn't sure. One evening he couldn't get to sleep and sat on the stairs, listened in on his grandparents in the room below. 'He's shy,' Grandma said.

'Nothing like his father,' Grandpa growled. 'Doesn't talk nonsense.'

'When he does speak, I like to listen,' Grandma said. 'I'll bet you were just like him at that age.'

*   *   *

Carrying his junior shepherd's crook, fingers wrapped around the ram's horn, Owen accompanied his grandfather evenings and weekends. After autumn rain one Saturday morning in September, walking back for breakfast from early inspection of sheep, Grandpa pointed his crook at circular white eruptions from the grass. Field mushrooms. Owen scuttled from one to another, raised them gently with two fingers, slid his penknife under and cut the stalks. Turned them over. The overnight perfection of their fine brown gills. He held them to his nose, inhaled the smell of earth made flesh. Grandpa took off his cap to carry them. Before they entered the cottage he passed it to Owen to give to his grandmother. She took the cap from the boy, smiling.

'Beauties,' she said. 'Early, though, isn't it?'

'Had 'em earlier than this,' Grandpa replied.

In a moment she had cut them on her board and they were sizzling in her pan. The three of them relished the succulent flavour and texture.

'Grandpa loves a fresh-picked mushroom with his bacon,' his wife announced. 'Don't you, Gwyn?'

Owen turned to his grandfather. The old man said nothing, only ate greedily.

*　　　*　　　*

It was when she realised Owen was being taught to imitate the calls of certain birds that Grandma's mood turned. Grandpa would stop when they were walking, his hand across Owen's chest, and repeat the sound of a distant curlew, not its musical bubbling trill but the yelping alarm note. Owen

30

understood he was to attempt the same. His early efforts provoked disdain but his grandfather persisted, obliging Owen to. Sometimes they paused and all they heard was an ambulance siren or a church bell carried on the wind, or the whine of an all-terrain vehicle, one of the Honda three-wheelers advancing across the hills. Grandpa spat—at their intrusion upon his silence, at their unstoppable encroachment.

'Oil runs out,' he said. 'Forgot how to walk, see. Who'll round up then?'

He gobbed into the wet grass and strode on, grimacing. He must have been feeling early twinges of the pain that would see him and Grandma, less than five years and two hip replacements later, in a brick bungalow down in the valley, from where he'd gaze with grey eyes up to the tops. How many thousands of miles of walking over rough ground, of jumps off brick walls to sun-baked earth, of slipping in mud and off rocks in streams, of jarring collisions and juddering falls. But for now he suppressed the pain of grating bones.

*   *   *

'What are you doing?' Grandma demanded. 'Why are you teaching him calls?'

'Nowt for you to fret,' he said.

'You promised,' she said. 'Not again. Not here.'

'Keep out of it,' he said, his anger building.

Grandma turned her attention to Owen. 'He knows he couldn't do it on his own.'

'Leave the boy alone.'

'Wouldn't consider it if you weren't here.'

31

Owen had no idea what they were talking about. In the evenings, sat outside, Grandpa would freeze, finger pointing into the dusk. Although whatever he heard was out of sight, his eyes moved around their sockets like the pupils were some essential part of his sonic radar. Owen listened. The ghostly quavering hoot of a tawny owl. Grandpa immediately imitating it, Owen following. He felt his grandfather's hand, ruffling his hair. The rough fingers cupped his face. 'Good boy.' Owen hoped his grandpa couldn't see his grin: he couldn't hide his happiness, hoped the twilight might.

The two of them then performed a duet, one calling, the other answering, in open defiance of Grandma. 'You stupid man,' she said. She went back inside, slamming the door on them. The leaves were turning.

*   *   *

Above, clouds scudded across the face of a hunters' moon. They walked over the upper fields. A packet of silver sheep parted for them. Owen trotted every few yards to keep up with his grandfather, whose stride was loose and eager. They skirted Corndon Hill. Wood pigeons had come at dusk to roost in the oaks by Fishpool. They passed beneath the orbit of a bat's insect-devouring circuit: once, twice, three times Owen saw its veering flight. The night was alive with movement. They walked fast. The surface of the earth—rough rolling pasture, streams flowing through sombre woods, heather, gorse, high bracken—prickled with the same excitement the boy had felt gathering in his grandfather for days. All hunting animals were on the prowl, their nervous prey ready to betray themselves. Men too tonight, Owen sensed, far around them, had slipped into the dark like guerillas, a countrywide uprising.

It was no revolution. Grandpa seethed at the fact of his position, not its injustice. He hated no one more than the man whose land he farmed, whose rent he paid, but had no thought to overthrow him. Desired only to get back at him, inflict a visceral measure of revenge.

They walked close by Nind, but no dogs barked, and entered the woods on Pellrhadley Hill. After that Owen lost track, his attention taken up with sticking to his grandfather in the darkness, pausing at every sound. He was in a state of ignorance, had no idea what they were doing, what could possibly happen. Grandpa should have had the twelve-bore, holding it high up the barrel, his arm held up, the gun resting horizontal on his shoulder, as it was yesterday when he carried it to the shed to oil it in preparation. But the gun was gone this morning. Grandma had taken it in the night and refused to say where she'd hidden it.

'You tell me!' Grandpa snarled.

Grandma stood at the kitchen sink, her back to her husband, shaking her head.

Grandpa grew visibly hot with anger. His voice deepened into something grit-laden, nasty. 'Tell me, woman.' Owen sat at the table, his breakfast growing cold, congealing on his plate. Something terrible about to happen. Insanity in the room. Which one of them was the more crazy? He didn't know. The brink of violence.

33

Grandpa turned and walked out of the cottage. They heard a clatter of metal. One of the dogs squealed. Grandma turned around, leaned back against the sink, exhausted. She shook her bowed head. 'Too much to lose,' she said quietly, to herself.

And now Owen wondered what they were doing out here without a gun, his grandfather's stubborn madness, seeing his plan through. He felt the hand on his chest. 'Down.' They knelt on damp pine cones. 'Up ahead,' Grandpa whispered. 'Need to walk around to the right. Out of the wood, skirt it a hundred yards, come in and walk slow straight back toward me. Send it my way, see. Can you do that?'

Owen felt the dead weight of his grandfather's hand on his shoulder. It was almost pitch-black here in the trees. 'Send what, Grandpa?' he whispered.

His grandfather breathed deeply. 'Fallow deer. Forty yard upwind of us.'

Owen walked in a trance. Unable to imagine how on earth he could possibly find his way in the darkness, he gave himself up to the instruction his grandfather had given him, believing it to be so absurd that it could hardly be his fault if he wandered round till dawn and found himself ten miles away. He went out of the wood, walked through heather in moonlight, re-entered the trees, walked in a line, turned left towards his grandfather. Or so he envisioned.

With his arms held in front of him, Owen stumbled slowly through the darkness. In these woods were badgers, foxes, wild cats. There were snakes underfoot and likely hanging from the branches that scratched his face. He began to tremble, a terrified child blundering through a dark wood seething with beasts. A black panther escaped from a zoo. Wolves released from captivity. Owen realised that he was sobbing with fright, though he made no sound: shivering, tears slid from his eyes, he carried on blindly forward. The sudden sound of movement just ahead. He was convinced that whatever it was was rushing towards him. Owen began to weep, but then he became aware of another sound: the long, wailing cry of a deer in distress. It stopped abruptly. Owen aimed towards it.

When Owen found them, Grandpa had killed the doe with his knife and was already hauling it over his shoulders, holding two hooves in each hand, a great scarf of meat around his neck. The way that events had unravelled one into another seemed to the boy inconceivable: that he had taken the correct route, that the deer had bolted in this direction, that his old grandfather had fallen upon it. What kind of demonic explanation was there? They reached the edge of the wood.

'Go first. Wait for me by the bridge. Anyone sees you, run. Catch you, say nothing. You see anyone: owl sound, remember?'

They made their way back in a leapfrog fashion, together under cover, separately in the open, Owen sent on ahead to warn his grandfather of other men loose in the night. After a while he began to get sleepy. He'd never stayed up anything like as late as this. There were fewer clouds than when they set out, the open land was like moon fields, the earth had been abandoned, there were no people here nor anywhere else, Owen could

35

relax in the silver land. All he had to do was sleepwalk home.

He was woken by voices, and dropped to the ground. Moments later two men walked by him. How could they not have seen him? One was tall, lean, the other broader, had a gun. He lay on his side and watched them amble towards the tree behind which his grandfather waited. Perhaps they wouldn't see him. He'd hear them, wouldn't he, and keep out of sight? Then he saw the dog, joining them from some exploration of its own off to the side. It would, he figured, smell the deer for sure. Owen stood up and made the hooting sound they'd practised often. He thought he did it pretty well. The men turned round.

'Who the?' said one. 'What are?' said the other, the tall one, and he started coming towards Owen, standing straight and clear in the moonlight. The boy hooted again. The tall man paused for a moment, spooked maybe by this eerie being, half owl, half child. 'Stop,' he said, and began walking again. Beyond, the fat man called the dog to his side. 'Stay where you are,' the lean man ordered. Owen turned and ran.

He sprinted. Panic-stricken. Only, though, for the first minute. Then, glancing back, he saw the tall man was further away than he had been, and struggling across the field after him. The man ran as if he'd been handicapped, hobbled because he was an adult, chasing a swift eleven-year-old boy. Owen was fast and in that moment knew it. His lungs seemed to bloom, become twice as large, so that he wanted to laugh as he ran, then realised that he was doing so, giggling to himself as he galloped clear, the distance widening between him

36

and his pursuer.

With one hand on the top rung he hurdled a gate, cantered across another field, through a spinney. He was clear now, unless they set the dog loose. He trotted into a pasture where bullocks did double takes at his presence and scampered away. He jumped a fence and ran through a marshy piece of woodland. He didn't know where he was but he wasn't bothered. There was a large puddle ahead and he ran through it. He was halfway across when he realised it wasn't water but mud, or slurry, or quicksand, and it was over his knees. He staggered on and in two steps it was up to his waist. He tried to turn, and with a great effort managed to do so, but the swamp was up around his stomach. He reached out. There was nothing to get hold of except loose swilling mud. He tried to scrabble, to swim with his arms, but could get no traction. His feet were on some half-solid ground that gave slowly beneath him. He was up to his chest now and sinking.

Owen would soon say goodbye to this silver glade and sink into the darkness of mud. This was where he would die, and this was how, choking on sludge. He stopped struggling, but then he could feel the slime sliding, inch by inch, up over his shoulders. The boy put his lips together, arranged his tongue in his mouth and yelped the alarm note of a curlew. It sounded good. It meant, 'Help.' He made the sound over and over again, until the mud came to his lips and he could make the sound no more, then it came over his nose, and his eyes. He knew that when he opened his mouth to breathe the mud would pour in.

Though his eyes were closed beneath the mud

there came a murky vision: on a hill stood a boy, Owen himself, surely, yet he could not be certain, the boy stood with his back to him. Sound, too. Birdsong. The plaintive, haunting call of a lapwing in flight. P'weet, pee-wit, pee-wit. Could the boy see it, the bird's tumbling aerial display? No, Owen realised: it was the boy who was making the sound.

Owen had to interrupt. He could not breathe. His lungs were on fire. Gagging, he needed to open his mouth. The mud. Instead he felt a stinging in his scalp, a terrible pain in an unexpected place, which seemed brutally unfair—he was preparing himself for the agony of choking suffocation, not for this searing of his skull—as his grandfather grabbed hold of Owen's hair, bunched it in his fist and hauled him out of the bog.

CONSCIOUSNESS OF A LOST LIMB

Occupational Therapy
East Midlands Rehabilitation Centre
                    17 November 2000

Dear Sue,
    I think I told you that I agreed to give a talk at the conference next month: to tell the story of phantom limb pain, and the introduction of the mirror box. If you've got a minute I could really do with some feedback.
    As the audience is going to consist of health professionals across the board, I've interwoven a case history as a way of personalising the subject.
    I'm not used to writing at such length. Remember how much detail we put into case histories when we were training. Then you qualify and of course there's no time, everything's abbreviated. Anyway, it'd be great if you have any ideas for improvement.

    Andrea

CONSCIOUSNESS OF A LOST LIMB

Ninety per cent of amputations are to lower limbs. Most are caused by peripheral vascular disease—old smokers' arteries harden, ageing diabetics lose feeling in their feet—and the legs are compromised, being the limbs furthest away from the heart.

When meningitis strikes people in their late teens their bodies, in a desperate defence against the disease, can cease sending blood to the extremities: if gangrene, or meningitic emphysema, develops, the sufferer may lose all four limbs.

About 10 per cent of amputations are to upper limbs. Most of these involve young men who've sustained trauma, usually in a traffic accident, although Owen —— was thirty-five years old, and he'd been inside a car rather than on the more usual saddle of a motorbike. He came to our department in 1996 having lost his right hand. The surgeon involved had assessed the possibility of salvaging the hand, hoping to reattach it using microsurgery, but in this case nervous and circulatory function had been severely affected. In addition the hand itself, I understand, was badly damaged.

Owen —— had a short transradial amputation, that is to say one between the elbow and the wrist.

Postsurgically, the limb was encased in a rigid plaster of Paris dressing: such a cast prevents the formation of oedema and so reduces postoperative pain and hastens healing of the residium, or stump. It may also serve as the foundation for a temporary prosthesis: the sooner after surgery a client uses an artificial limb, for simple grasping actions or merely from a cosmetic point of view, the more likely their acceptance of a permanent prosthesis.

Owen —— spent five weeks in hospital while the wound and other lesser injuries healed and the swelling reduced. He was given a referral letter to our centre two weeks after the accident, and came to see me on a visit from hospital. Although we don't operate strict specialisations here, I'm particularly interested in upper limb loss and rehabilitation, and so receive most such referrals.

I remember Owen well. He had home-made tattoos on the fingers of his remaining hand, but he was a gentle man, reserved. He spoke quietly, a distinct trace of his upbringing in the Welsh borders in his voice.

The first interviews with a client are of vital importance, as we try to find out their expectations, their psychological as well as physical requirements. When I first met Owen he appeared still to be in a state of shock, or rather numbness. I established that the right hand he'd lost was his dominant hand, but he showed no interest in the choice of prosthetic limbs put before him. Did he want more of a functional or a cosmetic hand? How much did he care about what others thought? At our first sessions Owen was monosyllabic and withdrawn.

The individual's psychological response to amputation is the key to their rehabilitation, and basic personality is of great significance. Self-confident individuals generally adjust better to the loss than self-conscious ones. Naturally cheerful people adjust far better than depressives, who are

41

likely to avoid social contact following their loss, which in turn compounds their isolation and depression.

On a practical level, those whose jobs or hobbies and general independence are badly affected by the loss of a limb will have more difficulty coping than those who can adapt more easily. Men often fear impotence or sterility with the loss of a limb.

Clients usually dream of themselves as possessing all their limbs. Getting out of bed at night, those who have lost a lower limb quite often forget their loss, and fall over.

I'd been told of the circumstances of Owen's accident. It was no wonder that he was shut down, closed off. He had other issues. But it's my job to concentrate on occupational therapy: emotional or psychological therapy is between the client and counsellor. The boundaries that are in place have to be respected, otherwise things get confused and none of us are able to do our particular jobs properly. That doesn't mean that if Owen had started talking I wouldn't have listened. I would have. That's part of my job as well. But he didn't. He never said a word about the accident.

I understand Owen declined to continue seeing the counsellor after their third or fourth session.

*   *   *

Each prosthetic device is bespoke, made for the individual client. There are two types of artificial upper limb, or terminal device: the hand and the hook, either of which is secured to a plastic socket that encases the residium.

Most clients are keen to replace their lost hand

42

with a replica, of which there are two sorts: a passive, fixed hand or an active hand with a grasping mechanism that moves the index and middle fingers, and the thumb, towards each other, while the fourth and fifth fingers remain fixed.

An active hand is commonly operated myoelectrically: the prosthetic socket has two electrodes which connect with flexor and extensor muscles in the residium. When the wearer consciously contracts the appropriate muscle, the electrode transmits the microvoltage generated by the muscle to a small motor that enables the hand mechanism to open or close the fingers. Sensors in the fingers stop them grasping objects too tightly.

Hands are laminates made from glass-reinforced plastic and acrylic resin. They are covered with a flexible 'glove' that matches the hair colour and skin tone of the client's other, real hand. A cheap PVC glove may cost as little as £80, while a high-definition, ultrarealistic one made of silicon can cost £3,000–5,000 for a whole leg or an arm.

People often wear rings, wristwatches or other jewellery on their artificial hand. One of my clients has found it so difficult to come to terms with his amputation that he sleeps with his artificial arm on.

*   *   *

It was at first impossible to determine what kind of prosthesis Owen wanted. As I've said, he showed no interest in his future. But then things changed. He came to his fourth meeting with me—he was now out of hospital, back at home—and brightly

43

asked me to show him the hooks again.

Hooks are lighter than other types of device; they're tougher and more durable. Most amputees, however, care very much what other people think. They resent and are upset by people noticing and staring at their artificial limb, their disability. A very few clients don't give a damn, and care only about the functionality of their prosthesis. I knew I should be wary of Owen's leap from depressive lack of interest to a gung-ho attitude: if this was evidence merely of denial then it would not bode well for recovery. My reservations, however, were overcome as Owen spoke of his determination to resume as active a life as possible. He worked as a self-employed gardener, and together we looked into the array of gardening tools modified for disabled people; he spoke of his young son and his wish to do everything with and for him that any father could. The only thing he didn't want to consider was motor vehicle adaptation for disability: Owen said he had no wish ever to drive a car again.

Hooks generally operate by a steel cable attached, via metal links in a cuff running the length of the arm, to a trunk harness. The client puts tension on the cable by flexing his shoulder; the cable pulls and operates to either open or close the hook's two steel or aluminium digits. These digits can act either like a finger and oppositional thumb or like two adjacent fingers. Their grasp force is determined by rubber bands encircling the base.

Because the tips of the fingers of a hook are small, the client can see the object to be grasped more easily than with the thicker fingers of a prosthetic hand. They're also much cheaper than bespoke hands, and although our priority is to provide whatever an individual client needs, he or she may well reject an ill-chosen prosthesis and simply not wear it. If it was one of the most expensive types, then we've clearly wasted money. And we were already at that time working to a tightly controlled budget at the Centre.

Owen took to his hook with relish. He subjected it to all kinds of tests, challenging it and himself to do pretty well everything he could before the accident. Within a short space of time he was able to operate tools, though for other reasons was unable to return to work. He also liked gimmicky aspects of having it: holding a cigarette between the claws, or trying to juggle with soft balls. He was always making jokes.

'Sorry to keep you waiting,' I said once, when the previous appointment had run over.

'No problem,' Owen said. 'Having a good chat I was with the other cybermen out there.'

A proportion of clients—particularly men—make light of their condition with such flippancy, but Owen was intelligent. He understood, for example, that I must have heard all such cracks many times before, and he'd add an ironic touch. He once greeted me as he came into my office by raising his hook and saying, 'Can you hear the clock ticking, Peter?'

Now I used to look younger than my age, and with my short hair I could be described as boyish. And most actors who play the role of Peter Pan are boyish women, aren't they? So Owen was making the almost obligatory such prosthesis-wearer's reference to himself as Captain Hook, but playing with it to include me. And the question itself referred not only to the clock swallowed by the crocodile, who you'll remember was after Hook, but also perhaps to time that was after me. How long would I remain a boyish, young-looking woman?

Perhaps Owen was also flirting, in a mild way.

I became aware, however, of two possibly contradictory aspects of Owen's behaviour. He made out he didn't care what people thought, making jokes at his own expense, yet one always felt that he was hiding something—which indeed he was: the loss of his hand was as nothing compared to his greater loss. I was never sure, to be honest, whether the rehabilitation with which I assisted him was also helping him come to terms with his grief, or rather offering him a peculiar form of denial.

*   *   *

Such was the speed of Owen's recovery that I stopped seeing him after three months. When he telephoned the Centre a further six months later, however, to book an appointment with me, I was not surprised. The pattern was a common one.

The persistence of sensation in and awareness of limbs after they have been amputated has long been known. A French surgeon wrote of the phenomenon in the sixteenth century. Admiral Lord Nelson lost his right arm in 1797, and thereafter felt the fingers of his absent hand digging into his palm. Pondering this survival of the hand's spirit after its physical loss, Nelson decided it was direct evidence for the existence of

46

the soul.

During the American Civil War thousands of wounded soldiers developed gangrene and had their infected limbs sawn off in field tents. A Philadelphian physician, Silas Weir Mitchell, later worked with many of these veterans of the war who retained the 'sensory ghosts' of their lost arms or legs. Weir Mitchell coined the term 'phantom limb'.

For most of the twentieth century the phenomenon remained mysterious. Explanations ranged from a patient's wish to have his or her limb back inducing the phantom in their imagination, to inflammation of nerve endings in the stump. In 1887 the eminent psychologist William James conducted the first survey of phantom limb amputees and found that 'many patients say they can hardly tell whether they feel or fancy the limb'. He also wrote, in an article 'The Consciousness of Lost Limbs', that phantom limb sensation tells us absolutely nothing which can practically be of use to us—except, he believed, the approach of storms.

Nowadays it's generally agreed that the causes are complex and to be found in the neurology of the brain. Parts of the body, including limbs, are mapped on to the cerebral cortex, and when a limb is lost the corresponding area of the map appears to adjust to receive signals from another part of the body, but the person feels the sensation as coming from the lost limb.

Women who've had a radical mastectomy have phantom breasts. Men who've suffered a carcinoma of the penis and had it amputated have experienced phantom erections. One patient

47

who'd had his appendix taken out suffered the pain of phantom appendicitis. He refused to believe that the surgeon had removed it.

* * *

Owen came into my office. 'You've got to help me. My hand,' he said, holding up his hook where the hand had been. 'It's killing me.'

I was shocked by the state that Owen was in. He smelled of tobacco and alcohol.

I assured Owen that there was nothing unusual in what was happening to him. I had him sit down, fetched a cup of tea and a biscuit, gave him time to settle, before asking him to describe the pain for me.

'It changes,' he said. 'Like burning, see, my hand's in flames.' He held it up, as if I might see the conflagration. 'It tingles, like pins and needles. Then there's shooting pains, like, up and down the nerves from the wrist to the tips of my fingers.'

'How often do these pains occur?' I asked.

Owen looked at me as if to ask why I might imagine he'd come to see me. 'All the time,' he said. 'It doesn't ever stop.'

* * *

'Almost every amputee experiences phantom sensation,' according to Gustav Rubin, MD, FACS, 'but statistically only 5 to 10 per cent have varying degrees of phantom pain.' According to Jack W. Tsao MD, DPhil, 'Phantom limb pain occurs in at least 90 per cent of limb amputees.' Steven King, MD, MS believes that 'as many as 50 to 80 per cent of patients who undergo amputation report experiencing pain in the missing body part'. In this country, the Pain Relief Foundation, based in Liverpool, reckons that 75 per cent of amputees develop phantom pain. At the East Midlands Rehabilitation Centre we ask all our clients about their personal experience of phantom sensation: the anecdotal evidence is that 80 per cent experience phantom sensations, of whom 75 per cent (i.e. 60 per cent of the total) suffer pain.

I've enumerated these conflicting figures in order to indicate not only the lack of scientific agreement on the matter but also the subjectivity of the phenomenon.

*   *   *

I tried to ask Owen how his family were, his job, his marriage. It was clear that there were other issues. But he was uninterested in anything except the symptoms.

'Stabbing pains,' he said. 'Like a knife, or then a skewer, piercing and twisting in my flesh. The flesh that isn't there.' His descriptions were vivid, and I wrote them down. 'Then this raking pain,' he said. 'Like cheesewire, it is, running up my fingers. The feeling changes. But the pain, see, it stays the same.'

I asked him whether he felt like someone was inflicting this pain upon him.

'No,' he said. '*It's* doing it. My hand is hurting itself. My hand is killing me. And I can't stop it.'

We discussed the various treatments available. It's a truism in medicine that when there are many ways to treat a condition, none of them is much good: an effective treatment soon becomes the sole method used. Most treatments for phantom limb pain available to our clients were shots in the dark which had appeared by chance to alleviate symptoms for some sufferers; we knew—and still know—so little about the neurological mysteries of the brain. The typical human brain contains over one hundred billion neurons. Each neuron is able to make contact with thousands of other neurons at points called synapses. It's been calculated that the number of potential brain states—the number of permutations and combinations of activity that are theoretically possible—inside one person's head exceeds the number of elementary particles in the universe.

What we now know—which is a good deal more, thanks to increased research and to magnetic resonance imaging (MRI) and other types of brain scan, than we knew the few years ago that I worked with Owen—is that it is through the complex working of the sensory and motor neural pathways, the reorganisation of the 'mapping' of the body on the cortex and the neural plasticity of the brain that phantom limb sensations occur.

So Owen began what would be a long and, for him, increasingly pointless itinerary. Our doctor began with prescription drugs (painkillers like ibuprofen and paracetamol have little or no effect on phantom limb pain). The antidepressant amitriptyline helps some sufferers, but caused Owen only the unwelcome side effects of a dry mouth, constipation and nausea. We moved on to anticonvulsant drugs carbamazepine (developed to treat epilepsy, it occasionally alleviates other nervous system disorders and nerve pain) and gabapentin, but again these gave no relief and only negative side effects: drowsiness, a rash on his good arm.

I told Owen of various complementary therapies, or what are sometimes referred to as psychologically based modalities, that seemed to help certain patients. Owen went away and tried them all: acupuncture, reflexology, biofeedback, hypnosis, with practitioners around Birmingham. I'm not sure how he paid for these treatments, to be honest. He had little work during this period, and he gave me to understand that he was no longer living in the marital home, though without offering further detail. Suffice to say that none of these other methods seemed to help, although to be fair I'm not sure Owen gave any of them more than one session.

I showed Owen how to massage and to gently percuss the stump. We also used TENS, transcutaneous electrical nerve stimulation, which involves placing electrodes on the stump to cause a tingling sensation, and reduces the pain for a proportion of sufferers.

None of these treatments helped Owen. I grew increasingly despondent on his behalf, as well as my own. Although at least these methods weren't destructive. In the past, treatments have included cutting the stump back further, cutting the nerves to the stump, cutting the roots of the nerves near the spinal cord, chasing the pain deeper into the poor patient's body, cutting the nerve pathways in the spinal cord itself and even cutting out parts of the brain.

It's difficult to imagine being in constant pain. It's easier to empathise with emotional pain than with physical suffering. But I've worked with a number of clients who lived with it and I understand how miserable, how debilitating it can be.

* * *

V.S. Ramachandran was a world-renowned brain researcher who a short time before Owen had his accident applied himself to the question of phantom limb sensation and pain. He speculated on the problem of patients whose phantom limb was paralysed. 'What if,' Ramachandran wondered, 'the patient could send a message to her phantom arm and every time she did so she got back a visual signal that it was indeed obeying her command and moving? Could we trick her eyes into "seeing" a phantom?'

It occurred to him that virtual reality could be used: a computer might create the illusion that an arm was restored. The cost of such technology, however, would exhaust his team's entire research budget. Ramachandran came up instead with a low-tech alternative: mirrors.

Owen was the first client with whom I employed mirror box therapy. The pair of us may well have been the first in this country, after one of our technicians constructed a box from a description in Ramachandran's newly published research paper.

The pain in Owen's phantom left hand had been increasingly fixed in recent weeks, his hand contorted in a clenched, agonising spasm. Today, however, things were if anything worse: 'My nails are digging into my palm,' he said. 'I swear there must be blood.' He was by this stage, I should add,

52

understandably sceptical of any progress. But Owen was also clearly making a great effort to hold himself together: I could smell alcohol on his breath, but he was clean, his clothes were always clean and pressed.

The box was of strong card covered in black material, and was separated into two, shoebox-sized compartments. The dividing wall had a mirror on one side—in Owen's case, the left. The right side of the box—where Owen would place his residium—had a lid placed upon it, the other side remained open. There were two holes at the front of the box. Having removed his hook, Owen inserted his residium—and, so to speak, phantom hand—through the right-hand hole, where it would remain hidden from view. Then he placed his good left arm through the hole on the left side. I explained what we were going to do. Owen smiled in a sardonic way I'd come to recognise, particular to shy, clever people.

'We're going to use magic now, are we?' he said, and then, as if speaking about me to someone else in the room, 'The occupational illusionist steps forward.' It struck me that this was really my, our, last chance.

Owen could now see his good left arm and, instead of the hidden residium, the reflection of the left arm, which created the illusion of being able to see two complete hands, left and right. I asked him to make his good hand mimic the posture of his phantom. Sure enough, he clenched it tight, grimacing, digging his fingernails into his palm. It now looked to him as if he were looking at two intact hands, the fingers on both bunching, squeezing hard into themselves. Then I asked him

53

to slowly, very slowly, unclench his good left hand. He began to do so. For a while there was silence. I watched Owen: he was gazing at his hands—his good left hand and its reflection, both of which were unclenching—with mounting intensity.

'Oh my God,' Owen said, as his hands opened out. 'Jesus wept.' He stared at his hands and gradually flexed individual fingers. 'Sweet Mary, Mother of God.' Owen was literally open-mouthed in amazement. 'It's working,' he said. 'I don't believe it, but it's working, see? My hand's stopped hurting. It's doing what the other one does.'

It remains the most privileged moment of my career so far. Dr Ramachandran's invention was indeed magical, and I was able to witness its effect. We continued the session. Using the mirror, Owen was able to persuade his phantom hand to mimic whatever he did with his good hand. The pain stopped. If he removed his hands from the box, however, or closed his eyes, the pain returned.

The next day we had another session, with the same results. 'I feel like one of the Marx Brothers, you know?' Owen said, smiling. 'Groucho Marx, and his reflection?' I nodded, though I didn't really know what he was talking about, until I happened to watch the film *Duck Soup* with my children some while later, with its wonderful mirror scene. But I guessed at the time that as the pain diminished so Owen was rediscovering his sense of humour.

Afterwards, I gave Owen the mirror box to take home with him. He proceeded to use it whenever he was in pain, half a dozen times a day. The relief would continue after he stopped using it, for varying lengths of time. He occasionally rang me up to tell me how well things were going or to express disappointment that he was unable to get rid of the pain for good: however long relief lasted—hours, a day—the pain always reasserted itself in the end.

The last time I saw Owen was a year or so later. A Thursday afternoon in March, about a quarter past three. I was driving along Chester Road. The day had been a wet one. It had only just stopped raining, and although there were still black clouds on the right-hand side of the sky the sun had come out on the other. The light was dramatic: it was as if everything to one's right was a giant stage, lit up for performance against a thunderous backdrop.

I caught sight of two figures on the right-hand side of the pavement up ahead, striding along. One was Owen. In his hook he held the handle of a spade, whose shaft rested on his shoulder. A boy, his son, I presume, walked beside him, holding his father's left hand. The boy carried some small tool, a trowel, I think, in his left hand. Unlike other dishevelled pedestrians around them, Owen's and his son's clothes were dry. The two of them strode along in the light that comes after a storm.

*   *   *

The mirror box was an extraordinarily simple therapeutic tool which had profound implications for our understanding of how the brain adapts to the loss of a limb, and how phantom limb pain occurs and can be controlled. At the Centre we're now, in partnership with researchers at Manchester University, at the stage of moving on into the realm of technology that Dr Ramachandran first envisioned: computer graphics imaging. Mirror box therapy did not cure phantom limb pain for good, but we believe that it was a vital step towards that eventual aim.

THE BURROWS

The first time he saw them it happened by chance, after dusk, one warm June evening.

It was two summers after Owen's long stay on the hill. He'd been back a few times since, increasingly useful, with an appetite for work, and stamina, fortitude. Becoming a countryman: less comfortable indoors than out; no more wish than his grandfather to return to the homestead with light fading around him. Eyes dilating in the twilight, and Grandma's dimly lit cottage was too bright, the men forced to blink like owls as they stepped inside.

Owen was pulling thistles in the pasture furthest down away from the farm towards the Malt House. He'd volunteered to clear a few when his grandfather limped inside for tea, knowing it would please the old man, wanting to stay out. Daylight like food you craved more of, greedy for the last dregs.

The heads of the thistles were still tight, purple; they had to be got now. Later the flower heads would open and a breeze scatter the down, benevolent fairy-like flurries of it, drifting across the hillside, carrying their evil seeds. Creeping thistle was the exception: it spread through its roots, extending underground. 'Can't beat that bastard,' Grandpa admitted. Fortunately rare in these parts. The air had been damp and drizzly, the ground was soft, so long as he didn't yank but gave a gradual tug to the weed its roots yielded. Owen laid the stringy carcasses out on the grass to perish and wilt. He understood by now the interconnecting chains of species essential to each other, the intricate interdependency of life forms on the crust of this earth, but there were some species whose value was obscure. Thistles were one. Wasps another. Colt's foot. Mosquitoes.

Everything was food for something else, or served a purpose of some kind. Few species self-sufficient, or purely parasitic.

He wore an old pair of leather gloves, protection from the spiny pricks. The pace of the work determined by the slow pull, it could not be hurried, immensely satisfying. By the time he'd cleared the lowest field and looked up, the moon, three-quarters full, shone on silver hills. The sun had long since gone down, leaving a fringe of burnt orange still in the western sky.

As he walked back around the flank of the hill, Owen entered the wood that covered the lower, steep slope on that side, down to the creek by The Graig. Squat twisting stunted pillars of oak growing on the steep bank; the air some degrees cooler under and amongst their branches. The phrase 'Open-air Mass' came to him: it suggested an image of worship in a bare field; better in a wood, Owen thought. The atmosphere here had the same quality as the church in Welshpool, of something he couldn't quite identify. Of sanctity? No. Of quietness, contemplation? What was it? There was a feeling of expectation within him, obscure and real as an illness coming. It was the sense of something about to happen, about to materialise. He sat on the ground, leaned back against a tree trunk. What time was it? After nine, for sure. Grandma would have kept his dinner in

58

the Rayburn. Maybe nearer to ten.

Owen's breathing slowed. There were sounds in the silent night but all, at first, indistinct. Faraway rustles in undergrowth, a murmur in the air, some vague thing's breath; a high-pitched shriek in the distance, out at the edge of his field of hearing.

Amazing how much moonlight seeped into the wood: he was in a grey glade, tinged with a mercury glow. Then it happened. He felt his skin bristle, the whole surface of his skin was suddenly switched on. Alert. Not knowing why. And then a creature lumbered past him, big as one of his grandfather's dogs but more bulky, padding within inches of him, then pausing, sniffing the air, moving on a little more quickly, while Owen sat there, his heart thumped to a halt.

The creature moved on and away, out of sight. A blobby, sidling beast from deep in human dreams. A creeping thing from Owen's unconscious, slipping into silver visibility for a moment. No. A nocturnal animal, he told himself, that's all. What on earth was it? A badger.

Owen stumbled back to the cottage, certain of two things: he would investigate further, and make no mention of the matter to his grandfather.

* * *

Thirteen years old. The boy's voice had changed: like honey over sand. He used it sparely. Tall as his mother, he wouldn't grow much more. His father had gone for good the previous autumn and it was as if other men knew this was the cruel clean final severance; as if his territory were no longer marked, they closed in on his woman. Men came to

59

call. Some were strangers, others Owen knew, vaguely. They'd give him things. A penknife. A fifty-pence coin. One man, with a permanent kink of a smile at one side of his mouth and jet-black eyes, took Owen to the football in Shrewsbury. His mother was feckless, sweet. Accepted her husband was gone, and let go. She seemed to her son to do nothing to discourage or encourage the men, was available, that was enough and they knew. He headed for the hill when he could.

*   *   *

The badgers' sett Owen found the next day, Sunday, further down the slope, deeper into the steep wood. The half-dozen holes were larger than rabbit burrows, and so were the spoil heaps below each one, of sandy soil excavated by the diggers. Stones too big to have been dug out by rabbits amongst it. He studied the ground and found footprints, and coarse hairs trodden into the soil. In the evening he ate supper with his grandparents then said he felt like a wander, walked up the track till out of sight then cut back over the shoulder of the hill to the wood, just in case his grandfather was not viewing TV but having a smoke outside.

The boy sat downwind and watched the entrances to the sett, and saw the animals emerge from their burrows. It seemed to be a colony of six adults and three large cubs. He saw no discernible difference between male and female; the cubs stayed close to one adult, presumably their mother, even if they no longer suckled from her. The animals came up out of the ground and the adults directly set off, in various directions, along

60

well-worn paths.

*   *   *

Back in Welshpool Owen bought a camouflage
jacket from the army surplus store and paid a visit
to the small town library he'd not been to in years.
He hunted along the shelves, found natural history
books, but not what he wanted. Kept browsing.
Eventually one of the two women at the desk asked
what he was looking for.

'Badgers,' Owen said, shy eyes cast down.

'You want a book about badgers? Let's see
what's available and order one, shall we?'

It came a week later—newly published, Owen
this copy's first reader—and the boy stared at the
pages and soaked up their contents like a sponge,
to his mother's amazed witness: this was something
new. Owen told his mother that badgers were close
relatives to weasels, polecats, mink, martens, sable,
otter. Omnivores, he said. 'They'll eat mice, rats,
moles, shrews, hedgehogs and rabbits,' he recited
in his voice of grit and oil. 'All kinds of insects.
Daddy-long-legs. Beetles. They'll eat frogs, toads,
snails and slugs. In the autumn there's blackberries, strawberries. Fallen apples, pears. But you
know what their favourite food is, Ma?'

'I don't.'

Owen scrunched up his face, an expression of
delighted disgust. 'Worms.'

*   *   *

He couldn't wait to get out, every weekend, and his
grandfather was glad of him, the old man's right

61

hip hurting now, bone grating bone. Inside his flesh, under his skin, you couldn't get at it. The boy's young wiry legs scampered up on to the tops, checking the sheep. His grandfather considering a quad bike. He had a catalogue and chewed through it, full of resentment. Went on the waiting list for a hip replacement operation.

Owen's grandparents gave him a little money for the chores he did; he resolved to save it all up for a pair of binoculars. Aimed to have them by Christmas.

With the summer holidays Owen was out there the whole time, a young farmhand. After an early dinner with his grandparents he went off, always up the track and skirting around to the wood, the pattern set. The badgers spent almost all night foraging for food and Owen followed them as and when he could, taking care to keep beneath the breeze: badgers lacked the good eyesight of foxes, but their sense of smell was many hundreds of times keener than humans'.

Owen watched one pad across pasture with its nose to the ground, sniffing for worms, whipping them up quickly, snapping the whole worm into its mouth. Worms were full of water, and gave badgers all the liquid they needed if they caught the number they required: two hundred in a night.

It was a damp July, and continued into August, food plentiful, and the badgers returned to the sett. The cubs were almost as large as the adults now: one chased a fox off. Owen saw them grooming each other, and sometimes sharing food brought back, members of the group jostling each other like comical rugby players, barging one another out of the way with their ample flanks. He began to perceive the pecking order, at least those at the top and bottom. One slunk around in the background; if he or she came close to shared food any one of the others would turn on it, bite it if it didn't scarper fast enough. The clearly dominant boar sprayed his scent around the sett, and elsewhere on his territory, and even on the other badgers in his colony. Owen could smell its musky aroma, milder and more pleasant than his grandfather's pungent ferrets.

Even as the hidden creatures and their habits became familiar to the boy, there remained something uncanny in the observation. He assumed it would be the same with any animal; allowed a glimpse into one of the infinite workings of God's creation.

At first the boy overdid it, stayed out too late, engrossed, crawled into the cottage in the early hours. Up unsparingly early the next morning, he was soon exhausted; some nights he stayed in, yawned, crawled to bed first. At least his grandparents had no curiosity, didn't bother him with questions: where was he going, where had he been; whether he did or didn't want to watch television with them before turning in seemed no concern of theirs.

Then one evening at dinner, 'By the way, lad,' his grandfather said. 'Been meaning to say. See a brock on your rambles, let me know.'

Brock. Another name for a badger, Owen knew. Was the old man aware of how he spent his evenings?

'Terrier man I owe a favour to,' he said.

Owen nodded. No more was said. But then a couple of nights later, as they ate in silence,

63

Grandpa suddenly spoke. 'Be no use, see.'

'What's that, Gwyn?' Grandma asked.

'Brocks,' the old man said. 'Even afore they spread TB to cattle. Do no good, do they?' He slurped half a mouthful of tea, and swallowed. 'Cull 'em. Used to gas. Trap and shoot now.'

Owen understood it was he whom Grandpa was addressing.

'Terrier man always happy to nab a badger. Sells them all over.'

Owen asked why.

'Baiting,' his grandfather said. 'Good fighters, see, stand their ground. No braver animal.'

'But baiting's against the law,' Owen said, betraying his interest.

The old man nodded. 'Been illegal hundred and fifty year. Doesn't mean it don't happen, see.'

Owen envisioned a scene of men setting their slathering dogs to fight a badger, a crowd of baying punters waving banknotes, his grandfather among them. As if reading his mind, the old man said, 'Won't catch me going to one a they.'

Owen's relief made him blink, slowly, but his grandfather continued, 'How d'you know it's not fixed?' He grinned at his food, the expression so rare it was both radiant and macabre. Shaking his head. 'Not Gwyn Ithell. Oh no. Won't catch him out.'

*   *   *

That year's lambs were weaned in August, turned onto grass on the low fields left after hay and silage crops had been taken. Owen helped his grandmother in her garden, dead-heading roses, planting the bulbs of autumn-flowering plants, cutting back the straggly growth on pansies and violas. Unlike his grandfather, who seemed to think advice freely given to the boy was unearned, Grandma passed on all she knew and more.

*   *   *

One night Owen was watching the sett. Most of the badgers had returned with food and were eating, and two of them, he realised, were in communication with each other. It was hard to tell at first in what way: they drew close then apart, snuffled and growled. It could be playful, or amorous, but gradually the volume and agitation of their movement increased, an ill-will between them became apparent. They whickered at each other, moving around now at a wary distance, as if anticipating the other's attack. And then suddenly, as if at some prearranged signal, they hurled themselves forward and tried furiously each to bite the other's tail, within a moment were wheeling around in a crazy rotating dance. They didn't stay in one place but rather ploughed across the ground like a spinning top or gyroscope, oblivious to undergrowth or anything else in their way.

The fighting badgers went away from the sett, disappearing into the darkness of the wood, but Owen could hear them, their growls giving way to awful ominous screams. Then they were back, one clearly in retreat. It scuttled into one of the entrances, closely pursued by the other. For a while Owen heard the fracas continue, deep rumbles of anger underground.

Eventually there was silence. The violence had

sucked all the boy's attention towards it. He looked around him. The other badgers were feeding, unperturbed.

*　　*　　*

Owen had long since made his last visit to the Catholic church in Welshpool, soon after his confirmation. His mother had taken him, in those early years, to gain his lifetime's membership rather than for her own sake. He became an altar boy. She stopped going, and after some time so did he. If there was holiness in the world, the boy found it more easily in the wild than inside a building, between the words of a liturgy.

Sunday mornings Owen's grandmother went to church early, down in the village. Upon her return she set her shoulder to the great meal of the week, roast beef or pork or chicken with vegetables, Yorkshire puddings, gravy, food the three of them tucked into like the starving or condemned. Afterwards they would sit stretched out on sofa and chairs, snoozing, immobilised.

This Sunday the boy's mother joined them. There were no buses; she must have been given a lift. One of the men, Owen guessed, dropped her at the bottom of the lane; would be sitting in some pub now, be back there to meet her later. The two women spoke, adult inanities, flowers looking lovely, the lack of rain.

Grandpa spoke. 'I seen a badger once, stranded by the rains, swim across the River Lugg.' He ate systematically, piling a morsel of each component—meat, potato, carrot, cabbage—on his fork, parking it in his mouth, chewing slowly.

66

'Thought the bugger'd drown, but he didn't. Fought his way across.'

'If he had've drowned,' Grandma said, 'the others would have found his body and dragged it home.'

'Is that right?' Owen's mother said. 'Did you know that, Owen?'

The boy shook his head.

'Oh yes,' the old woman insisted. 'Badgers bury their dead. Give them a proper funeral, they do.'

Her husband, to Owen's surprise, did not contradict her, though what she said was surely nonsense. The boy was coming to the conclusion that his grandmother was not particularly intelligent. Either that, he thought, or did she— and his mother too, now he considered it—make themselves out to be ignorant, in some tactical act of self-effacement?

*　　　　*　　　　*

It was odd, these parallel activities: Owen furtively watching the badgers, his taciturn grandfather bringing the species up in conversation, as if the old man had just discovered a subject he felt able or desired to talk about. Was he toying with his grandson, the way he kept raising the subject up from underground?

Owen's observation becoming more methodical, he'd got his mother to bring a notebook with her. 'Miss you, my lovely,' she told him when she left. 'Come back when school starts. Look after your mum.'

There was only a fortnight left, but he began to record what he saw. In daylight he found the remains of a hedgehog, all gone but the spines; a rabbit skinned inside out. While one or more members of the badger colony took two nights to devour a wasps' nest: on the first night they took most of the grubs, but returned to finish off the rest and as many adult wasps as they could, presumably unaffected by the insects' stings.

Then one night Owen watched one badger mount another, and though it chewed the other's neck hair he realised this was not a fight, exactly. A boar copulating with a sow. He'd seen other animals mate, a process usually over in seconds. This pair of badgers remained coupled for an hour; he wondered whether humans could possibly take that long.

*   *   *

Owen returned to his mother and school in Welshpool at the beginning of September. His grandfather said nothing, but it was clear he was pained to see the boy go. There was talk of getting someone else up to help with the sheep, or cutting down on their number. In the evenings his mother drank slowly, steadily, to a good-natured slump.

It wasn't until half-term, at the end of October—when by chance his grandfather was in Shrewsbury for his hip operation—that Owen went back. The ewes had been dipped, the wool around their tails clipped, and they had been tupped by the ram; wether lambs had been sold. Another farmer came along the track, over the top from Priestweston, to help out. Owen understood that since he'd gone his grandmother had been tramping that long winding hill.

68

On his second day the boy found time in the afternoon to visit the badgers' sett. There was a light drizzle of rain on the green hills. When he saw the tyre marks on the wet grass, a Land Rover driven across his grandfather's field, up to the fence before the trees, Owen ignored them. You saw all the evidence you needed, but you wouldn't allow yourself to draw a conclusion.

In the wood, rain collected in the canopy of the trees and fell to earth in thin streams, or tiny puddles spilled from where they'd collected on leaves until overbalancing.

Owen knew by now of the world of terrier men: assisting lurchers after hares or deer; working their dogs against foxes, rabbits and rats. When a sett was dug, a badger would be baited by a young terrier—restrained or injured so that it didn't kill the dog—or it might be put into a sack alive and taken to a secret pit, where men collected and cash was wagered. The boy knew that illegal activities were interrelated: not just badger but dog fighting, cock fighting, the selling of protected birds. So that he understood what it was he found.

It looked like the sett had been bombed. A scene from a First World War battlefield, trenches gouged by artillery. This destruction, though, had been wrought by hand, by men with pickaxes and shovels, and their dogs. The badgers' tunnels in all their impressive excavation were laid bare. Owen could see the cul-de-sacs, winding corridors, spacious lairs, all exposed, and ruinous. He saw that the colony was destroyed. His badgers were almost certainly all dead. He turned and walked out of the wood, and back towards the cottage, perplexed with grief.

69

FINGERS

Dr Macintyre referred me. I never asked her to. You know that, I suppose. I'll tell you the truth: I wouldn't touch drugs as such. The stuff I've took is all prescription, they was in the bathroom cabinet. Drink I give up when I had kids. Never missed it.

Doctor reckons I don't need them. She may be right, all I need to do is talk. Says I need to see you before she'll do me any more. I don't mind talking, never have.

I worry. What bothers me is he'll do something bad. I feel sick when I think what he might do. But what can be done about it? You tell me. I'd like to know. What can anyone do if a person makes up their mind?

You need to remember the good times. We met in 1987. There were this pub, the Red Lion, me mates and me used to go to for a change. A Friday night. I'd notice him, this bloke sat on his own in a corner. Spoke to no one. Dressed smart. Only ever wore a white shirt but it were fresh ironed. Black trousers pressed, black shoes shining. His hair wet still from a shower. A man with no sense of fashion but who took pride in his appearance.

On the table in front of him a pint of slow beer, tobacco pouch, packet of green Rizlas, yellow box of Swan Vesta matches, the red-tipped ones. Never had nothing to read or occupy his self, apart from the matches, which he played between his fingers. That's when you noticed his hard-worked hands.

He'd placed himself in the corner, with a view of the whole bar, but he give the impression he had no interest in anyone. See a young bloke like that once in a while, ignoring everyone. Like he's being rude on purpose to a roomful of strangers, waiting until someone better turns up.

Once or twice our eyes met, for one second our glances collided, but then he'd look past me, like I were in the way of something more interesting— the spirit bottles up behind the bar, or the lighting fixtures on the ceiling. The bloke hadn't even registered my presence.

I can't remember how did I get to talk to him? Might have been we met when he come to the bar. A word about the weather, the way you do. Or the music on the jukebox. The landlord were ten year older than his clientele and the day he stopped listening to new music were the day he reckoned everyone else should: the pub were one of few still had a jukebox, only every song on it were fifteen year old.

Yes, I remember now, short conversations while he were putting his money in, selecting a disc. Got as far as knowing each other's name. 'Mel.' 'Owen.' Awkward. He made you feel like you was intruding, interrupting some important thought he were sharing with his self.

I didn't even know, while I did it, why I were persisting. He give me no encouragement. It were like this secret mission I demanded of myself, whenever our gang stopped by the Red Lion. I kept an eye open, made our paths meet. Words was exchanged.

'All right?'

A nod from him, 'Not bad,' and that were that. Mission accomplished. I'd persuade the girls to drop in early of a Friday evening, whatever else we

71

was doing later. Then one of them realises what I'm up to, they mocked me rotten.

'The weirdo in the corner?' says Janice.

'Mr Lonely?' says another. 'You, Mel Broughton?'

True, it weren't like there were no shortage of men. I never had to work hard, never had to work at all, and most of the men was no good. I were nothing neither. Had no family but a brother in Dudley. I were twenty-two, worked in an egg-sorting factory. Half the gang were mothers, tiddlers back home with Grandma while we girls went on the razz. We'd all wagged it through school. If we wasn't pretty, we was free. Let ourselves be blown about. Bints like me, and young mothers who hated the men what treated them like dirt.

I knew I wanted different, only I never knew what.

*　　　*　　　*

It were hopeless. I'd say a word to him, he'd mumble some reply, I'd talk a lot of nonsense and tootle back to me teasing mates.

I nearly give up, then I go there on me own. There he were, rolling his self a Golden Virginia fake at his table in the corner. What the heck's I doing here, I thought, as I stood at the bar. To hell with him. I'll have this half of cider, I'll be off, I'll not be here again. Without the girls I must have stood out, felt even more foolish than with them. Like everyone in that bar knows why I'm there, sniggering behind their drinks. Then I realised someone were standing beside me. I turned. It were him. He were only an inch or two taller than me.

'You weren't here last week,' he says, so blank you couldn't tell whether he were saying how disappointed he was or telling me off or just letting me know how brilliant was his powers of observation.

'Gerrout,' I says. 'You must have missed me,' I says, lightly, like how funny, what a joke that were.

He looks at me, Owen does. I look at him, and for the first time he holds my gaze. 'Yes, I did,' he says.

*   *   *

His hands was rough, a gardener's hands, I liked the feel of them. They had scars. One was a bite off a ferret, so he said. Another he says, 'I cut myself shaving.' Owen learned how to make me laugh. Soil in his fingers like fingerprints, not with ink but earth. And he had home-made tattoos, little ones, across his knuckles. Letters and symbols: a cross, a yin and yang. I says I could tell him and his mates was pissed when they did them.

He says, 'I did them myself.'

*   *   *

Owen were self-employed, he tended rich people's gardens out in the suburbs. That was why he were spruced up on a Friday night: he had that look of a man relieved to change out of dirty working clothes and dress up, but also, although he'd been in Birmingham ten year near enough, he were still a country boy. He had that reserve. Did things

73

deliberately. Took his time. There were something old-fashioned about him.

I told Owen that, that he were spruce. He called it a true compliment, being as it is the name of a conical evergreen tree, useful for timber and paper pulp, and the flavouring of beer.

*   *   *

Let me come along to watch him work. He were slight but made of wire, stronger than you'd think—he'd work for hours without a break. Takes confidence to work on your own. Every decision you make has to be made alone. You might not have thought such a quiet man would have it. He cut some old bush right back, I thought he'd killed it, but three month later, in the spring, it blossomed in this spray of vivid yellow. He pruned a knobbly apple tree with them rough hands with such precision, so delicate, it were like he were scared one wrong snip might sever an artery, sap come spurting out the wound.

In the garden of a large house off Sutton Park Owen planted an empty bed with one after another identical-looking, tiny green plants. Took me back there in July. You couldn't believe what had grown in the blank space of brown soil: flowers of all shades of every colour, different sizes and shapes. The most beautiful thing you ever saw. A painting made of petals. It hadn't never occurred to me how a person creates such a sight, but someone had, this quiet man. He planted something in me too.

*   *   *

He were hard work, were Owen Ithell, but once he relented he give his self to me without holding nothing back. That were when I realised I'd been waiting to do the same.

* * *

He got the thing for flowers from his grandma, Owen says, and the need for solitude from his Welsh grandad. He told me all about the two of them, like they was his family, brought him up, I were surprised when he says he spent odd weeks or months with them.

I know things is meant to skip a generation, I says, but what about your parents?

Owen told me he didn't know whether his father was dead or alive and he didn't care. No brothers or sisters. His mother lived east, over King's Lynn way. He'd drive there to make sure she were all right, slip her some cash, drive back. Spoke of her like she were his responsibility. After his father had gone for good he went home from his grandparents' place and spent the rest of his childhood looking after his mother. Taught his self to cook and clean.

I said once it were funny he were in Birmingham, the big city, between Wales where his heart was and his mother over in the Wash, and he said it weren't funny at all, just an unfortunate coincidence and that was all there was to it.

* * *

Strange thing it were, watching my friends change their minds about Owen. He were reticent, polite

75

to them. Janice says, in her mocking voice, 'He worships the ground you walk on,' like how sad were that, and got a lot of laughs. 'Waits on you hand and foot.' They saw how he were with me, began to think there might be some use in it. He affected a lot of us, not just me. Sounds silly, but a year after we got together I looked around one night, half me mates were with decent blokes.

*   *   *

He come gradually out of his self when it were just the two of us. Like it were a surprise to him that he could trust me. We laughed a lot in bed. He'd pretend to be other people. Pretended we was animals. Going to bed were an excuse to fool around. Mess about in there like kids we did.

*   *   *

He'd been an altar boy for a while, Owen had. Said how much he liked it, said it were somewhere to go. Mass on Sundays, helping out at weddings and funerals. An empty church. He loved being in there on his own. Priest were a nervous man, Owen says, needed a smoke before taking a service: people going in the front of the church, Father were out having a gasper round the back. Owen told me you don't think you're listening, you don't think you're taking it in, but then you catch the smell of incense or a snatch of a hymn and it all come back. It's all in there.

*   *   *

We had our wedding in a barn on this hill in Wales. Owen organised it, drove over, asked the farmer what owned the land if we could borrow it for the day. Hired two coaches to take the gang over. We and a few mates went the day before and got this old barn decked out with balloons and streamers like Christmas. His mother come, my brother too. Owen's grandad come up from his bungalow down below. I were expecting a giant, there were this miserable old widower hobbling about on two sticks, moaning about being dragged up on to the tops. He give Owen a bag of old tools, though—pliers, a kindling axe, a knife—and Owen were well chuffed.

A great party. We had music—generator and decks, big speakers—and dancing. Plenty of pills and drink. The little barn were full of our mates, townies every one apart from Owen, there in the middle of nowhere, it were what you'd call odd. But it worked. I'll tell the kids about that.

*   *   *

Sara were born in 1990. Can't imagine there were ever a prouder father. Nor better husband, let me say. Turn his hand to anything. Never claimed there's a job a man shouldn't do: he'd stay up late, ironing all of our clothes, ready for the morning. Polished shoes, laid them out in their pairs, in a row in the hallway of the flat. Then he'd sit in the corner of the living room, smoke his last fake of the day, wonder how his life were turning out so good.

When she were a toddler, Sara wouldn't let me help her walk. She'd stumble, little mite, she'd

77

bash herself, but push me away. If Owen were there, though, she'd hold on to one of his rough tattooed fingers, grasp it tight in her tiny hand. He'd walk behind her, bent right over, guide her along. The look on Sara's face: happy, proud.

Sara seemed to have inherited self-confidence from each of us, Owen's with the natural world and mine with people. We couldn't see our weaknesses in her, like it were a miracle. Maybe they would have emerged in time. Or maybe not. You just don't know.

After Sara we had Josh, who were just like his father. Born shy, my little prince. Hardly look his own mum in the eye, never mind other people. Deliberate like his dad. Hated to be rushed into anything. We moved from the flat to the house, with its own garden, a tip what Owen transformed into a jungle playground.

*   *   *

Soon as Sara were born I says to Owen we have to visit his mother. Owen cleaned out his car the night before, put his tools in the lock-up garage; I made sandwiches and put them in the fridge. We got up early in the morning and drove east. Liz lived in a block of flats on the outskirts of King's Lynn. We took her out for the day, a picnic up around the coast.

Liz were all made up and waiting. She give us a big hug that smelled of sandalwood and Polo mints. She were in her mid-fifties, worked in a shop. She wore hippyish clothes, though when you looked closer often there were just one paisley-pattern blouse or orange Indian trousers. The rest were normal high-street stuff had somehow adapted itself to her. She looked like a funky grandma, a little glamorous, a little doolally. After that we did it regular, three, four times a year. It's spectacular over there, them great flat beaches and marshes and dunes, that high wide sky; though she lived so close it were as much a novelty for Liz as it were for us Brum dwellers.

She were great with the kids, nuzzled and nudged them, spoke baby language like she'd been relearning it at evening class, just for their visits. As they grew she'd sit in the back of the car between Sara and Josh, ask them questions, then lean back with a smile on her face and let them natter at her from either side.

After our picnic Owen would wander off with Sara. He'd found a telescope in some charity shop, must have been about the only thing he ever bought for his self, and he'd keep one eye on Sara and watch birds with the other. Thousands of them on mudflats at Snettisham, pushed by high tides into the lagoons. Harriers flying low over reed beds at Titchwell Marsh.

While I fed Josh, Liz and I would talk. She told me how it had been with Owen's dad, how hard she'd tried to cling on to him.

'Nothing like Owen,' was her words. You couldn't quite tell which were the one she were most fond of. There was other men. One brung her to King's Lynn, then drifted off and left her there.

Once or twice it were mizzly weather and we'd mooch about the town, more often it were glorious. One spring visit, Sara were six, end of March, we braved a trip to Holkham Bay. With the tide out all you can see is sand. Pine trees behind.

Take you hours to walk from one side to the other. Can't be a finer beach in the whole world, not that I've been. There were no wind that day, the sky was nothing but blue stretched over us.

She were sweet-natured like her son, were Liz. Owen always packed a bottle of white wine. I didn't drink none, and the most he supped were one can of beer. Liz worked her way through the bottle, getting slightly more barmy, till she'd fall asleep on the rug. She were lovely with the children and they was fond of her, but you knew you wouldn't leave them with her. She weren't equipped to take care of people. I told myself to talk to Owen about getting her over to live with us.

Josh were snoozing on one side of me, my mother-in-law on the other. I thought, This is what a family can be like. I weren't looking for a mother, but Owen had given me one. I could see Owen and Sara in the distance, the air were shimmering the way it does on a beach. They walked back across the sand, hand in hand. We'd just discovered I were pregnant with our third child. I thought, People come together, the born and the unborn, it's a sort of survival unit. One scar, then another, begins to heal.

We was lulled. We never considered things could blast apart.

*   *   *

There were life before the accident, and life after. They are two different lives.

I tried not to blame Owen. I tried to look after Josh. I tried to think about the child I were carrying.

80

I couldn't get why she were sitting in the front. He were driving her home from her dance class. Why weren't she in the back? I tried not to blame him. You go numb. You breathe deep, you think, I'll wait for it to pass over me. Owen did three things. First he were numb too. Then he tried to tough it out. Then he fell apart. I said people don't change, but Owen did. A bitterness appeared what hadn't been there before. Both the loss and his part in it. The falling apart that's not what I blame him for.

*   *   *

It were his right hand he lost, his dominant hand, the one he used to operate a tool, to write his name, to shake hands with.

He hated people staring at the hook. People thought he were cool with it cos Owen were the first to mention it, wave it around, make a joke. That were an act. They didn't know him like I did. He says to me, 'I wish we was living after World War One, Mel, when there was loads of blokes had amputations. It were a common sight. No one thought nothing about it.' A mixture of guilt and rage were in him but he tried to hide it, it were like a toxic cocktail in his gut.

*   *   *

There was two court cases, one after the other, on top of everything else. It's the last thing you want after what happened, whether you're in the dock or on the other side, and Owen had to do both.

81

*   *   *

We'd lost Sara then I had Holly. Owen tried to help, he wanted to do like we'd done it before. But you can't scoop up a baby with a split hook. Owen couldn't hardly prepare her bottle, never mind hold her in the bath, or change her nappy. You could see the frustration building in him.

*   *   *

He wanted sex. He needed to be reassured. I couldn't do it. When he took his hook off, I couldn't stand to be touched by that stump. He says we have to find new positions, that's all, we have to adapt. I told him to keep away from me. I didn't want to hurt him. It were like Sara's death right there in front of me.

*   *   *

Then the pain in his hand what weren't there started. He never drank bad till then. It were like someone had given him this magical potion: Owen drank and the pain were drowned, for the hours of oblivion.

He kept pulling his self together, says, 'I'm all right now, I'll not let go again.' He couldn't help it, you could see the pain and the thirst build up. Like his fingers on the hand that were left was trembling to get round a bottle. He'd slump on the settee, a man whose heart had stopped. Still stagger up in the morning, make his self presentable. But then he'd slip out the back door and be gone on a bender, two or three days at a time, return like a dog, stinking of mud and stale liquor.

I were left to look after the kids. It were like I were watching two people I used to know. We was holding on and hitting out. Shifting apart. I wanted to help him but I couldn't. What could I do? No one told me. Does anybody know? I were so mardy with Owen, so mean. Never hit no one before. I'm not proud of it, especially what Josh saw, don't nobody think I am.

*   *   *

Owen tried dope, it only made him feel the pain more keenly. The doctor at the rehabilitation centre prescribed drugs for him. You know about the amitriptyline. They only give him side effects. Don't give me none. You can't tell the doctor I've not taken this serious. You can't say I haven't talked.

Nothing worked for Owen like alcohol. The cheapest booze he could get his hands on, drank till he couldn't feel.

We kept seeing Liz, she come to stay with us. She couldn't say nothing to him.

*   *   *

We got used to not having money, but the thing people don't realise about poverty is that it can always get worse. He got a few months sickness benefit but not disability living allowance—you need to lose a leg for that, he'd say. He were self-employed. After the accident he couldn't work. Said he could still use the tools with his hook, but he had no way to get with all his kit to the houses.

83

Refused to drive. I says to him, Go for a job with the council. Parks Department. It weren't no use. Claimed he couldn't work for no one else, have some gaffer tell him what to do. Like he weren't working for them blasted rich folk whose flower beds he tickled and lawns he mowed. There was one or two close by he could walk or bike to, spade strapped to the crossbar. Reckon they liked having a one-armed gardener. Novelty value.

*   *   *

A brown mongrel dog run across the road. Chasing something, he said. No one else saw it, this hound of hell.

*   *   *

I never wanted another man. Never wanted no one else but him. But you don't know what lonely is till you're sharing your house with a ghost, disappearing, and when he reappears all you do is fight. Johnny was his friend more than mine, he come round to see Owen. 'He's out,' I says. 'Don't know where. You're welcome to wait. Kettle's on.'

'You all right?' he asks, and it all come out. I never planned it. Don't think I did. None of it was what I wanted.

Owen had to leave. I thought that might shake him back together. Then it all got legal, and took on a life of its own. I weren't trying to do nothing but look after Josh and Holly. Probably messed that up too but you tell me what else I should have done.

*   *   *

He were homeless for a while. Moved into a slummy flat in an old high-rise. Refused to discuss a divorce. When he come to pick the children up I could smell the drink on his breath but he were smart. Josh told me his father had one other white shirt and pair of black trousers hung up just like the ones he were wearing. His wardrobe. Josh and Holly stayed the night there once. When they woke up in the morning all their clothes was washed and ironed, folded on the table beside their dad's.

Physically Owen changed. Filled out. The sugar in the alcohol. His clothes didn't hang off his wiry frame the way they had. His tough tanned gardener's face took on another colour, the ruddiness of a drinker, which made him look not old, exactly, but more, I know it's stupid, wiser. Alcohol give his face that look of wisdom more than suffering. I was the one marked sad, not him, and I weren't the one driving the car. They say sorrow steals your looks quicker than time itself. Heads no longer turn. But I don't dwell on me.

The children was always confused after they'd seen him. Josh all silent, moody, rude to Johnny and angry with me like it were my idea for his dad to be broken. I had to put a stop to it, it weren't good for no one. Everyone agreed. May have been underhand, the way we done it, but I were trying to get things stable.

Owen's complied with all the court orders. I've took care not to embarrass him. I don't talk to old friends, or tell Liz. Never said nothing to the school. If he's humiliated it's not by me.

85

Even now he phones. Isn't meant to but he does. Now Johnny's not around I let him talk. You wouldn't believe it was that shy, proud man he used to be. Begging me to get back together, to bring the children round, to let him see them. What can I say? I know I can't say yes. Then he goes all silent. 'You still there?' I says. No reply, but you can sense him. Brooding. Sobbing to his self, his hand over the mouthpiece.

Me just as bad at the other end, after I've put down the phone.

I don't see what he's got left. He's got nothing, has he? I'm worried sick he might do something bad. Something terrible. It makes me feel sick in my stomach.

Truth is I don't know if I want him to or not.

SNOW

It was one of the last long, cold winters. First the rain, on the edge of frozen, cutting into buildings, clothes, skin. In the high exposed places the wind collected the rain, whirled it around and hurled it, endless frozen arrowheads of water, flying in horizontally. It hit the old man's face in stabs of pain. It drove into the last of the stone walls criss-crossing the hillside: at night the water, turning to ice, expanded; a section of wall would explode in a distant unheard rumble.

*   *   *

Owen had come out at Christmas. Some man, with young children of his own, had invited his mother, Owen a complication who anyhow had no wish to get to know another man's brood. He was fifteen now. 'I'll go to the hill,' he said.

A memorable visit, it was when he learned to swing an axe. Mild days at the end of December Owen hitched a trailer to his grandfather's tractor and the two of them scoured the locale for fallen trees. For other men it was a summer job, but Gwyn Ithell had his own ideas. The old man chainsawed trunks and thick branches into logs, which Owen piled in the trailer; the boy drove back to the farmstead, emptied the logs into a pile by the woodshed—green wood to one side—returned. His grandfather wore neither goggles nor earmuffs. The angry whine of the power saw assailed him; occasional sharp chips flew at his face, drawing blood, like shaving nicks; clothes, hair, eyebrows became coated in sawdust.

When the pile by the shed was a pyramid the height of a man they progressed to the second half of the operation. For an afternoon hour in the last of the pale sun the old man swung the axe. Owen lay the chunks of wood on top of one another in the shed, as instructed; his grandfather demanding the wedges were laid neatly.

'I'm a dry-wood-waller,' Owen whispered to himself. As much as he could he studied his grandfather. The old man took a second to appraise each log as he placed it on the great wooden block, judging its knot and grain. When he swung the axe he did it slowly, with little seeming effort: he gripped the end of the handle with his right hand, with his left grasped the shaft up by the axe head and lifted it up and over his shoulder. Then he offered the axe head gently up into the air, as it rose letting his left hand slide down the shaft until it met his right hand at the end of the handle. The axe head was now directly above his grandfather's head, the shaft vertical, and for a fraction of a second it seemed to hover there, gathering latent energy, before beginning its easy descent.

What was hard to see was how fast the axe head fell, the sharpened edge of five pounds of forged steel slamming into the log along a line of grain, such was the functional, perfunctory grace of the action. Most often the log was split with one blow. Sometimes it took more, depending upon the species of tree.

When Grandma called Grandpa in to take a telephone call from a dealer, Owen tried the axe himself. It took all his strength to lift and wield, and by the time it fell onto the log there was barely enough momentum in the swing to make a mark. He became quickly furious, throwing himself into the action, but there was no improvement in its effect. He knew he was fighting against the axe and what he had to do was to collaborate with the tool, to work with it.

So Owen experimented, feeling his way into each part of the choreography—the legs-apart stance, the lift of the axe, the fall. His grandfather could not be still on the phone: he always gripped the receiver as if by its throat, like an animal he mistrusted, and spoke so tersely that whoever was on the other end must put their receiver down wondering what it was they'd done to old man Ithell that so angered him. But he remained in the cottage.

Grandma peered into the dark, as if trying to see that sound: of wood cracking. 'Leave him,' the old man said. The light had gone by the time Owen came inside. The boy was beaming.

*   *   *

The next afternoon Owen split the logs, his grandfather content to let him, to be the one to pick up the chunks and fill the shed. Owen had the knack, rode the paradox—did he generate or harness this effortless power?—and now he got to know the different kinds of wood. Ash split clean and easy. Beech past a certain age was obdurate. Oak, too, was tough: you had to choose the right grain to attack, and then be patient, confident of your choice—make little impression with the first

89

two or three blows, have to work the axe head back out of the log each time and reset it on the block, yet feel the log break apart under the fourth.

The old man rolled a cigarette. 'You should have seen the elm I got after the disease,' he said. 'Went over and took it from the Powis Castle estates over there. Tough? You couldn't bloody split it with an axe.' He coughed and spat a gob of phlegm. 'Had to *saw* the damn logs, into cubes.'

Green wood they stacked against the outside wall of the shed, on its sheltered side, under the eave, for use in two or three years' time. Laid down like wine. When the pyramid was gone, Owen saw his grandfather's satisfaction. 'See us through,' he said. Fuel for the Rayburn and the sitting-room fireplace, to last the winter. Owen returned to Welshpool.

*　　　*　　　*

After the rain, the air froze, the earth solidified, and still the wind blew, finding gaps around windows, doors, through the thick stone walls of the cottage. Owen's grandparents saw each other's breaths condense as soon as they went up the stairs.

The old man's left hip was hurting. He expressed no gratitude to the surgeon who'd performed the first operation, replacing his right hip. 'Don't work as good as the old one,' was all he said; did not appreciate the pain gone. And now the other one.

It was Grandma who rang Welshpool, before the February half-term. 'He could do with some help,' she told her daughter-in-law. 'He'll not ask for it himself.'

*   *   *

The day Owen arrived the temperature seemed to fluctuate: he could not, with the use of his human senses, tell whether it was rising or falling, it seemed to be doing both, somehow. Up on the hill it was cold to Owen's bones but the sun warmed what it reached, weakly. Then the ground felt soft, the frozen earth apparently attempting to thaw, except that his nose and ears stung, the air prickly and brittle.

What happened the next day did so in silence: snow fell thickly from daybreak to sunset. They watched it from indoors. The following morning Owen rose early and went out with the dogs. The sky was blue, the land white, the snow hard, encrusted. He walked across it, around the shoulder of the hill, and the snow was like a powder shaken over the ground to reveal the footprints of those who'd crossed it, all the animals who did not hibernate but persevered through the cold. The dogs scurried this way and that, noses to the ground, and Owen could see what they had always been able to smell. A badger had come up from below, a hare sprung across the field, a fox come skulking after what it could scavenge. He found spots of blood. A rabbit, perhaps.

It struck Owen that he'd heard foxes in the night. Incorporated the sounds into his dreams. Whether or not he'd ever actually woken it was impossible now to say. Up the hill had come a fox dog's bark, dry and staccato, and the yowling of a vixen, their hot rut a part of this cold season.

*   *   *

Owen drove the tractor across the snow to feed the sheep sugar beet, sheep nuts, hay. Their clamour in time of hunger was overwhelming: a hundred ewes, Owen thought, mimicking chainsaws. By this time of year they'd been brought down off the tops, to the less exposed pastures around the cottage. In addition his grandfather had been cutting back his liabilities: subletting the furthest fields to a young farmer at White Grit, reducing the count to a couple of hundred ewes. 'Not enough to make money,' as he said. Their time on the hill was running down. Owen's grandmother had put in train the move to an almshouse bungalow down in the valley, though she knew her husband wanted no part of the arrangement; preferred all talk of it to take place out of earshot.

*   *   *

The skies were dark, purple-black, but it was just too cold to snow again. A low sun forced its way between the heavy clouds, which loped sullenly on over the hills.

'One missing,' the old man said. 'Count them for me, boy.' He'd never sought Owen's second opinion before. The boy confirmed the number: sixty-four.

'We'll take these ones in,' Grandpa decided. 'Then you can come back to look for it.'

With the help of the dogs they drove the ewes, heavily pregnant now, into the large barn. It was almost time to scan them, see how many each carried, prepare to sort them into lambing groups.

Owen walked back around the flank of the hill to where the small flock had been, the first of the fields between the badger copse and Malt House Farm, and followed the perimeter of the field for places the ewe could have escaped. One section of wall had lost its upper stones; a stretch of fence had sagged a little. Shreds of wool had snagged along it, no doubt where sheep had scratched themselves. She could have clambered over. Would hunger drive a single ewe to separate herself from her flock? Owen wasn't sure. Perhaps pregnancy made them erratic, or more daring. Owen traipsed haphazardly, in approximate, ever-widening circles beyond the field, his attention wandering.

He heard a piercing whistle overhead and looked up. A pair of buzzards, wheeling in the blue sky. The beak and claws, their calm killer's eyes alert to any prey that might emerge from hiding: rabbits, rodents, robbed of cover, snow a bare white betrayal. The sound the birds made seemed one of glee.

The whine of the tractor grinding up the track to the other flocks brought Owen's attention back to the search. 'Where are you, sheep?' he yelled.

*   *   *

Owen returned to the cottage for lunch, admitted the failure of his mission. He assumed the incident was over, a loss to be absorbed. When they'd eaten, to his surprise his grandfather said, 'I'll join you.'

The old man began by recounting the ewes in the barn: sixty-four still. Then he whistled the dogs

93

to him, and they trekked back to the emptied field. Meg was limping, Owen noted, as if in imitation of her master. Getting on now herself. Pip would be the last of the mothers and daughters of their line to work these hills with Gwyn Ithell, would end her days in domestic tedium, twitching in her sleep, dreaming of the wild running up above.

Grandpa gave his unintelligible instruction and the dogs took off. Pip bounding over the broken wall, Meg stumbling after.

'Damn sheep's going to be camouflaged by the snow,' Owen suggested.

'Hear the bugger bleating fore you ever see it, won't you,' his grandfather told him. They walked rapidly up one side of the cut in the next cwm, down the other, then further over the hill again, the old man never stopping to think or plan. Ordering Owen to walk thirty yards across from him, commanding the dogs to sniff out some other area. As if there was an obvious way to proceed in such a search, a definitive formula, though Owen could not find its logic.

*   *   *

They came home at dusk. 'Check them sheep in the barn, would you?' Grandpa asked Grandma. 'Should be sixty-five. We can only figure sixty-four.' Owen went with her. Switched on the electric light, bare bulbs hung on wire strung from one beam to another. Yellow, buttery light. A half-hearted murmur of bleating. His grandmother walked into the pens, where the pregnant ewes milled waist-high. Unable to escape this intruder in their midst, they affected to ignore her. She confirmed the count.

*   *   *

When Owen came to breakfast he found his grandfather at the table, staring into a gloomy corner of the room. The grey and scratched, heavy plastic Ever Ready torch beside his mug of tea.

Grandma dolloped ladlefuls of porridge into the bowl in front of Owen. 'Been out all night,' she said to her grandson. 'I told him, Will there not be enough sleepless nights for you with the lambing?' She banged the lid back on the pan. 'You can't tell him.'

'Did you find her?' Owen asked.

The old man gazed at the wall. He shook his head. 'Not yet,' he said.

*   *   *

Owen fed the sheep, first those on the hill, the tractor's great wheels carving through the snow. No more snow had fallen in the night, everything icing up. He broke up the bales of hay and scattered it for the frantic ewes. They seemed less important to him this morning, somehow: mere numberless beasts, while their lost sister was taking on a singular identity, a significance. When he fed those in the barn he counted them yet again. Each recount was more absurd than the one before— they could hardly have kept on getting it wrong— yet each one had a little more of a peculiar kind of hope: that there was something magical in the ewe's disappearance. Perhaps it wasn't the sheep that had been misplaced but a number itself, and

95

this number was what he would refind in the counting. Not this time, though. Sixty-four once more.

*   *   *

Owen walked out to look for his grandfather, looking for the sheep. His feet crunched on the frozen snow. Climbing halfway up Corndon, he turned, scanned what he could see of the crooked hills around him. No sign of man or dogs. He raised his gaze. The day was extraordinarily cold and clear: he could see across to Cader Idris, that great throne of its summit. The morning had been still, but as he stood there Owen could feel that change was coming. It was less cold than it had been an hour or two before, and the crystal air was subtly agitated, as if across the visible landscape the giant Cader had woken after a night on the mountain and shaken out his blanket, and the disturbance of air rippled eastward. Owen lowered his gaze and was startled to register russet on white: some twenty, twenty-five yards away a fox was sitting unperturbed, staring coolly back at him with its amber eyes.

*   *   *

At lunch, Grandpa shook his head. 'Can't figure it,' he said, speaking with his mouth full of stew. 'If it's trapped, why's it not bleating?' He swallowed, contained a burp in his throat. 'Would someone steal it? Isn't worth it, see.' He shrugged. 'Maybe out there, but the dogs haven't found her. Maybe dead, but it's not like sheep go off to die, like.

She'd have laid down where she stood. Can't figure it, can I.'

The puzzle had rattled around his head while walking. He was baffled. 'I'll count 'em in the barn again.'

You're wrong, Owen thought. That's the only explanation. There never were sixty-five. It was always sixty-four. If you knew them individually, or numbered their ears, or wrote down how many were in each parcel or flock we'd not be trapped in this error, with no way out.

*　　*　　*

Grandma joined them in the afternoon, and the three of them went up the track past the forestry plantation and came back around the side of Corndon, spread out between the stones and the heather, the dogs scampering across the white crust then sinking, and breasting through soft snow like aquatic mammals, whiskery snouts showing. The old man was limping badly, his face contorting with pain whenever his leg jarred.

They dropped down to the lane between their hill and Roundton, snow packed down by tractors, the road surface a slab of ice now, a frozen river, the snowplough not yet reached the back roads out here. Grandpa asked at Woodgate Farm; Brithdir. A sheep could escape not through intention but by accident, lose its orientation instantly, skittle along bleating in any old direction. Then it would attach itself to any flock it came across. Such had been known. But the folk the old man consulted had noticed nothing.

'Wolves come back, is it?' Morgan said, his

mouth, barely half-filled with teeth, cracking open in a sly grin. 'Heard tell of a panther other side of Stiperstones. Come a-roaming, is it?'

Grandpa walked down to The Graig lips tight with anger at being mocked by his neighbour. The trio clambered up through the steep wood where the badger sett had been. When they emerged from the shelter of the trees back into open pasture the wind surprised them, and new snow falling too, tiny hard flakes of it swirling around like grains of salt on a shaken planet.

They fanned out to move up the vale to the abandoned cottage, losing sight of each other intermittently in the mounting blizzard, calling, their voices thrown deceptively around. Back on the track below the plantation the old man told his wife to go home, by way of Lan Fawr, then took Owen to the disused quarry, with its mini slag heaps of granite and lunar indentations and depressions in the ground. All this they'd covered before.

Owen gave up looking for any dumb ewe. The boy was shivering and miserable, shrinking inside his inadequate clothing, intent upon his own survival as the snow drifted against the banks. He kept close to his grandfather, and even the dogs did likewise now. The old man was so tired he fell asleep as he walked; stumbled awake. It was almost dark when they got back to the cottage.

*　　　*　　　*

Owen's grandfather was in bed before the other two that night. 'Let this be an end to it,' Grandma said. But in the morning he told Owen to take his grandmother and the dogs, it was time to bring the rest of the sheep in. Yes, Owen thought. It was time yesterday, should have done it then.

Grandma tried to halt her husband, laid her hand on his arm as he reached the door. He took her hand by the wrist and firmly lifted it away. 'I'll not lose this one, see,' he told her. 'I'm their shepherd, aren't I?'

* * *

No snow was falling but the sky was grey with threat looming. There were two separate flocks needed bringing in. The first came down the track entire, fast, from sheltered pasture, but the other was in a south-west-facing field that looked like the blizzard, with planning and intention, had gyred and swirled and funnelled snow here, piling it in great drifts against the bank on one side. The sheep had huddled against the bank as if it would give them shelter even as the snow mounted upon them. Owen looked upon the scene, and the creatures' stupidity dismayed him. It was neither intelligence nor habit that saved them, he was sure, but luck: there was an overhang to a good stretch of the bank, and the wind-blown snow had sculpted a cave into which the animals pressed, their body heat in such proximity keeping them alive. Owen and his grandmother dug an exit tunnel with shovels and sent Meg in: she snapped around their legs; one after another the ewes barged noisily into the open.

Grandma walked in front, the dogs brought the flock downhill, Owen idled the tractor along behind. He tried to work out why his grandfather was devoting so much time and attention to one lost ewe. The old man seemed to have taken it as a challenge out of all proportion to the value of the animal. A challenge thrown down by what, or whom? Did he know it was his last winter here?

It seemed to Owen that in his grandfather's opinion human beings were no different to any other living thing. Ate, like other animals, what grew from the earth. Like stunted trees the wind had shaped the old man. He was weathered by the sun and the rain and hemmed in by limitations: heard less than his dogs, smelled a fraction of what badgers did, saw less than a buzzard overhead.

We pass through the world, the boy thought, how much of it teems around us, outside our senses, beyond us?

*   *   *

They steered the last ewes into barn, sheds, pens. The sky was clearing, the threat of further snow or hail today dissipating. The dogs sat panting by the back porch, steam rising from their wet hair. 'Look,' said Grandma. 'Here he is, by God.'

Owen looked up and saw his grandfather limping awkwardly across the near pasture towards them. Beside him was a sheep, tied around the neck with a length or two of orange baler twine. He wasn't tugging the creature along but walking at its pace, as if it were a bemused old aunt who'd lost her bearings and wandered and was being brought home.

'I'll get her some food,' Grandma said.

The three of them watched the ewe eat with a steady greed as sheep always do, their hunger

100

patient, endless.

'Well?' Grandma said. 'Will you tell us, Gwyn Ithell, or will we have to squeeze it from your tongue?'

Owen's grandfather smiled, set to rolling himself a cigarette. 'Found her in the far corner of the copse,' he said, nodding eastward. 'Must have passed within yards of her a dozen times, boy. She took a step into the wood and there's a hollow, where a tree root was or some such. Must have lost her footing and rolled over into the hollow, the perfect shape it was to hold her. Lying there on her back, all we'd have seen would have been her four thin legs. Wouldn't bleat on her back, see.' He took a long drag of smoke, held it, exhaled. 'Undergrowth kept snow off. Lucky nothing come and killed her.'

Owen saw his grandmother put her hand on his grandfather's. 'You found her, you stubborn Welshman,' she said. 'You did it.'

'Aye,' he said. Owen looked at his grandfather's face. Pleased, the old man looked almost boyish. Vindicated. Freed of something, Owen thought, some weight of obligation. 'I did, didn't I?' Grandpa said.

Statement by Owen I, Birmingham.
April 2002

Statement refers to marriage and children.

Myself, respondent, 41 years old. Up until 1998 had been with now estranged wife for ten years.

Solicitor said to keep a record, see. Had enough of courts, I had, but hardly begun.

          *   *   *

In my mind we had a successful marriage and a happy family life. Believe that if it had not been for the accident we would all be together.

Dog flew across the road in front of us. Put my foot on the brake. We struck. The car spun.

Wife blamed me. She had the right.

          *   *   *

Wife. In my mind, cross my heart. Last week I saw a flock of plump, raucous starlings, in the middle of them was one bird of a different species. Lovely yellow wagtail. First saw Mel when she came into a pub I'd gone to. She was with a bunch of her girlfriends. Could hardly take my eyes off her.

Her mates a kind of guard around her. That's what it looked like. Went back every night for

102

months, and I never did like pubs. She was there twice. I wasn't one for talking, see. Didn't want to scare her off. Sit there thinking of things to say. Witty comments. Comical observations. Sometimes could hardly keep from chuckling to myself in the corner.

Never see a way to get her on her own. Choosing a record on the jukebox. Mechanism gripped the 45, levered it around, placed it on the turntable. A hiss as the needle struck vinyl, a hiss that said, Hush! Listen! The air in the room prickled like skin with expectation. Into the atmosphere, electrifying sound waves, the tangled thrill of 'Layla'. Eric Clapton and Duane Allman's incredible guitars.

'Good choice,' said this voice beside me. Turned and there she was.

Not that she'd noticed me, hid in the corner. She was just friendly. Talk to anyone, Mel.

*   *   *

Wasn't used to company, was I? Used to being on my own, doing what I wanted. No one would ever let me down, see. Had everything I needed, then Mel walked in and I knew I'd been living half a life. Empty man, I was, with a heart the size of a pea rattling around in my chest. She gave me her hand in marriage.

*   *   *

We had a daughter, S, and then the boy. Heart swelled inside me. My wife was six months pregnant. She got on with my mother, preparing

103

to ask if we should invite Ma to the city, I was. You think you're ready for anything, invincible, like. You think you're blessed.

*　　　　*　　　　*

H born in 1996, three months after accident. I'd lost my hand. We should have helped each other but we did not. Nativity play at school, Josh in reception class. Wouldn't take a speaking role, who could blame him? Teacher had a friend ran an animal sanctuary, Joseph brought Mary into the playground on a real donkey. A cold Christmas evening, parents shivering. They got to the stable, Josh had volunteered to lead the animal to the back. The donkey following this tiny figure drew a spontaneous round of applause, it did. Josh glanced across to see if we were proud of him. I couldn't clap my son.

*　　　　*　　　　*

Found it hard to cope, I admit it. Fell away. Then the pain came. This mirror box helped for a while.

Wife unable to help me, she had enough to deal with. I try to understand it. Could not bear to be with me, could she? I'm trying to explain. Out of our depth and we still are.

*　　　　*　　　　*

Doctor offered me anti-depressants, practically forced them on me. Wasn't me it was this world that needed changing, see.

Went to the woods to drink, into the bushes of Sutton Park. Not the kind to seek succour on the streets, with comrades of the bottle. Wished to be alone. In my stupor I saw things. Creatures of the night would come and sniff me as I lay. Foxes, stoats, wild cats in the middle of Birmingham, passed through my dreams.

* * *

Wife comes from broken home. Her mother divorced three times, died, stepfathers disappeared. Her natural father and sister live in Canada. Split families are what she knows.

* * *

In May 1997 wife told me she was seeing another man—a 'friend' of ours—who gave her more support than I did. She told me to leave the family home. I refused.

Tried to discuss our marriage on several occasions. Wife said time for talk was over, see. Don't know what I said when intoxicated. Discussion ended with blows. Had to be given stitches to a head wound on one occasion.

* * *

My wife petitioned for divorce on grounds of unreasonable behaviour. I contested it. She went to court in October 1998 and was granted an ouster order. I was ordered not to remove anything or take anything with me. Homeless, really. Granted access to my children (voluntary agreement made in magistrates court) every Saturday. But subsequently wife, encouraged by the 'friend', refused to let me see them.

*   *   *

Advised to apply for contact. Wife's solicitor used every delaying tactic. By the time welfare officer became involved, children's routine had been established, deemed in their 'best interests' to be disrupted as little as possible. I requested children's wishes be listened to but judge refused, like, saying they were too young. Contact set at one Sunday per month.

*   *   *

Favoured, we thought we were, that was the problem. Blessed. We were punished. Not by the God of Mary and Jesus, the Lamb of God, who took away the sins of the world.

Who blessed the poor in spirit, the meek, the peacemakers.

But the other one, the older God I sensed, as a boy, still lurking in the shadows of the church. The vengeful God of the Old Testament who looked down on mankind from high up on his hill of judgement, ready to smite any man foolish enough to think he had it made.

This God swung an axe in his hand, smote our child, split our world in two.

*   *   *

Found a flat. Children came on day visits. Held

myself together, see. H was a sweetheart, her visits were holidays. J more moody. I was the one who'd been kicked out but he resented my leaving.

*   *   *

Access difficult. Wife claimed contact left children upset, better for them to make new family with 'stepfather', now living in my house. Sometimes I agreed to this, did not visit, then regret. Wife also drew in professionals such as Child Guidance Service, not to help children but to be professional witnesses to their anxiety.

*   *   *

I applied to the court to have right of access imposed. Two court welfare officers assigned, neither dealt with case for six months.

*   *   *

Mel let me take Josh camping once, big site in Sutton Coldfield. Got a bloke to drop us off there, came back to pick us up. Cadged a tent, sleeping bags, a gas stove. We did everything together, nice and slow. I let Josh watch and copy me, all in his own good time. My one hand, his two. Pegging the tent, blowing up the mattress. Frying bangers in the morning. There was fishing there, and birds. He used my telescope, mostly to look at insects.

When I dropped him back on Sunday afternoon, Josh said, 'Can we do that again,

Dad?'
  Said, 'Of course we will.'
  More than two years ago now.

*   *   *

One Sunday, wife would not allow me to see children, saw H through window of family home crying. Forced my way into house, didn't I? 'Stepfather', Johnny, was there. Only tried to get past him, see. He knocked me out, but 'self-defence' as I had delivered 'initial blow'. A hook's no good for scrapping. Whoever heard of a one-handed fighter? Janice—wife's friend—witness. Did wife set it up? Cannot believe she did. Following day received an ex-parte not to assault/molest/ interfere with petitioner or children or friend, with power of arrest attached. Ordered to keep off estate. Judge being satisfied I had caused actual bodily harm and likely to do so again.

*   *   *

Appealed. Blatant perjury by Johnny and Janice. Also I believe by professional witnesses. I was described as violent, not only to Johnny but also children, which is untrue, have never struck either of them. Again, refusal by judge to allow even the older child, J, to correct this.
  Ordered to keep paying mortgage payments in full. Wife not working, debts building, council tax and other arrears. Johnny now living in family home but this denied, wife claimed he was resident elsewhere.

108

Ordered to make maintenance payments. £190 per month for children's keep plus half cost of children's clothes. Solicitor's fees I estimate £1,200 per annum over three years (solicitors quote approximate costs and exceed them threefold). Ex-wife on legal aid.

Attitude to courts and justice after the accident cases, before the divorce, was good. Realise now I was naive. Judges in two interim maintenance and one ancillary relief hearings considered it their job to squeeze as much out of me as possible, in the name of 'what is best for the children'.

The law is all to hell. Judges do as the mood takes them.

Divorce a three-way split: mother–father–children. But courts adversarial in tradition and can only deal with oppositions: children are grouped with the mother, to create two opposing forces: mother/children versus father.

*   *   *

Want to take them wild camping. In the hills of my homeland. Theirs as well, see, though I've never shown them. There's a place I know we could peg a tent where no one would see us, a cave we could hide in when the weather breaks, in a stream runs water that tastes like rain and a person can slip from God's sight.

*   *   *

Flat I live in now condemned. Currently seeking

109

income support owing to harassment from Child Support Agency. Have no car, just trailer attached to bicycle. Have cycled from Old Oscott to Thimble End to work, from Kingstanding to Perry. Nothing I will not do if I can get it. Desperate. Cards printed: *No job too small, no grass too tall*. Have no fixed income being self-employed and not entitled to unemployment benefit or disability allowance having use of one arm and prosthesis.

Have paid mortgage religiously and now the CSA are demanding £2,500 arrears and £272 per month. A nightmare I do not understand, see.

*   *   *

Not seen children for more than twelve months. In one month eligible to appeal for contact order. Light at the end of the tunnel, have never taken my eyes off it. Josh eleven, judge has to listen to him now.

Had heard from mutual aquaintance that wife and Johnny's relationship is over.

Yesterday given two weeks notice that Mel is moving with the children to Canada. House has been sold. Even if given access: air fares, accomodation. Impossible.

The tunnel is blocked now, black. There is no light.

*   *   *

Am posting this on forum now. It may be finished, see. Bitterness, in my mouth, but also shame. I have two children, they are mine. Josh is too much like me. Holly is a child who makes you smile. I do not know her. The longer I go without seeing them, fear I will forget what they look like. Have they forgot me? This brain can't get a handle on it.

Full of energy, see. Energy is rage. Must do something, walk in circles, chew on ways to make it change. But how? Sit down, energy evaporates, hours later still sat there. A day goes. Another. Night comes. I will never see them. I have a knife.

*   *   *

Not necessary, see. Here but superfluous. Have reached the end of the tether.

PART TWO

Abandon

HE COMETH UP, AND IS CUT DOWN

In the dream the lapwing flies around the summit, its green upper plumage irridescent in the sunshine. It makes its mournful, haunting cry. Owen turns away, unwilling, unready. He sees the boy, who runs, arms outstretched, down the hill, away from him. He cannot follow.

*　　　*　　　*

Sunlight streams through the window, the bare room is brittle, obliterated in brightness. Owen wakes. He is lying in a cloud made of glass. As he wakes a plan appears. The plan carries its own charge. It's possible he dreamed it but it doesn't feel that way, it feels like deep inside the cells and out along the neural pathways of his brain the plan bloomed in the moment of waking.

He lies still a while. His eyes are closed but he is aware that at some point the light alters. It's some time around eight a.m., on a Monday in the middle of April. The sun has been sucked deep into a blue and grey coagulating sky, and a plan to deliver him from all his offences blossoms in his mind.

The flat is on the top, ninth floor. The tower is scheduled for demolition. People have been moving out ever since Owen slipped in, their apartments boarded up with brown chipboard, not just doors but upper windows too, as if the authorities are afraid that some group of rock-climbing squatters might scale the sheer concrete like spiders. Parachute onto the flat roof and abseil down from there. The flat is in someone else's name. For months one window after another in the grey block has been sealed, the tower looking as if it is slowly suffocating.

He blinks. Walls the colour of winter heather; the ceiling like dirty ice cream. A shallow built-in wardrobe, its doors long gone. His few clothes neatly stacked. Clean, bare floorboards.

The bed is a metre from the window, and there is half a metre between the end of the bed and the wardrobe. No other furniture. In their house in Wylde Green Mel used to keep her clothes in a chest of drawers in their bedroom but her dresses in the built-in wardrobe in the children's room. Owen's stuff too was spread between rooms. The arrangement had evolved. Getting dressed in the morning the pair of them were required to perform an interconnecting choreography. Moving in various states of undress from one room to another. Meeting in doorways. Illogical, annoying, intermittently erotic.

The muddle and make-do of a marriage, before it is put asunder.

*   *   *

Owen has a plan but he cannot move. There is one photograph Blu-tacked to the wall: himself and Mel on their wedding day. They'd got married in a register office, but this image was of them arriving in the late afternoon for a party, on the side of Corndon Hill, the two of them, seen from the waist up. Mel looks past the camera: out of shot, behind the photographer, sixty people mill around. Mel has a broad and lovely smile. A white dress. A

116

diaphanous shawl. A tiara of white flowers—irises, carnations—on her full, rich head of red hair. In her right hand she holds a bouquet with one huge red rose, one yellow one, and lots of smaller flowers.

With her left hand Mel holds the right hand of some skinny, short-haired oddity standing at her side. He wears a bright new white shirt. You can see clearly the fat ring on the finger of his left hand, placed there that morning. It would be hard, Owen thinks, for a stranger to make sense of this photograph. Why is this lovely woman, in her finery—long grass blowing from right to left in the wind that also seems to have pushed the couple to the left-hand side of the frame; the valley behind them attired in fields and trees and tiny buildings; above, bright cotton-wool clouds that you sense must have been shifting and turning across the gusting sky—what, you would ask, is she doing with this plain, dull-looking man?

They'd mown a serpentine path up through the long grass from the gate at the bottom of his grandparents' old field, marking it with bamboo poles. Attached to the top of the poles were strips cut from plastic agricultural bags. Green, blue, yellow and red, flapping in the wind.

*　　　*　　　*

Owen thrusts aside the duvet and rises from the bed. At once he sits back down to save from staggering, a tornado spinning in his skull. It settles, his brain pulsates, a steady rhythmic throb against his cranium. He is so hungry that he can feel an emptiness in the middle of his body. A

117

nothingness, a vacuum. He can visualise it. It would show up on a body scan. If he does not eat, the hole will grow.

Two dessertspoons of coffee beans pour into the electric grinder that Josh and Holly gave him for his birthday two years ago. When the kettle boils he puts a little hot water into the small cafetière. He likes the sound the grinder makes, a kind of crackle through the electric engine whirr that in another machine would suggest serious internal dysfunction, but in this case reassures you it is doing its job. Gradually the crackles thin out in the sound, until the beans have been fragmented to a sandy consistency. He transfers the hot water from cafetière to mug, switches the kettle back on, and pours the ground coffee into the cafetière. As soon as the kettle clicks off, he fills the cafetière three-quarters full, producing a good head, an inch or so of froth, which will give to the eventual mug of coffee, after milk has been added, a richness of texture and taste.

Owen leans on a stool in the empty kitchen. The hot drink in his mouth, taste on his tongue, the warm liquid easing into his stomach, the caffeine working its way along the nerves of his arms and up into his brain, where it has a rousing effect, a concentrating, energising influence.

*   *   *

Grey nylon rucksack. Owen puts in a compass, a lighter, a torch, his grandfather's knife and sharpening stone, his own multi-tool, a mug, a small camping pan, a ball of string. From the bathroom cabinet, an out-of-date bottle of Calpol, shampoo. A towel. He tightly rolls two plastic groundsheets, ties them to the bottom of the rucksack.

The shower is tepid, the towel is damp. Owen shaves, wielding the razor in his left hand, holding the skin tight over his jaw with the stump of his right arm. Strapping the holster over his shoulder, he attaches the prosthesis to his right arm and dresses in a fresh white shirt, black trousers, socks and shoes, and a grey jacket. Puts his khaki cap on his head.

Owen runs the kitchen tap for a long time until the water is cold, then fills a plastic bottle, and puts apples, tea bags, sugar, a lump of cheese and the end of a loaf of white bread in the rucksack.

The door hangs open behind him. There will be no turning back. Four flats on this landing are boarded up, two including his remain occupied. It is much the same on the other floors. He descends the wide echoing stairs. The last of the children, he thinks, left long ago. Some of the remaining residents are single, others in couples; Owen has been unable to work out quite who is who. He sees people come out of flats he didn't think were theirs, only to turn and lock the door. Sometimes Owen is convinced that everyone in the tower knows everyone else, and is involved in a rigmarole of all kinds of intercourse. But when he actually speaks to anyone, he often finds them shy, ill at ease.

There is the sound of feet trotting up the stairs, and a man he's not seen before comes into view. They meet on a landing. When the man sees who it is he looks surprised. 'You on your way out, chap?' he asks.

Owen nods.

The stranger shakes his head. 'Looking a lot better.'

Owen is unsure whether the man refers to him or to the world outside. 'Feel good,' he says.

The man brings his hand up before his face and points his index finger at Owen in a conspiratorial way, narrowing his eyes as he does so. 'The power of positive thinking,' he says. Then he climbs on up the stairs, and the sound of his footsteps recedes into the air above Owen's head.

*　　　*　　　*

He walks towards the shopping centre. Cars browse the streets. A dog slouches along the opposite pavement. A van with its front corner staved in, immobile beside the pavement. Uncollected skips, piled high with rubble and rubbish.

Muddy pools on rugby pitches. Owen cuts through a small park, an old cemetery. Headstones, unearthed, are propped up against the outer brick walls. Lopsided tombs have been left in place. Brown ducks scatter, laughing. A perfume of roses.

He heads for the post office. Owen has a plan that involves a number of steps to put into operation. He must be calm, methodical. He needs a drink. He must pull his mind together.

The sky is made of clouds, layers of light grey and darker grey. He hears a slapping noise, repeated: an elegant young woman runs, her flat heels flapping on the pavement. In a car park a lorry lies on its back, its big wheels in the air.

Behind a supermarket two men rummage through a large refuse bin: inside it, their heads bob up and down, intermittently into view. Owen stands and watches, wondering why he has not thought of doing this himself. One of the men climbs out with an armful of out-of-date packets of food. He doesn't seem to see Owen, who resumes walking.

An office block is being built. Up high, two workmen lean on a horizontal scaffolding pole like the railing of a promenade, enjoying the sea view.

Owen switches on his mobile phone. A moment later it throbs in his pocket.

A text from Josh from yesterday. *we 1. i scored*.

He stares at the phone, then places it on the flat top of a fence post and walks on. Josh still secretly texted his father, though he knew that Owen was not allowed to reply. Well, they would see each other soon enough now.

He buys a can from an offie, just the one, pulling it loose from the plastic rings of a four-pack. Outside, he holds the can with his hook, pulls the tab with thumb and forefinger of his left hand. The can opens with a pleasant hiss. He sinks the lager in one long slow draught, stands still on the pavement. His thirst is endless. His body is like a sponge, he can sense the beer spreading through him, his flesh, every cell drenched in booze. Then, eyes closed, he savours the alcohol rising from his body as, carried in blood, it reaches his brain, swims there a moment until, like the last thin vestige of a wave on sand, it washes through his head, and is gone. Owen opens his eyes. The world is shining. He drops the can in a bin and walks on.

*   *   *

121

Owen turns a corner and enters a street. Houses set back from the road. Along each pavement men in yellow fluoro jackets run away. With gloved hands they pluck black bin bags from the pavement, carry and drag them into piles every twenty yards. Some bags are ripped, their contents strewn: bones, yoghurt pots, bread crusts, bones.

Behind him, a lorry comes into the street. More runners. He lets them overtake him. They hurl the black bin bags into the mouth at the back of a foul-breathing vehicle, which grinds past him.

A sound carries, of the tide hitting a pebbly shore, the sound of waves crashing in a nearby road, a different lorry, swallowing glass.

He takes a left, a right, once more the emptiness.

Electronic noise bursts out of an open window, a bedlam of various beats. It sounds like someone inside the house is throwing metal balls down the stairs, musical juggling; a racket of repetitive precision. It dissipates behind him. Owen feels jittery. He wants to hurry up.

*   *   *

The bicycle is a white racer, leaning against a silver birch tree. It has no lock. Owen stops, looks around. He squeezes front tyre, full of air, back one too. The brakes function. The bike has no accessories—no mudguards or lights or basket—it is naked, skeletal like a bird. The next thing Owen knows he is riding it along the wide pavement, his hook clamped to the handlebar, his left hand ready to brake. Weaving in and out of trees, then sliding onto the road and pedalling hard.

Out of the suburb and into the urban entanglement of metal, noise, velocity. Free as air, veering in and out of nervous traffic. The vast roundabouts on the inner ring road. Sailing under the wheels of juggernauts, pantechnicons, the suicidal frailty of a bicycle, a sailing dinghy in these shipping lanes.

*   *   *

Owen enters the main post office. Inside, the queue is long and layered back onto itself like an intestine. Owen is moved intermittently forward by some kind of peristaltic shunt. Television screens on the wall above the row of serving kiosks advertise a succession of commercial products and services. Red numbers on a counter high up on the wall rise gradually higher. 'Cashier number five, please.'

In front of Owen are two women. They address each other every now and then, while they gaze around the room. 'So obvious,' the dark-haired one says. 'Who's she think she's fooling?'

There is a long pause, as the other woman, with brown-blonde hair, tries to imagine exactly who she does think she's fooling. In time she replies, 'Makes her look a lot younger though, don't it?'

Now it is the dark one's turn to ponder. 'Bob said he'll get me one for my birthday,' she announces. 'But that's years off.'

Owen enjoys the stately pace of their conversation. It reminds him of childhood. There is something old-fashioned, rural, about it.

'I don't mind having stuff taken out,' the blonde

woman resumes, dreamily. 'Wouldn't have nothing put in, mind.'

The dark-haired woman nods at the ticket in her companion's hand, says, 'About time,' and they advance upon a vacant kiosk.

When it is his turn Owen clears his post office account. One hundred and seventeen pounds and fifty-nine pence. The young man behind the counter presses his knuckles against the wad of notes and turns them over with his thumb, counting them at incredible speed.

*   *   *

In the library there are two long rows of computer monitors, back to back. People peer into them, bathing their faces in the pale glow. Owen is fortunate to be given a slot when the person who'd booked it fails to show up. A moderate amount of mail. Spam, mostly. Using the index finger of his left hand and a pencil in his hook, Owen taps the keyboard with two digits. He sets up an auto out-of-office reply. *Owen Ithell is no longer to be found at this address*.

Owen looks for a book to take on the journey. It would need to be something he could share with the children. He wanders up and down the aisles. *Children's Guide to the Wildlife of Britain*. People sit and read, study. The illusion of peace. Their minds within the mind of the library. He has heard of a library in the shape of a human head. Windows in the eyes and ears, was it? No, it had walls of glass. I am in it now, he thinks.

*   *   *

Mid-morning. The clouds break up. The rucksack presses against Owen's back, he can feel the sweat on his shirt. The straps bite into his bony shoulders. He leans back. An aeroplane rises in a blue sky, like a toy thrown up by a child in a distant suburb. The smell of asphalt. On a cricket ground, out by the side of the wicket, an irrigator: on a tripod a long bar from either end of which water shoots upwards. The bar spins on its axis on the tripod, first this way, then that, so that the jets of water are made to describe helices. One double helix after another, repeating, dissolving.

* * *

Owen enters the school by the back entrance, through the cramped staff car park. The little playground is empty. Crisp packets, snack wrappers, rustle and stir in the brisk morning. A hard sun rises above the climbing frame. He screws up his eyes. The sky is white. He walks round the side to the front entrance and rings the bell.

The school secretary opens the door. Sally is a large woman in her late forties or early fifties. She wears what look to Owen like colourful pieces of material flung over her body. Her body a piece of furniture covered in drapes, in throws of fabric. It is difficult to guess her shape beneath. She perspires along her upper lip.

'Come in,' Sally says. 'Come in.'

Owen stumbles into the reception area.

'Would you like to sit down?' Sally asks.

Owen doesn't want to sit down. He isn't sure what to say.

125

'Is everything all right?'

He hadn't thought about what he would say. He hadn't considered the need to say anything. The head teacher comes out of her office.

'Won't you sit down, Mr Ithell?' she asks.

'Can I fetch you a glass of water?' Sally offers. There is a long pause. They lean towards each other, as if the three of them are praying together. There is the smell of something organic in the vestibule. A machine in Sally's office comes to life with a quiet belch, followed by animated squeaks. Owen realises the smell is coming from a large brown paper carrier bag in the corner: an uncollected bag from the PTA fruit and vegetable scheme.

'I'll fetch him a glass of water,' Sally decides. 'He's white as a sheet.'

Mrs Okechukwu takes Owen's arm. Before he knows it he is sitting down, next to her, on one of the easy chairs in reception, under the cross. Everything is quiet. There is an odd hush, a peculiar quality to the sound inside the school, with two hundred and fifty children in their lessons. Owen had never noticed it before. The air seems to contain their suppressed energy. He hears a distant teacher's remonstration. A quick convulsion of laughter in a different classroom. Then the constrained quiet once more.

Sally bows before him with a white plastic cup of water. 'I'm fine,' he says, taking it from her with his left hand. The water is lukewarm. He drinks it down, slowly, every last warm drop.

'I need to take Joshua and Holly out of school,' he says. 'I've come to collect them.'

Mrs Okechukwu asks, 'Has something . . . ?' She

126

stops, keeps the shape of her mouth around the last syllable.

'Their grandmother,' Owen says.

'Has she . . . ?' Sally asks.

'She's not well, see,' Owen says. He shakes his head. 'Doesn't look good. May be our last chance to visit.'

The two women look upon Owen with tender wariness. It occurs to him that they'd rather look after him than entrust the children to his care.

'She's very calm,' he says. 'Looks like the end is close but she's not ranting. Mean a great deal to her to see her grandchildren.' Owen squeezes his eyes closed, and gulps, and opens them again. 'Mean a lot to them as well, see,' he says. 'Times to come.' He looks from one to the other. 'Wouldn't want to deprive them of the chance to say goodbye.'

Mrs Okechukwu rises and says to Sally, 'I will get Joshua,' and the two women go off in different directions. Sally comes back first, clutching a green jacket and a pink rucksack. Holly walks ahead of her. She's not seen her father in a while. Recognition blooms suddenly on her face. She grins at him. Every few steps she skips, tempted to run yet restraining herself, aware already of appropriate behaviour. So grown-up, his little girl. Her sixth birthday just a few weeks away.

Owen stays seated, but reaches out, and Holly lets him gather her to him. 'Daddy,' she says.

The head reappears with Josh, her solicitous hand high upon his spine. He is shaking his head. 'What are you doing here?'

'Nana's ill,' Owen explains. He makes a solemn face. 'We'll go and visit her.'

Owen feels Holly's body give a little wriggle beside him. 'On the bus?' she asks, wide-eyed. Her father nods.

Josh is frowning. 'Does Mum know?' he demands. Josh's frown darkens. He looks troubled, angry. He looks like he is doing a comic impression of his father, but it's not supposed to be funny.

'Your grandmother's not very well, Joshua,' Sally tells him.

Mrs Okechukwu says to Owen, 'Their mother knows about this?'

'Of course.'

Josh has always hated disruption to or a break in his routine. Eleven years old now. When he was younger, Owen would remember too late the need to warn or remind his son of what was about to happen. *We're going to the park in half an hour. Tomorrow you're seeing the optician: I'll take you out of school mid-morning, and return you after lunch.* Josh found it hard to cope with being surprised. Clearly, he hasn't changed.

'I don't want to go,' he says. His resistance is palpable: perhaps Mrs Okechukwu is exerting pressure on his neck, and he is pushing back against her. 'I can stay here,' Josh insists.

'It's your grandmother, Joshua,' Sally tells him.

'Let me ask Mum if I can stay here,' Josh says. His countenance has become clouded by suspicion.

'Is their mother going?' Mrs Okechukwu asks.

'No,' Owen says. The notion of panic occurs, without actually afflicting him. 'It's fine. Joshua can stay here. You stay here, Josh. Holly and I will go. I'll tell Mummy to collect you as usual. That's fine.' He stands up.

'Are you sure you're all right, Mr Ithell?' Sally

128

asks.

The vestibule lurches. It feels as if the school is a raft, floating on water.

'You're trembling,' says Sally.

Owen steadies himself against the wall, until the blood has returned to his brain. 'I'll be okay outside. Thank you.' He takes Holly's hand.

'If it's arranged that Joshua should go,' Mrs Okechukwu says in some confusion, 'I believe he should.'

At that moment lessons around the school begin to come to an end. Morning break. There is a rustling sound, and something like breathing. The school building is like a skull inside of which the brain of a great creature stirs from sleep. The children are thoughts. They distract the head teacher.

'We'll give Nana a kiss from you, okay?' Owen tells Josh. Josh nods, relaxing, the threat of disruption to his day being withdrawn.

Owen and Holly walk out of the front door and back around the side of the school. Children are bursting out of doors, hysterical, each intent upon some course of action. Girls of various ages skip over to ask Holly why she's being taken out of school. Gratified by the attention, self-important, she tells them she is going to see her nana, who is ill. Owen keeps hold of her hand, moving her along, urging himself forward too, afraid of a shout behind them, calling them back, reining them in; a phone call having been made, Mel berserk at the other end, a male teacher, others, summoned urgently to corral the out-of-control father.

But no yell comes. They make it out of the playground and through the staff car park, only then do they hear the sound of running feet. Owen stops and turns. Josh reaches them and begins walking, obliging them to resume doing so. He doesn't want to make a scene, he's just changed his mind, that is all. Given a little more time, he'd been able to assimilate the information and decide for himself that he'd like to come on this expedition.

They take a left and a right and cross the humpbacked bridge, and once they are on the towpath of the canal Owen begins to breathe a little easier.

* * *

Electric-blue dragonflies blur across the water. Male and female mallards float: they seem to be waiting. A smell of parsley. Owen wipes his sweaty hairline. Holly's hand is slippery in his. Josh walks beside him, black rucksack on his back.

The sun is above, everywhere and nowhere. Owen raises his head with relief. He knows this is only the beginning, the initial step, the first hurdle. He feels euphoria, like the sky above him is his to float into. The vapour trail of a jet aeroplane curves across the blue sky, as if the pilot has discovered a navigational error, and is discreetly correcting it.

I AM A STRANGER WITH THEE, AND A SOJOURNER, AS ALL MY FATHERS WERE

People pour into the city, tired and hungry. They arrive and are lost, look around for guidance. Others are leaving. The concourse is a jostling swarm of criss-crossing paths. Owen and his children queue ten minutes for a ticket. Josh goes first. The barrier swallows his ticket, spits it out, opens its wings to let him through.

The waiting room is in the middle of the platform. Its walls are thick transparent plastic. Outside, old people tow trolley cases, their breath in the harsh sun condensing before them. Families huddle around bulging bags: bulky, shapeless men and women in sports clothes, children either too fat or too thin. Young men in oval mirrored sunglasses. Alternating tannoys—one voice computerised, female, the other a live man—clamour for attention. Inaudible information.

Owen, Josh and Holly are the only occupants of the waiting room. They sit apart, a triangle of passengers. Holly must have turned towards her father: he can tell from the sound of her voice. 'Mummy said you're sick.'

Owen looks at his daughter and shakes his head. 'She didn't mean it,' he says. Holly comes over and climbs onto his lap. Josh is across the room, kneeling on a chair, looking out. Beneath her green jacket Holly wears a red T-shirt with two black embroidered dogs on the front, a blue denim skirt, odd socks—one purple, one pink—pulled up as high as they will go, almost to her knees. Sturdy

131

shoes. Sweatbands on her wrists, her hair in plaits, hairgrips holding them to the sides of her head. Owen is grateful that at their school the children do not wear uniform. That bit less conspicuous.

Holly squirms around until she gets herself comfortable. The hook does not bother her. She lets her body relax into Owen's. With his left hand he strokes her arm. Holly takes it as her due: an expectation of sensuality. Owen realises she is studying his face, inspecting it closely. He breathes in through his lips and Holly peers into his mouth. 'What happened to your tooth?' she asks.

Owen feels with his tongue, finds the gap at the front of his upper jaw. Lost it a month or two ago. 'Sold it, like,' he tells his daughter. 'Get good money for a decent tooth, know who to go to.'

Holly stares at him a moment, then seems to realise she'll get no sense out of him on this and says, 'Let's talk about something. What shall we talk about?'

'Anything in the whole wide world, girl.'

Holly thinks for a moment. 'When you did meet Mummy . . .'

Owen frowns. He thinks, Anything but that, but says, 'Yes?'

'Before I was in Mummy's tummy . . .'

'You mean when you were just a twinkle in my eye?'

'No. Before.'

'Before Josh?'

Across the room, Josh's body stiffens, alert to the conversation behind him.

'Yes, fore Josh. Fore our sister. When did you meet Mummy?'

Owen sighs. 'She was so beautiful, see,' he says,

132

shaking his head. 'First time I saw your mother,' he tells Holly, 'she was wearing a dress so tight I found it difficult to breathe.'

Holly frowns. 'But when?' she says impatiently.

'When? Let's see.' He calculates, and decides, 'Fifteen year ago.'

Holly grows exasperated. 'But *when*?' she repeats.

Owen plucks a date at random. 'The twentieth of November.'

Holly flushes with anger.

'Tuesday, Holly,' Owen says.

Holly's small hands bunch into tight fists, and she raises one of them. Her eyes well up. Her skin is the colour of raspberry milk. She is about to strike him. But then she seems to pause, to steady herself, as if taking pity on his obtuseness. 'But were it *after*?' she asks.

'Yes,' he says. 'Yes. That's right. It was after.' This, bizarrely, seems to satisfy her.

Josh turns around. Looking at Holly, he says, 'Owen doesn't even *know*.'

Owen wonders what she meant. Did Josh know what she meant? He looks at Josh, who turns away.

Outside, families haul their items of dead luggage for ten or twenty metres, dump them down again and look around in every direction, unsure of where their train might come from.

Owen recalls when he and Mel married, his feeling of relief. And pride of conquest. She was his now, as he was hers. He knew—he was certain—that her brother, their friends, his own mother, considered him fortunate. At a certain moment during the wedding party he took a break from dancing and stepped out of the barn. He

133

looked down into the valley from up in those hills he planned to take the children to now. Behind him the beats and the rapture. It struck him (and as it did so he knew that he would remember this moment forever, the cloudy sunset, silhouetted hills, shuddering music), it struck him that in pledging herself, her future, her very life to his, that in some strange way Mel had evaded him. The girl he had pursued was not, could never be again, the woman he had captured.

Outside, a train comes. Another leaves. The waiting room begins to fill with people. Lone travellers, they speak into their mobile phones. The sound is different from the murmurous babble of conversation: composed of interwoven, overlapping monologues, it is more theatrical, with odd emphases and pauses.

'This is ours,' Owen says.

Shuffling on his knees, Josh backs off the seat, turns and walks across the waiting room, pulling the supports of his rucksack over his shoulders. 'I thought we was going on the bus,' he says, frowning.

'Take the train for a change, is what I thought.' Owen stands up and half-lifts, half-tosses, Holly over and around his right shoulder so that she can cling to his back like a monkey. Josh shrugs. He lifts his sister's rucksack and loops it in his father's hook. Owen is able to carry it along with his own rucksack, leaving his left hand to cradle Holly's bottom behind him.

They walk to a platform, climb onto a train. Josh walks along the centre aisle. At the end of each carriage Josh pushes a button and the door hisses open. There are plenty of empty seats. The

134

train had arrived from somewhere; people have spread out. Laptops. iPods. Paperback books. Companionable magazines. Dainty paper bags of coffee, sandwiches from the buffet car. Sachets of sugar, tiny tubs of milk. People gaze out of the windows.

They reach an empty carriage at the front of the long train. The driver, whose bull neck and the back of whose bald head they can see through a window in the door of his cab.

Josh sits, silent. Holly empties her rucksack on the table. The flotsam of a five-year-old magpie. A plastic beetle, a hairgrip, one dice, a pink pony, odd crayons, they tumble out, a domino, dented ping-pong ball, one of her mother's rings, which Owen suspects may be valuable. Holly's bags were not bad places to look if you'd lost something. The last thing to fall out is Owen's old toothbrush. It disappeared around the time of the children's last visit, after which he'd had to get a new one. Why Holly had filched this he has no idea—she is too proud to admit theft, it would be no use confronting her, she'd deny taking it and become angry. Memento of him or merely a momentary covetousness? Neither makes much sense, but Holly is five years old, and she has her own logic.

Josh draws something in his notebook, shows it to Holly. Owen sees them exchange looks. About him? He feels aloof from them, superfluous. A paternal superfluity. The absence, the two of them, the broken triangle. He will mend it.

*   *   *

The lurch of a train. The judder and sway. It is

hard to write by hand. Josh lets out little grunts of frustration when his pen slews across the page. Owen expresses his sympathy. The boy puts down the pen. It rolls over the table.

'I want to text Mum,' Josh says. 'Left my phone at school.'

'It's okay,' Owen says. 'She knows where we are.'

'I want to talk to her,' Josh says.

'And me,' adds Holly.

'I don't have my mobile,' Owen tells them. 'We'll call her later, from a phone box.'

*　　　*　　　*

Their train rumbles through industrial yards: stacks of iron, mechanical shapes of indecipherable purpose, parts less of machines than of giant puzzles; piles of sand, grit, gravel, like spiceyards, the ingredients of industrial civilisation. The yards appear deserted.

Josh watches with a brooding gaze. The train passes a park. A fluoro-jacketed gardener with red earmuffs is agitating leaves with a blow vac, tidying the lawns by means of small tornadoes. You don't need two hands to do that job, Owen thinks. Bare trees, their trunks like stalks, look like they've been stuck into the ground rather than grown from it. At the corner of the park more trees have been planted, hundreds. They look like war graves, like the trees have died, but sticks and rabbit guards remain, a memorial for each dead sapling.

Windows cut into the roofs of houses. Suburban back gardens. Plastic toys abandoned. An upturned boat. 'We've passed this way already,' Josh says. 'We're going round and round.'

Is there an accusatory tone to Josh's voice? Does he blame Owen for being thrown out? He is disappointed that Owen did not stand up for himself more effectively. He witnessed his father assault his mother's boyfriend, receive a bloody beating and lose his last right of access as a consequence.

Holly has repacked her bag, is carefully zipping it up. 'Look,' says Josh. In a large field, deep in long grass, white in the green, the letter H. A single set of rugby posts? Or all that is left of a HOLLYWOOD-type sign? 'We've been here before,' Josh says.

Holly looks up. 'Definitely,' she says, slowly, so that Owen can hear where the syllables join, each link. Her latest longest word, to be used at any opportunity.

'You wasn't even looking,' Josh tells her.

'I *were*,' Holly claims. 'Don't be horrible.'

'Whatever you say's whatever you are,' Josh says, in a faint sing-song.

The train begins a long skid to a halt. It stops beside an empty platform. The doors open. No one gets off. Other passengers stand up, look around. One or two step out, gaze up and down the platform, pull up their collars, hugging themselves. Light cigarettes.

The driver is reading a newspaper. Owen knocks lightly on the window, and when the man looks up Owen opens his arms as if to ask, What's going on? The driver shrugs: I know no more than you, mate.

Owen and Josh stand on the platform, shivering smokers on either side. Holly joins them. It is always colder, Owen thinks, on railway platforms, there's invariably a cold cutting wind blowing through the station. He doesn't want to be stuck here. He wants to be moving. Is it easier for the police to find someone in hiding or in transit, on public transport? There is no announcement, nor sign of a guard. Every twenty metres stands a T-shaped streetlamp, like those crosses in certain crucifixions painted without the top section.

The wind tosses objects into the air—a crisp packet, a sheet of newspaper—and plays with them. The wind is solid, like the sea; birds are like fish, swimming through chunky air. A black hat reels above their heads. The children watch it, then look at Owen, as if he might explain it. Behind them, the train grumbles, and stirs. The driver must have received the order to proceed. 'Come on,' Owen says. He takes Holly's hand, the trio climb back on. Passengers return to the same seats they'd occupied a quarter of an hour before.

The train pulls out of the empty station. Josh shakes his head, then he says to his father, 'Are we going to see Nana?'

Owen finds he is unable simply to say, Yes. 'We'll call her,' he says.

'Why didn't we go to the coach station?' Josh asks. 'We could have gone on the coach, couldn't we?'

Owen tries to remember whether or not you could get to King's Lynn by train. He thinks you can, changing at Ely. He knows they have visited his mother without him, more often than he has. He'd withdrawn from everyone.

*　　　*　　　*

Holly stands up. 'I'm going to the toilet,' she says.

138

Owen begins to gesture in the right direction, to save Holly walking towards the driver's cab, but she cuts him short with a smile. 'I know, Daddy.' She sways past his right shoulder.

Josh gazes out of the window. Back gardens, divided by fences, like the frames of a film. He looks like he is asleep with his eyes open. Utterly still. Spellbound by nothing. In a trance, Owen thinks, like the stupor he himself achieves with alcohol. Perhaps the wish to enter it has nothing to do with circumstances: a narcoleptic tendency, a genetic need.

They pass a small breaker's yard where parts of disparate cars are neatly stacked: bumpers here, tyres there, doors of different colours. A square, with green shrubs and green metal benches, no one in it. The train passes beneath overhead motorways, the pillars that support them like cloisters coiling through the city. In the centre, a new tower block, with the words SKY LIVING FOR SALE. Holly has been gone too long.

'I'm going to look for your sister,' Owen says, standing up. A nod of acknowledgement from his son.

Owen makes his way to the end of the carriage. The toilet is engaged, so he waits outside. After a minute the door slides open. A middle-aged woman emerges. He continues on along the train, scrutinising every seat. He checks each toilet, waiting, if it is occupied, until a stranger emerges. The train stops once or twice, people get on. When he reaches the rear of the train he realises that he must have missed her; in all probability she'll be back in her seat by now.

Returning in the opposite direction, it seems

like there are many more passengers in each carriage than when he came through just now. That, Owen reckons, is what happens when you are searching for one particular person: you don't notice everyone else. Lurching in the same direction as the speeding train feels faster than did walking towards the back of the train, against its momentum.

After a while Owen starts to count the carriages he passes through. He begins to suspect that it is taking longer to get back to his seat at the front of the train: there are more carriages than there were just now. No sooner does Owen dismiss this absurd thought from his mind than it is replaced by another.

People are looking at him. Not in the idle way that everyone does at someone swaying down the centre aisle, but with a distinct, knowing gaze. He isn't sure how or when exactly it happens, but at some point Owen realises that they know where Holly is. At first him, that man in the suit, on the mobile phone, the way he watches Owen come towards him, as if reporting on his progress to someone on the other end of the line. Then her, an elderly lady lifting her gaze lazily towards him in his panic, on her thin lips a contemptuous smirk. But soon everyone whose eyes he meets, they all know: this is the idiot who has lost his daughter.

The train stops again. More passengers climb on board. A steady flow of them come through the carriages, looking for a seat. A female train manager pushes through, calling, 'Come along. Plenty of room in carriages Gee and Haitch. Toot suite. Move along there.' Many must have squeezed into the front of the train and now they are dispersing. He begins to smell the toilets as he approaches the end of each carriage.

People are standing in the aisle, sitting on their suitcases or even on the arms of seats occupied by others. Owen pushes awkwardly past. He wrestles his way around them. The smell of people. Of their clothing. A gradually rank aroma is filling each carriage: bodies sweat, clothes warm up and give out the oversweet odours of the flesh inside.

The carriage begins to swoon. To sashay, as if the train has left the tracks and is dancing into a disastrous waltz. There appears a vacant seat, into which Owen slumps. The dance slows. Owen remembers that he hasn't eaten in a while. The blood returns to his brain. The train resumes its normal momentum. They pass the chocolate factories, the university. The train runs alongside a canal; a pair of middle-aged women paddle a canoe. In searching for Holly, Owen realises, he has abandoned Josh. The older brother is still a young boy. He lost Sara, is he trying to lose the other two as well?

No, no. Calm down. They'll be drawing pictures together at the table in the carriage at the front of the train.

An elderly man stands close to where Owen is seated, beyond a pair of tattooed youths, whispering to each other. The man holds on to a partition upright with a frail grip. Owen stands up, catches his attention, and offers him his seat. The old man's expression of surprised relief. He struggles past the youths, who contort themselves around luggage and furniture to give him space. When Owen turns sideways to usher him into the vacant seat, he finds that it is occupied. Someone else has slipped into it behind his back.

'I'm afraid that's my seat, isn't it,' he says. The woman ignores him. 'I'm giving it to this gentleman,' Owen explains, gesturing towards him with his palm, turning his body a little to the side so as to afford her as full a picture of the old man as possible.

She doesn't look up. 'I've got it now,' she says.

'Yes,' Owen says. 'I believe he needs it more.'

She is a hefty woman. It would take some effort, Owen surmises, to lift her from her seat. Her face reminds him of some actress, but travelling in disguise, hiding behind the chubbiness. Her pretty, child-like face registers a brief tremor of annoyance, across the bridge of her nose and around her eyes. 'I said, *I've got it.*'

If the woman is ill, why doesn't she say so? It's so hot in the crowded carriage. 'But it's my seat, see,' Owen makes clear, 'I offered it to him.'

The young woman stares straight ahead. 'It's not yours now, is it?' she says.

It takes Owen a second to register that the fragile sound behind him is that of the old man, speaking: 'It doesn't matter.'

Owen can't think of anything to say. He looks around the other three people sitting in this quartet of facing seats, hoping for support from them. Each one gazes out of the window, into the far distance. No one gives any indication that they can see or hear him.

'It's the gentleman's seat,' Owen says. He can hear the finality in his voice, the acceptance of defeat. He is aware that he is sweating profusely.

'She needs it,' says a man standing beside Owen. He'd not noticed him there, not as an individual in particular in the crowded aisle. His voice is without aggression, is in agreement with the underlying tone of Owen's utterance. Owen senses the man's relationship to the young woman. He is also dark-haired, also good-looking beneath a fancy dress of corpulence.

'It's all right,' the old man says. Owen sees him turn away, prepare to squeeze back past the tattooed youths, as if he could resume his place and this episode might not have happened. Owen steps towards the old man and grasps him by his bony shoulders, arresting his movement.

'I'm going that way,' Owen says, holding the old man in place so that he can push past him, and the two youths, and on through the carriage and into the next. Bit by bit he puts the incident behind him as he presses, apologises and manoeuvres his way forward, towards the front of the train.

Finally, after what seems like twice as long a train as before, Owen catches a glimpse between passengers of Josh's head in the next but one carriage, and, at the far end of it, the door to the driver's cabin. At this moment the train begins to decelerate, abruptly enough to oblige Owen to grab the top of a seat to keep his balance, and to make the people ahead of him lurch backwards, as if they'd each received a tug from behind.

The train comes to a halt. Owen peers out. He can't quite make out the name on the sign on the platform, only the last two letters: RY. He assumes that people will get off, but no one does. The opposite happens: more passengers are getting on. Around him, people do not communicate, exactly, since they avoid eye contact, but what everyone does is to express their feelings, with disapproving

143

little tuts and exclamations of breath, with discreet sighs or shakes of the head, fatalistic gestures that speak of many things (What a sorry state of affairs this is, what happened to this island? Disgrace. But we've been through worse than this, and we shall endure.) Then people squeeze a little closer.

Of their own free will at first. But then they are shoved up against each other as more people come into the carriage from either end, pressing their way in, using their suitcases as battering rams. People who didn't think they could get any closer to their neighbours find themselves barged up against them.

It occurs to Owen that they are being forced to take part in a game—there'll be a prize for the carriage with the most people in it—the kind of game Josh and Holly will want to play. Children are being lifted onto the tables between some seats or even up into the luggage rack. There they lie, looking down, anxious, wide-eyed creatures.

A whistle blows. There are angry shouts. The sound of doors being slammed. It is then Owen sees Holly, alone, out on the platform. How did she get there? Why? She is trotting up and down the train, looking in through the windows, searching. She looks terrified, lost.

'Let me past,' Owen yells, panicked fury surging through him. 'I have to get out.' He thrusts a young man aside, heaves past a middle-aged woman, but the aisle is clogged with bodies. Even if people want to make way for him, they can't. Owen climbs onto an armrest. The only space is up above people's shoulders, that is the only way through. Where to put one's feet is the problem. The tables and armrests are occupied, so that he is forced to step on people's laps, thighs, knees.

'Let me through!' he shouts. 'My daughter's on the platform! Let me by!' He clambers over people's shoulders. Packed together as they are, there isn't much they can do but let him, as he puts his hand and hook on their heads for balance, and leverage. Occasionally a hand shoots up and slaps or grabs at his ankle, but he kicks and shakes them off, and he has to be careful of his fingers where people try to bite him as he presses upon their skulls. His hook is clumsier but less vulnerable than his hand.

Suddenly the train lurches backwards, and like a single serpentine organism the jam of people in the aisle seems to suffer a simultaneous convulsion. Owen grabs the rail of the luggage rack just in time. Immediately he realises that he should have done that from the beginning. Hand over hook now he speeds along, putting his feet he knows not where. He passes a sign saying EMERGENCY—PULL CHAIN, and wastes time bending to reach it. It comes away in his hand. At the end of the carriage it is difficult to get the last few yards through the vestibule to the door, but he is determined. The train is moving forwards now, but this fact has little relevance to Owen at that moment. He reaches the door and pulls down the window. The man who had been standing by the door points to a sign.

'Don't open that,' someone else behind Owen says, in a loud voice. 'The train's moving.'

Owen leans out of the window, grabs the handle, turns it, and the door flies open. Owen swings with it and lands on the platform, spun round once but taking no more than a step or two to regain his balance, before looking along the platform. Holly has seen him and stands immobile, staring at him. Owen realises that he has retrieved her, and in getting her has lost Josh. Did he make that choice? A surge of anger like a lightning bolt shoots through him. He turns and sprints on past the next carriage, to the front one. The train is idling out of the station. Owen reaches halfway along the carriage. There is Josh, on this side of the crowded carriage, fortunately. He is gazing out of the window, as he was when Owen had set off in search of his sister.

Owen hammers on the glass. Josh blinks at his father, who gestures to indicate to Josh that he should get to the door. As if a spell has been broken, Josh leaps into action: as if the knowledge transmits itself from father to son in some arcane manner the boy climbs straight up to the luggage rack and swings like a monkey along it, stepping on people's heads when he needs or is forced to. Owen follows his progress, jogging along the platform. In twenty seconds Josh has reached the door, which Owen opens. He pincers and grabs hold of his son's clothing and drags him off the train, hugging him, the pair's combined momentum taking them into a pirouette along what remains of the platform, Josh's shoes two feet off the ground.

Owen holds his son in a tight embrace, breathing hard, the boy rising and falling off his father's chest. The train drifts slowly out of the station. Owen remembers his rucksack, he glances up to see it and the children's too hurled at that moment out of the train door window.

When he gave Josh a hug his son's body felt stiff. He kept his distance, a certain formality, rarely allowing himself to let his guard down, but now Josh squeezes his father's neck. Owen's hair is sweaty. Stubble scrapes against Josh's cheek. His father smells smokey and tangy and sharp. Josh feels himself being lowered to the ground, as Owen kneels on the platform. As the sound of the train recedes Owen can hear the sound of running feet, coming closer.

Holly slams into their embrace, demanding space within it for her. She is crying. '*Why* did you do that?' she demands. 'I were so scared. *Why* did we come here?'

Owen kneels down in front of her. 'I'm sorry,' he says, drawing her to him. Josh eases himself away and stands by, as his sister weeps.

The only other person in the station is a man of indeterminate age, with a satchel over his shoulder. He stands by the doorway to a deserted ticket office. He wears a suit that had belonged either to someone else or to himself when he was smaller than he now is. His hair is combed flat on his head, and he grins as Owen, Josh and Holly approach him, his small eyes contracting into their plump sockets behind pebble specs.

'That is the twelve thirty-seven,' he says. 'Running eighteen minutes late.' He appears amused, by the train's erratic timekeeping or by the accuracy of his calculations. 'The twelve fifty-four's almost caught up with it.'

Owen ushers the children out.

'Nice to see someone get off here,' the man says.

*   *   *

They walk through suburban streets, which after a

while begin to widen, houses set back from the verge. A road sign says 40, and the traffic that passes them speeds up. They walk past a mansion with a huge empty car park around it; its roof is charred and the windows have been replaced by metal sheets.

A boarded-up filling station, a warehouse behind locked gates.

They are not yet clear of the city. They could be stopped at any moment.

I WILL TAKE HEED TO MY WAYS; THAT I OFFEND NOT IN MY TONGUE

The road climbs gradually, towards fields, trees. At the top of the rise they look around: the city spreads itself out as far as the eye can see, south, north, east, west. They are still surrounded. To the south-east is the centre, towers rise like the stalks of flowers about to bloom. Smoke rises from somewhere north-west. West Bromwich. Wolverhampton.

Holly looks nothing like her mother. She walks, intoning a tuneless song to herself. Her features—pert pinched little nose, cupped jaw, thin-lipped mouth, eyes like blue buttons—are petite. Mel has wide cheekbones, full lips, almond eyes. Yet Holly does resemble the girl in the school photograph of Mel at five years old. The code for her physical destiny buried deep in her genes, instructions to be issued in adolescence, a transformation. As would have happened to Sara.

Will happen to Holly.

*   *   *

They stumble along the verge, a grassy bank on the left-hand side of the road.

'Where are we going?' Josh asks.

'It's a surprise,' Owen says. 'An adventure.'

'What about Nana?'

'I'm hungry,' Holly complains.

It must be lunchtime, at school. 'We'll eat soon,' Owen assures her, holding her right hand. Few cars

149

pass. He puts out his hook as he walks, turning when he hears an engine, in time to catch a glimpse of a driver's glance at this suspicious trio. Immigrants, tinkers, New Age travellers, the man holding out not a thumb but a claw. Who would stop for them? The breeze that precedes rain unsettles the air. The earth trembles like skin, trees shiver. Josh hugs his jacket self-protectively. 'I'm cold,' says Holly. Owen keeps walking, towing her forward.

*　　　*　　　*

A white car slows down. It is a low vehicle and the verge is high above the road, so that they cannot see the driver and it's as if the car itself is inquisitive, sidling along beside them.

The passenger window slides calmly down. Owen, Josh and Holly stand still as if on command, and the car, though barely moving forward now, stops with a visible lurch. Owen bends down. The driver, a woman, the vehicle's only occupant, turns towards him. 'Get in,' she says.

'Thank you,' he says.

The car is warm. It smells of mints, and plastic, and a faintly cloying perfume.

Such is the relief to be cruising along an open road, it's a minute or two before Owen remembers to introduce himself and the children. The woman says, 'I'm Claire.'

Owen tries not to look at her. Conversation gives him the opportunity to. 'No school?' she asks.

'Doesn't hurt to take them out once in a while, like.'

She has short, dark hair, sallowish skin. She is

150

almost good-looking, Owen thinks. Each of her features is a little exaggerated, she's not plain.

'You shouldn't pick up hitchers,' the woman says. 'But I used to hitch myself. Spain. Greece.'

'Good of you,' Owen says. 'Appreciate it.'

'Heading south?' she asks, glancing in the rear-view mirror.

'Taking them to see their grandmother,' Owen says.

'I'm going to Devon,' Claire tells him.

Owen studies her surreptitiously. No earrings, but you can see where her earlobe, and her left nostril, have been pierced. A scar above her eyebrow. No make-up, only the thick perfume. Brown eyes. Her nose naturally imperfect, or perhaps once broken. It's hard to tell how tall a seated person is, but her legs look long. She wears a black T-shirt, skirt, tights, black pumps. She stares at the road ahead, glancing in the mirror whenever she says something. 'I'll be looking to stop for something to eat soon.'

She is forced to slow down for a tractor trundling like a toy along the road; overtakes it when the way is clear.

'We'll be hungry,' Owen says.

*   *   *

The road runs straight, curves around a scarp or chasm, runs straight again. Past an almost empty field: one horse, poised, patient as an athlete. A convoy of motorbikes comes the other way: old chromey beasts, ridden by portly men.

'Harley-D's,' says Josh with authority. They pass, one after another, each with a throaty burp.

151

After they've gone it seems almost silent, the white car's engine rendered quieter than before. Rain is falling in the fields.

*   *   *

The motorway is chock-full with traffic, stuttering south. In two lanes container lorries, one behind another, like the carriages of an endless train, dwarfing the occasional car sandwiched between them. Josh opens the window. The terrible urgent roar of tyres on tarmac. He closes it again.

Josh invites his sister to spot a particular shape or make of car—'Red Mini: that's five–two to me'—widening criteria to keep well ahead of her.

White caravans towed by saloon cars occupied by white-haired couples sucking Everton Mints and barley sugar. Top-of-the-range vehicles in the outside lanes, stopping and starting with everyone else: motionless across the carriageway, a blockage, then everything shunting on again.

Heavy eyelids, heads droop. The children drift in and out of sleep. The slurred consciousness of travel.

*   *   *

'How about here?' the woman says. SERVICES. She presses the indicator lever attached to the steering wheel, a green light on the dashboard blinks, they pull off the motorway.

The cars in the car park are so similar they might be at a factory: mass production, row upon row, line after line. Perhaps they're brought from the factory to this car park beside the motorway, to be collected and delivered to garages across the country. The white car joins them as the woman steers it into a snug parking space. Only the company symbols on the backs of the cars are different, identified by Josh as they walk towards the service station: Vauxhall, Honda, Citroën . . . The woman locks the car behind her. She presses her thumb hard on the remote key fob, muscle flexing right up her arm, an almost punitive gesture.

At the entrance to the service station Owen and the children pass men and women in different uniforms, selling membership of motoring organisations. They wander through the crowded, bright emporium.

Holly holds her father's hand. 'Look,' she says, dragging Owen towards a poster of the menu in one of the cafeterias, a photograph of each dish on offer. Holly touches the poster on a picture of sausage and bacon, eggs, waffles and baked beans, shinily succulent. 'Dinner,' she says.

The food when it arrives is less glossy than depicted. Owen expects the children to be disappointed, but they tuck in with enthusiasm. Everything is extraordinarily expensive, as if this place were located at the end of some coastal peninsula and not on a major artery of the road network. He calculates that he cannot afford to buy food for himself if he's not to run out of money on the journey, but sips an expensive cup of tea while Claire and the childen eat.

*   *   *

Claire goes to the toilets, saying she'll be back in a

minute. 'She said south,' Josh tells his father. 'Nana lives east. I know that.'

'Don't worry about Nana,' Owen tells him.

'Why not?'

'I'll explain later. I promise.'

Josh's eyes narrow. He nods at something behind Owen. 'There's games,' he says. 'Holly and me could go on them.'

'We can't afford to play games,' Owen says. 'Sorry, Josh.'

Josh gazes around. Unlike an adult, who would glance here and there, he stares at one particular person, then another, mesmerised. At length, looking at a counter with half a dozen computers, he says, 'We'll go on the Internet over there. It says there's free sites. Come on.' Holly gets up and follows.

*   *   *

The S-shaped central avenue of the service station gives on to various franchised cafes, retail outlets, toilets. Owen can see the entrance, as well as the children. He glances at them every few moments; sometimes one or other of them is checking on him.

Pale orange, green and grey plastic chairs and tables, many empty, some occupied by casually dressed pensioners. They look as if they'd been slobbing around at home and were called here unexpectedly. They wear floppy cardigans, sloppy tracksuit trousers. They sit in couples, saying little, their fallen faces suggesting a disappointment to which they are almost resigned.

There are no other children here on this

154

weekday. Owen knows his own must look suspicious. Will someone alert social services, the police? They rejoin him now, Josh letting out a dolorous sigh. 'They're rubbish,' he says. 'Only free sites are ones for you to buy stuff.'

'Yeh,' Holly concurs.

'Come on,' Josh says, and she follows him once more.

'Where are you going?' Owen asks.

'Look around,' Josh says, over his shoulder.

'Keep in sight.'

'Course.'

'Just a look,' Holly explains. 'That's all.'

*   *   *

Owen watches the children move towards a room of fruit machines. He is alert, tense, seeing everything. He sees Josh move stealthily from one machine to the next, slipping his fingers into the coin trays. Holly kneels, her head on the floor, peering underneath the machines. Each evidently comes up with pickings, for they become animated: put money into a machine which blinks and flashes back at them in multicoloured gratitude.

The coffee machine hisses and snorts like a horse. Ambient pop music plays, just loud enough to swim in and out of Owen's awareness. He finds himself humming a familiar tune inside his head without noticing it had got in there. The smell of cooked eggs.

Businessmen in suits and ties pay for their food and carry their trays to a carousel, where they help themselves to cutlery, serviettes, small sachets of ketchup, mayonnaise, pepper and salt. They sit in

155

pairs, converse excitedly, then hunch towards each other, furtive, wary of being overheard here, this anonymous meeting place. One will open a laptop, the other move around the table to join him, and stare at the screen together. One of them catches Owen's eye. Owen wonders if the man is comparing his face with a photo on the screen.

*   *   *

In their early days together Mel called Owen her beachcomber of the city. He couldn't pass a builder's skip without leaning in to poke about, pull out some piece of broken furniture or child's toy, weigh it in his hand. She understood he was mentally stripping it down, taking it apart, assessing the potential reordering of its component parts. 'I've got a use for this,' he'd say, as if he'd been searching the past half-year for precisely such an object. It endeared him to her, this talent for envisioning utility for something cast aside. Benches made from floorboards, pallets for bed frames; plant pots were parts of chimneys, pipes. Most of their furniture inside the flat came free. Once he took a bicycle apart, borrowed some bloke's welding gear, laboured in the backyard. Mel came home and he led her through to the kitchen with her eyes closed, put his hand on her head and tilted it towards the floor so that when she opened her eyes and Owen said, 'See what I made,' it took her a moment scanning the room before she raised her gaze and saw gifts hanging: from hooks on bicycle wheels hung pots and pans; in the lounge the frame had become a candelabra, with eight candles burning.

156

Their dinner service was a medley amassed from charity shops. Owen trawled them in rotation, alone then with Sara, then Josh, when they were babies, toddlers, on Saturdays. The children's clothes were cast-offs, their toys second-hand. He took them blackberry picking along the railway line, apple scrumping in the nature reserve, crayfishing in the river by the bridge.

Mel found it charming. Except that Owen had little discernment, a subtle failing that became evident with time, as the house filled up. 'It's like living in a car boot sale,' she told him, smiling at first.

He was nonplussed.

'I'm ashamed to bring people back here,' she said in time. 'It's a family home, not a junk shop.'

She was changing her mind, Owen understood now, about the man she'd fallen for, even before the accident. He wondered if he could have known this would happen, what he should have done.

'Sorry to take so long.'

Owen turns. Claire is standing beside him. 'I had to make some calls.' She holds two fresh mugs of coffee. 'Need one for the road. Keep the driver alert. Then we can go.' Claire sits and texts. Owen drinks coffee from the mug in his left hand, his hook resting on his lap.

*　　　*　　　*

A young cleaner calmly pushes her trolley from one abandoned table to another. She scrapes leftover food into a bin, stacks dirty plates, pours cutlery into trays which makes a sound like water through shells. She has a canister of pink detergent

157

in a holster on her belt, its trigger attached to a twisted length of hose: she unclips the trigger and sprays each table top, then slowly wipes it with a balled-up wad of kitchen roll.

The cleaner scrapes waste into her bin. Chips, baked beans, vegetables, toast, so much food ordered then left behind. Owen gets to a table before her, calmly carries a plate with a half-eaten fry-up back to his place.

He watches the children move into another room. Successful gamblers, they are using fruit-machine winnings on computer games. Josh is waving a large gun, shooting at a screen. Owen can read the words, THE HOUSE OF THE DEAD. Holly is driving a virtual car along a racetrack in some Nintendo game.

The service station seems to be filling up. Detritus builds up on abandoned tables. Owen becomes selective in his gleaning, picking portable items of food, slipping them into his rucksack. He glances at the computer room. It is empty. Owen's heart thumps in his chest, he looks around wildly. He sees Josh signalling to him, pointing outside, to a play area. Holly stands beside him. Owen nods and they trot out. He watches.

The play area is an adventure playground. Diminutive commandos, Josh and Holly climb netting, balance their way along a swinging, slatted bridge. Owen watches them, his heartbeat settling. Beyond, a man lets his dogs off their leads: two brown pointers run pell-mell across an ungrazed field towards a wood. A stand of silver birches.

*   *   *

Outside, the repetitive cars come and go, vacating spaces for one another, filled within moments.

In the playground Holly cruises down a slide. Josh leads an assault on a wooden turreted castle, spraying its defenders with imaginary bullets. Owen knows they must leave now, he no longer belongs, as if this station is becoming either more or less real than he himself, this transit area, where people are being sorted in some kind of selection process of which some are almost aware.

'Forecast not so good,' Claire says.

Owen had forgotten her. 'Maybe we'll stay in a hotel,' he says. 'I have a backup plan,'

She sips her coffee. 'What kind of plan?' she asks.

If I tell her the truth, Owen thinks, all will be lost. If I tell her a lie, she'll spot it. His mother once told him that his father, faced with a simple question requiring a straightforward answer, would rather spin a yarn. Whereas she, at the first thought of falsehood, would feel her vocal cords constrict, and squeak. Her son is the same. He says nothing.

'I had a plan once,' Claire says, and smiles at the memory, this gift from herself. She begins to tell him the story. It concerns her persuading a group of her teenage friends to do something none of them wanted to do. She had to change one person's mind after another. Owen is absorbed, though he doesn't follow the story. He's drawn into Claire's force field, her animated self.

It occurs to Owen that he and Claire are sitting slightly closer to one another than they were a minute ago, drawing towards each other by imperceptible degrees. He can feel her breath now, see the imperfections of her skin, blotches in each cheek. Variegations of colour, tone. She has become desirable, and he finds himself changing, his libido brought alive, a long-forgotten sensation. They speak, but it is in code, and even as he listens, or occasionally interjects, Owen cannot say whether or not it makes any sense, it is gobbledegook, nothing more than an excuse to watch her lips move, enticing, to look into her eyes looking into his.

Their fingers meet on the wiped-clean table, the fingers of her right and his left hand touch. Semi-independent from their owners' minds, the fingers stroke, caress, pinch each other, as their owners watch. Claire stops speaking. Her face is blushing. Beneath the table, Owen feels his knees push forward in search of hers: they meet as if underwater. Two bodies yearning towards fusion.

Suddenly, with his hook, Owen grabs his left forearm and yanks it aside. He stands up, looks outside. The children are still playing in the adventure playground.

Claire is embarrassed, irked. She looks at her watch, holds up her phone. 'I need a top-up. Be a moment. Right back.' She heads towards the newsagents. Owen watches her wide shoulders, her long legs. Her posture makes her look taller than she really is. It's a repeated visual surprise when slouching men pass her and prove to be an inch or two taller than her. She disappears behind magazine racks.

Strip lights on the ceiling. No shadows. Owen can't understand how there are no shadows on people's faces. The glare from the strip lights fall to the floor and bounce back, and off the tables and the walls, filling in where there should have been shadows.

*   *   *

'He's hurt.'

Josh is holding his elbow and grimacing, struggling not to cry. As Owen embraces him, Josh's eyes fill with tears.

'He fell off the log,' Holly explains.

'It were slippery,' Josh says.

'His arm hit the wood.'

Josh nods back over his shoulder. 'Vikings was after me.'

'Where does it hurt?' Owen strokes his son's elbow. Josh rests his head on his father's shoulder.

'We done the law of gravity last week,' Josh whispers. 'I hate it. It's too strict. Everything falls.' He's stopped crying, is absorbing himself in telling his father his idea. 'Why can't things just float down to the earth sometimes? It hurts when you hit the ground.'

'Where's that lady?' Holly asks.

Owen eases his son off his lap to the floor and stands up himself. His skin tingles.

The place is crowded, people make such slow progress it takes a while of observation to see that they are not stationary, as if in some jam-packed nightclub, but moving each in one direction or another. Countless negotiations every moment. Owen glimpses Claire in the far distance across the mall, in the company of three or four men and women in white shirts, the black police epaulettes upon their shoulders, talking into radios attached to their chests.

'Pick up your rucksacks,' Owen says. 'Back to the playground.'

They walk through the cafeteria, Owen bent forward, he hopes undramatically. Doors swing open, the coolness of the day a shock to him after air-conditioned warmth. 'Quick,' Owen says. He suspects he doesn't need to, that the children understand the urgency required. Holly is not dawdling as she naturally does. They follow him out of the play area and turn right, away from the service station, into the field where dogs are exercised. Owen is drawn to the silver birches, he can almost see the three of them half a minute hence dissolving into the wood. But the field is too wide, and in less than half a minute a police officer would be at a window and could spot them scarpering. He turns left instead, and they run along a hedge. One or two people are in the field, drivers stretching their legs, and Owen is conscious of a need to make their running look like fun, not flight, so alternates between leading and theatrically chasing his children.

They reach the cover of a thicket of scrub and saplings. Holly flops. They kneel. Owen crawls back and looks across the field. He can just see a man with a dog. He's standing still, facing towards the service station, which itself is out of sight from here. It's suddenly apparent that the man is listening to someone, someone is addressing him. A moment later he shakes his head, shrugs. He points away, to the far side of the field, towards the silver birch trees, as if to say, Maybe over there? Then police officers come into view, they cross the field at a trot. No dogs of their own, thank God, not yet at least.

162

Owen crawls back to the others. 'Let's move,' he says, taking Holly's hand. They walk through the scrubland towards the roaring sound. 'We're on the wrong side of the motorway,' Owen explains. 'We need to cross it, see, to the west.' The road is raised up high—they lose sight of the vehicles upon it. As they climb the bank it would be easy to imagine they're approaching a waterfall. When they reach the barrier and see the speed and the unremitting volume of cars and lorries hurtling across in front of them it's immediately obvious that any attempt to dash over between vehicles is out of the question.

They walk south beside the motorway. Josh yells, 'I'll have a look,' and runs ahead. The boy seems in the excitement to have let go of his misgivings, for the moment at least. For half a mile they scramble over fences, up the bank then down again into a field. Josh comes running back, shouting something it's impossible to make out above the noise. He beckons them, and they scamper after him, until he stops, peering towards the bank in front of him, then looking back at them, then looking at the bank. When they reach him they see a tunnel underneath the motorway. Sitting at the round mouth of the tunnel is a dog.

'We can go through,' Josh says.

'Wait,' Owen answers.

The dog has brown hair, and looks like some kind of cross, between a collie and maybe a Labrador. A mongrel. It seems to be staring calmly back at them. Then it turns and walks away into the darkness of the tunnel.

'Be careful,' Owen says, advancing, holding his arms in front of each of the children. He wonders whether the mongrel is alone, or one of a pack of wild dogs. As they reach the mouth of the tunnel they can see the dog in silhouette, sauntering away from them. They follow. It's oddly quiet here, underneath the motorway. Owen yells, 'Waaa!' and the sound resonates around them. The children copy, uttering their own loud syllables which echo off the concrete walls. The ground has a little dry mud on it, perhaps this is a storm drain of some kind, for the passage of water rather than animals.

When they reach the far side the dog is a further twenty metres away. It's stopped and seems to be waiting for them.

'Where's its owner?' Holly asks.

Owen shakes his head. 'Don't know.' When they walk on, the dog resumes its own journey. It too heads west, so that they can hardly help but follow it. After a while they enter a high-sided track, an ancient right of way. Josh opens his rucksack and produces three green apples.

'You bought these?' Owen asks. 'Back there?'

'He took them, Daddy,' Holly explains. 'When the lady wasn't looking.'

Owen bites into an apple. His mouth floods with saliva. The sweetness. Teeth crunching skin and pulp, sweet juice and saliva. How strange it is to be alive.

*   *   *

They follow paths where possible, or tramp along lanes. Owen aims to keep away from roads. There is a thrill in walking out of and away from a great urban conurbation, an escape. They enter a wood, follow a rabbits' path then find themselves on a

164

tarmacadam road laid in a straight line between the quiet trees. There's nothing to explain the road in this deserted place.

Soon they begin to climb. They sit and eat their last scraps of food that Owen had filched from the motorway service station, other people's leftovers: rolls, butter; grapes, a banana; biscuits. Water and juice from half-drunk plastic bottles. Then set off again, climbing easily. The dog is still with them, and sits a few yards away.

After a while Josh says, 'How do you know which way to go, Owen?' He has a suspicious expression. 'Have you been here before?'

'The sun sets in the west,' Owen tells him. 'We head for the setting sun. And if the sun is hidden, I've got a compass.'

Josh is suddenly excited. 'We're going camping,' he says, turning to his sister. 'That's the surprise.'

Above them, the sky is grey and thick as oil paint. Black birds swoop across like cinders shot from an underground fire. From the top of the Clent Hills they look back at the sprawl of the great city. Owen cannot see east beyond it; it spreads north and south. He turns and looks west, to Wales, surely, the far horizon. The thick grey canvas cannot stretch all across the wide sky: above the line of land or sea or mountains there are pale interludes, pools of light blue.

Holly tugs on Owen's right arm. 'Carry,' she says. Awkwardly, gripping her leg with his hook, he hoists her onto his shoulders.

The sky is opening up. The sun, getting lower, illuminates more. It seems to be enticing them towards it, out of sight but reaching towards them, laying a path of gold across the patchwork

165

landscape of hedges and fields. The girl on her father's shoulders, the boy with a stick from a hedge that is a gun, a sword, a lance. The mongrel loping ahead of them.

The pub is at the edge of a village, and they sit in its garden, surrounded by other families. The building appears sick: what look like three huge sticking plasters have been attached to the outside wall. Braces, skewered through the infrastructure, holding it together. Across a fence sheep graze. Children try to entice the animals to come to the fence. The sheep decline and after a while the children run off, but then some other child, watching, goes to the fence. Men and women sit at the picnic tables drinking gloomily, wrapping layers of clothes or their bare arms around them while their children run about, from climbing frame to fence to table, strangers communicating with each other by this criss-crossing of their random paths.

Food comes. Sausage, egg and chips. After this first day, Owen decides, from now on, they'll prepare their own food. As they eat, tiredly, Owen gazes out across the field. The dark seems to come in from the distance, so that against the gloom, trees and sheep and people in the foreground appear lighter than before, each object standing apart from those around it, which isn't really possible though it seems so and makes them magical, totemic, so that he peers at one and the next in the hope that it might deliver its significance, which most of the time remains hidden.

But then the dark has gone over them and twilight is silent and uniform across their portion of the earth. Night is falling, unarguable, finite. At the end, though, at the end of the dying day, as his daughter dozes against him and his son gazes from beneath lazy eyelids at some insect crawling across his shirt, only then does the sun, long hidden, skit between the clouds and the long horizon. The whole of it emerges in a moment, grey then white then yellow, like a single all-powerful film lamp, lighting up the garden. The world is rendered cinematic. He can see that people see themselves on a film set, spectators and participants simultaneously. It is like a secret brief performance, an occult drama in which the inhabitants of the garden collude.

Josh looks up at his father, and they exchange smiles. We sense it is at the same thing, Owen thinks. Maybe we're wrong. His son leans into him. Owen raises his face to the sky and closes his eyes, and as he does so he becomes airborne, aerial: he flies as if surfing the setting sun, so to see this darkening moment across the country, skimming over fields, above woods, into suburban streets. Urban allotments and tenement gardens. Waste-disposal sites and reclamation yards. Schools, municipal playing fields. He sees the yellow light dying in private swimming pools with their air of desertion. He climbs out of the shadow of hills and up to their blazing peak, from where the sun spills yellow grey liquid across the Irish Sea.

*　　　*　　　*

Owen carries Holly into the wood. Josh unties the groundsheets from his father's rucksack and spreads the smaller one on the ground. Owen lays his daughter upon it. In the moonlight he breaks branches and spreads the larger groundsheet over a crosspiece, constructing a simple bivouac. Josh ties down the corners, to bits of wood that Owen, grasping them in his hook, quickly whittles into pegs. Then they spread leafy branches across the triangular opening behind Holly's head, to inhibit a draught through the shelter. Owen leaves the front open.

'We'll light a fire in the morning,' he says.

Josh seems to be accepting surprises in his stride now. He lies down dreamily, across the groundsheet from his sister. Owen squeezes between them. They lie in silence for a minute, maybe two. Owen becomes aware of a particular, ominous sensation, like something approaching from a distance, outside him, though it is coming from deep inside: he can feel his right hand, his phantom limb, throbbing. Beside him, Josh's breathing is inaudible. Owen assumes he is asleep, so is surprised when he hears his son say, in a hoarse whisper, 'We're not going to see Nana, are we?'

'No,' Owen tells him. 'She's not sick. I had to tell the school that so that they'd let you come with me.'

'Where are we going?' Josh asks.

'I'm going to show you where I come from,' Owen says.

Owen waits for the next question, but none comes. Josh was satisfied with his answer. Or more likely exhausted. Owen knows that he himself is too, but there is no way that he could sleep. His right hand is there, though he knows it's not, throbbing at the end of his arm. Phantom limb

168

pain comes at night, always. The sensation alters: now it feels as if it is being shredded by some unseen sadistic device. The pain in his non-existent hand causes him to visualise it: it's all mangled and crushed, as it was in the accident, broken and bleeding, severed nerves exposed, veins, sinews, bone. And still being subjected to further stress. That's what it feels like, now as every evening of his life.

Owen crawls out of the shelter. In his rucksack is a bottle of wine. He bought it from the pub, along with white bread rolls and sausages for the morning. There's a corkscrew on his multi-tool. Holding the neck of the bottle in his hook, squeezing the bottle between his knees, he pulls the cork. He lifts the mouth of the bottle to his lips, and drinks, willing the alcohol to travel swiftly to the end of his right arm. To still the pain.

Owen sits on the ground, a few yards from the shelter. The children are safe. He drinks steadily. In time, when the bottle is empty, he will unstrap his hook, take off his shoes and crawl in between them. He's blearily aware that the dog is in there too, curled up beside Holly.

TAKE THY PLAGUE AWAY FROM ME

Owen wakes, shivering. He is alone in the shelter, the children no longer warming him. In the floor of his skull there is a sediment, of wine dregs, in its roof something pulsates. And there's an odd aroma in his nostrils. Groggy, he sits up. The children are squatting outside, watching him.

Owen blinks slowly, squeezing his eyes shut, then open again. 'Was I talking in my sleep?'

Josh looks away. 'Not much,' he says.

Holly crawls back in beside Owen. He opens his arm. 'I was awake first,' she says proudly.

'Look,' says Josh, moving aside so that Owen can see. The boy has built a campfire. Of course: the smell of woodsmoke. He must have found the lighter in his father's rucksack, not to mention dry grass, kindling, larger dry pieces of wood: the base of the fire is an amber glow. Now Owen can feel the heat of it.

'I've done the same you did that time,' Josh says.

'You've done it well,' Owen says.

'And sausages,' Holly prompts.

Josh holds up long twigs, each with a sausage skewered on its end. 'Now you're awake we can cook these,' Josh explains. 'Place your order, Owen.'

'Don't call him Owen.' Holly scowls at her brother. 'Call him sir,' she says, and turns to her father. 'What would you like for breakfast, sir?' she asks in a sing-song voice. 'Hot dog?'

'We've got no ketchup,' Josh says.

'Guess what?' Owen says. 'I picked up a few

sachets at the services, didn't I? Look in the side pockets of the rucksack.'

*   *   *

When Owen stumbles through the trees, he realises it's not just his throbbing head that hurts. His legs ache, muscles that had lain dormant inside his skin were thrown into reluctant action yesterday, and now complain to him in the only language they know, that of pain. How far did the three of them walk? His knees and hips, his back and shoulders, ache too. What was it Ziggy, who used to help Owen with large garden jobs, told him? 'In Poland we say, After the age of thirty, if you wake up and nothing hurts, this means you're dead.' The children walked as far as he did but seem not to be suffering, not even five-year-old Holly. Owen pees onto the forest floor, damp grass, dry leaves. The sound he can hear repeated deeper into the wood; by a stream, presumably, down the slope ahead of him. Pissing outside is entirely different from using a toilet, seeing one's evacuation drain into the earth. In his clients' gardens Owen preferred to find a secluded spot, behind shrubs, a tree, to discreetly pee, rather than ask to go indoors.

The smell of sausages, roasting. Holly holds one skewer, Josh two, each turning the sausages towards themselves, checking them every few seconds. Owen, bare-chested, straps on his hook. Josh glances round. 'You could put a holster on one of those straps,' he suggests. 'He could carry a gun,' he tells his sister.

'Cool,' says Holly.

171

'The name's Bond,' her brother says in a transatlantic grown-up voice. 'Josh Bond.'

'My tooth is wobbly, Daddy,' Holly says. With the tips of the fingers of her free hand she grips the tiny front tooth. It shifts this way and that. Owen winces. 'My first one,' she says.

*   *   *

They eat three hot dogs each, and feed the dog two as well. Owen boils water in his small pan and brews tea, adding more sugar than he'd like until it's sweet enough for Josh to drink a little. Holly prefers juice. The three of them lie on the groundsheet, replete. Stilled. After this breakfast, Owen fancies, he will need no more food. Only the children need eat from now on.

'I want to talk to Mummy,' Josh says.

'Me too,' says Holly.

'She'll be worried.' The boy's eyes cloud. 'I think I'm getting worried about her.'

'We'll call her,' Owen says. 'I promise. We'll pass a phone box.' The words come out of his mouth. 'We're bound to.'

'Good,' says Holly.

Josh is unsure. His eyes are momentarily bright then darken beneath his frown. The weather in his head. 'Okay,' he says.

*   *   *

While Josh helps Owen take down the shelter and roll and tie up the groundsheets, Holly looks around, trailed by the dog. She returns holding a length of black plastic piping, some six or seven

172

feet long. 'It's my telescope,' Holly says. 'Can you carry it for me?'

Owen takes it from her. 'Maybe it's a didgeridoo, see,' he says, and blows into it. No sound emerges from the other end. 'Stay there a minute,' he tells the children. 'I just want to check something.' Turning, Owen runs into the wood, carrying the tube like a rifle, disappearing down the slope, until the top of his head vanishes.

'Maybe it's a blowpipe,' Josh tells his sister. 'We could make poisoned darts.'

'Yes,' she says. 'It is mine,' she reminds him, to establish the fact.

The children hear a shout, and look at each other. Josh picks up Owen's rucksack, and they walk in the direction of the call. The slope soon becomes a steep bank. Holly calls out, 'Dad,' Owen replies, they adjust their direction. He is nearby. They find their father in a stream, just above a stretch that plunges downhill so steeply it's practically a waterfall. He has placed one end of the pipe in the stream; the other is propped up on a long, Y-shaped piece of branch Owen has found, like a thumb stick. Water trickles out onto the ground a foot or two away from the stream, at a height of about five feet.

'Want to take a shower?' Owen asks. The children frown and shake their heads. 'Please yourselves, like,' he says. Rummaging through the rucksack he finds a small plastic bottle of shampoo. He removes his clothes, unstraps his hook and steps, bending, beneath the trickle of water. It's freezing cold. He is determined to bear it, and after a minute or two the biting cold is no longer painful, but stimulating. A deep hot bath would be

173

better, and this alfresco shower possesses a puny flow, but still the water is slowly therapeutic to aching flesh. Owen puts shampoo in his hair. He becomes dimly aware of movement, childish commotion, before closing his eyes again, relishing the cold aquatic restoration of his body. Bending his head beneath the water, he lets it rinse the shampoo out. The next thing he knows there is the sound of giggling, and he opens his eyes to find Josh and Holly, naked, have joined him.

He suspects it was at Holly's prompting. She is shrieking as she hops around, not only from the cold, a bedraggled pixie. Josh, circumspect, enjoys himself in a more reticent manner. The boy's a skinny-ribs, all bony joints, sinewy limb. Holly is more fleshy. She must eat more than her brother.

Owen moves aside so that the children can receive the flow of water upon them. He reaches for the plastic bottle of shampoo and, making them promise to keep their eyes closed, washes the children's hair. He massages the shampoo into their scalps with his fingers. Josh's hair is short, and dry and wiry, and the shampoo lathers readily; Owen cleans his neck and ears as well. He has to empty the bottle into Holly's long blonde hair. It hangs untidily, knotted and sticking to her skin, a heavy rope of hair.

The weak shower slowly rinses the shampoo off; it slides down their pink pale bodies, long rivulets of foam.

Owen dries off Holly first, then Josh. By the time he gets a turn to use their only towel it's wet through. When he pulls on his clothes they stick to his damp, shivering skin. He realises Josh is looking at him, smiling. He stops dressing, looks at

174

the boy, expecting a sardonic observation.

'You're really clever, Dad,' Josh tells him.

* * *

They walk out of the wood, skirt a village. On either side of the road there are birds on the aerials of houses, nattering as if to each other across the street. It is spring. A car passes at speed, a thump of music like the vehicle's angry pulse. Then they head off away from the road along a footpath. The brown mongrel dog trails a yard or two behind whoever's at the back.

The sky is grey, and brown. Colours appear to have been drained from the earth. The one vibrant plant is holly. Its red berries are gone now but the deep rich green is visible from a distance—in a hedge, across a field—it renders all the hibernating plants around it pallid by comparison, feeble. Other conifers are dull. All else is dormant. But as they walk Owen begins to see snowdrops, then yellow and pink primroses, and yellow flowers in a ground-spreading plant. Aconites. It's far too late for them. He looks closer at the trees they pass, sees on the branches of hazel, elder, sycamore, leaves emerging from the wood of branches wrapped up in tight little bunches, like sushi. The new buds. It's as if the whole of spring is showing itself in a moment.

From a large white house in a wood full of daffodils comes an anxious, imperious cry. When Holly asks what the sound is, Josh says, 'A peacock, of course.' Owen wonders how he knows, when or where he might have seen one. On TV probably.

The path passes through a grove of slender

175

beech. Every trunk is wrapped around by ivy. Owen feels sorry for the trees, knowing what is happening to them. A creeping strangulation.

At times the path becomes pure sand. 'It's like being at the seaside,' Holly says. A long narrow beach threading its way through a wood.

Another time the path widens, on the ground are large pebbles, rounded stones, as if they're walking along a dry riverbed. On either side are the straggly remnants of last year's bracken and brambles.

The children walk in silence. Holly seems lost in her own thoughts. Josh is more watchful.

Sometimes the path is cut deep between banks, it's old, much older than the houses and roads, the pastures and arable fields around it. Old paths through the forest. At times they leave the path and walk along a lane a while before finding a new path westward, reconnecting to a network that Owen begins to visualise criss-crossing this island, behind, underneath, intersecting yet apart from all the monuments and machinery of civilisation. He wonders whether his brain, in constructing the image, does so with a similar network of pathways and connections. The image is a liberating one. A person might choose to be a wandering soul and be able to manage it, here, on these ancient paths. Kept open by whom? Owen wonders. An army of council workers and volunteers placing bridges over streams and stiles over fences, replacing gates and putting up signposts pointing the way here, and there. What a job, he thinks. That's what he should have done if only he could have taken orders; surely he'd have been happy to, directed to a stretch of path with a map, and a trailer full of fence posts and wooden planks, wire and tools.

'I'm hungry,' Holly says, and Owen is surprised to see from his watch that it's after noon already. They sit on a fallen tree trunk looking out and up across a steeply rising field. The children drink orange juice, eat apples. It must have been the perfect temperature for walking: now that they've stopped Owen sees goose pimples appear on Holly's bared arms; Josh shivers. They pull on their jackets. In the field in front of them a large brown horse appears. It raises its head and lifts its tail and there, right ahead and above them, prances along the high ridge. It wishes to show them that this is precisely how a thoroughbred trots, with just this much dignity and poise.

*   *   *

They cross the River Severn, waiting till there's no traffic on the bridge. The wide river flows silent below them. The children jog ahead.

A little further on there is a phone box at the side of the road, beside an empty lay-by. The three of them crowd inside. A smell like old machinery. Owen finds coins. Josh knows his home phone number, and presses the buttons, while Holly holds the receiver, ready to speak first. But there's no one there, only the answerphone. The children leave messages: Owen is relieved to hear their enthusiasm for the journey they're being taken on, even as they tell their mother they miss her, and love her. He wishes he could add his voice to theirs. When Josh holds the receiver to him, Owen shakes his head, and Josh places it back in its cradle.

*   *   *

During the early part of the afternoon the landscape is more open. They are rarely out of sight of some farm or other dwelling. Owen imagines people looking up from pictures in a newspaper of this man and the children he's abducted, or listening to the news on the radio as they do the washing-up and seeing through a window the trio of distinctive figures cross the rolling vista, plus an unexplained dog.

Is it possible to hide? Everywhere in England is known. Hasn't every pat of soil been trodden on, turned over? But this pessimistic appraisal is followed by another: actually, nobody sees them. They move like ghosts across the open country, this tamed land.

*   *   *

Walking, Owen recalls the conversation in the car. He'd asked Sara what she was going to be when she grew up.

'A teacher,' she said, without hesitation. She loved school, couldn't wait to leave the house in the mornings. Mel was even a little jealous of Sara's class teacher, whom the girl adored.

'I'm going to marry a doctor.'

'Really?'

'Yes, and I'm going to have children.'

'How many?' At the time Mel was pregnant with their third.

'I don't know. Maybe three. They'll run around in the country. One of them will ride a horse.'

178

'You're going to live in the country?'

Owen looked at his daughter. She was frowning. 'In a small town in the country,' she decided.

Up ahead the lights changed. He pressed his foot on the accelerator. The dog appeared from nowhere. An image of the life Sara, aged six, had envisioned for herself, and would not have, had stayed with Owen.

*   *   *

They walk without talking for some time. Owen becomes increasingly aware of birdsong. It's as if birds accompany them, passing news of their journey from one to another. The day is warming up now. Crossing a field in which sheep graze, Holly wrinkles her nose at the sweet-sour smell in the air, of greasy wool and shit. She forgets her distaste when she finds a horseshoe, and insists on carrying it with her. Josh tells her it's too heavy.

'No, it's not,' Holly says.

'You won't be able to carry it.'

'Yes, I will,' she insists.

*   *   *

Over stiles the path crosses fields, following a stream that has carved a deep gully in soft, red-brown soil. At its widest points the gully is maybe thirty feet across, and twenty feet deep: they look down from the short-cropped grass into a river landscape. Trees have rooted in the banks. Huge boulders force the stream to weave in lazy loops. There are waterfalls, lagoons, sandy beaches. Josh makes a frame with his fingers like a cameraman.

179

'There were this thing on TV,' he tells his father, 'how they used to film with models. A ship floats into view, and this tiny stream turns into a wide river. Everything suddenly changes whatsit.'

'Scale?' Owen offers.

'Yes.'

*   *   *

They walk through a noisy copse of tall trees. There's a rookery overhead, the birds arguing in the high nests.

'Birds can't talk,' Holly says.

'Yes, they can,' Josh says.

'Birds sing.'

'Those aren't singing,' Josh says. 'They're disagreeing with each other.'

'No, they're not.'

'Yes, they are.'

Owen is about to interrupt, to tell the children to stop bickering, when he realises that they are cawing the words at each other.

'Oh no they're not.'

'Oh yes they are.'

Holly is the first to break into giggles.

*   *   *

'Can you carry this, Daddy?' Holly says. She is holding the horseshoe, having carried it in her rucksack for miles.

'I'll carry you instead,' Owen suggests, letting the horseshoe drop back to earth, and he hoists her up onto his shoulders. He catches Josh scowling at them, resentful of this preferential treatment even

180

though there's no way he'll ask it for himself. No one's going to carry him, he's eleven years old and he'll walk as far as anyone.

*   *   *

The footpath they're on cuts straight through the middle of a mobile home holiday park. Closely packed trailers. The park is on the lower slope of one side of a wide valley. The hill has been landscaped, terraces cut, each plot barely larger than the caravan upon it. It's hard to see how defunct mobile homes can be removed, their replacements situated. Perhaps they're lifted in and out by a monumental crane. Or perhaps none of them are ever moved. Here each one stands, now and forever.

There's barely anyone around. Outside one caravan a white-haired man kneels on a tiny lawn, cutting the grass with a pair of shears. An old woman walks her Yorkshire terrier on a long lead. It stops by Josh, sniffing him; he shyly puts a hand down to pat its head. It moves on to their dog— each sniffs the other's posterior, moving around in circles—then breaks off and resumes its journey.

The sun shines. The park is virtually deserted except for a large population of small inanimate beings: around every mobile home red-clothed, white-bearded gnomes stand on plastic rocks with hands on hips, or fish in tiny ponds, or grin at the world from behind white-dotted red toadstools. Bird feeders hang from rods stuck onto caravans, but the birds haven't found them, put off perhaps by plastic herons, pigeons, doves and ducks with whom they'd be forced to mingle. There are signs on the sides of the trailers. A SWEET NATURED WOMAN AND A GRUMPY OLD MAN LIVE HERE, reads one. A grey rabbit appears to twitch. Then it scampers off between caravans—the mongrel in hot pursuit—as if a plastic animal has come suddenly to life.

Holly is enchanted. 'I want to live here,' she says. 'I *love* it.'

A mile further on they stop to rest, the children drink the last of their juice on a track beside a field in which brown bullocks graze. Josh counts them. 'Twenty-three,' he decides. The calves all face in the same direction, and each one moves gradually forward as it eats, one hoof at a time, the whole small herd advancing slowly across the green field.

'Looks like they're playing a game,' Owen says. 'Creeping up on something in the hedge.'

Josh nods.

*   *   *

They pass dull green fields across which are scattered bales tightly wrapped in black plastic, and then a large field covered in curtains of black plastic, the earth being blacked out.

*   *   *

The footpath takes them through a graveyard. Owen hesitates. The church is right at the edge of a village and beyond the graveyard the path looks to carry on away from the houses, but he wonders whether they shouldn't skirt the village in a wider arc. The children, the dog, wait as he watches, and

182

listens. There doesn't seem to be anyone around. A sign asks people to PLEASE CLEAR UP AFTER YOUR DOG. They advance slowly along a grassy path towards the church. Many gravestones lean at a mournful angle. There are a number of box tombs. 'The bodies are in there,' Josh informs his sister. 'They're not buried in the ground.'

Owen says nothing.

'Stone full of bones.'

The path passes the porch. 'Can we go in?' Holly asks.

'It'll be locked,' Josh says.

Holly looks dumbfounded. 'Why?'

'People who don't believe in God,' Josh tells her, 'steal things from his churches.'

Owen is relieved they'll carry on past without a quarrel, but then Holly walks abruptly into the porch and tries the door, turning the heavy iron ring-handle with both hands. She pushes against the door: it opens. She proceeds into the church. Owen steps warily forward. Who knows what might be going on inside? A funeral, a prayer meeting. He peers into the gloomy interior. Silence. Emptiness.

The dog stays in the porch. 'Good boy,' Josh tells it. Owen whispers in his son's ear, 'It's a girl, actually.'

Inside, the church is large for what seems to be a small village; it is many degrees cooler than outside, and has the smell of damp stone. There are pillars along each side of the nave. The children wander round together, walking along each pew, exploring the intriguing nooks and crannies—it's as if a church had been designed to engage their children's sense of mystery.

183

Owen studies the large font of white stone at the back of the church. It's ornately carved, with knotted, interlacing shapes as well as strange creatures: a griffin, a centaur. A lamb. The Lamb of God. Owen is sure the font is very old, Norman, even. He's not really sure, though. He's so ignorant. He curses his ignorance. Would it have taken so much education, self-learning, to be able to date such artefacts? Perhaps it was actually carved in the nineteenth or even twentieth century by someone purposely harking back to an earlier era.

'Come and see,' Josh demands. The children drag their father into the chancel. To one side are seats cut into the wall, for priests or servers, Owen assumes. Beside arches above them are two carved faces. Holly is pointing at one of them. It has horns. 'It's the Devil,' Josh says.

'Yes,' says Holly.

'What's he doing in the church?' Josh asks.

*   *   *

Owen sits in a pew near the front of the nave. The children have checked out the choir stalls and been up into the pulpit, and now they are rooting around at the back of the church.

A memory. He and Mel were in a cafe. It took up the whole of the ground floor of an old, wide, two-storey industrial building, a factory that had been converted. Sara was two, maybe three years old, Josh a baby. Sara was restless, Mel tired. Owen took his daughter by the hand and wandered round the large cafe. There were some stairs leading up to some kind of balcony. They climbed them, slowly, the small girl accomplishing one step, then another.

There was a door leading from the balcony. Owen tried it, it opened, and they stepped through into what seemed to be some kind of rehearsal room. It was empty except for a drum kit, some speakers. An ashtray on the floor, loose pages of a newspaper. When they tried to go back through the door to the balcony they found it locked: some kind of security catch had clicked. At the far end of the rehearsal room was another door, which was unlocked. It gave onto a hallway or landing, with a lift and a dark stairwell. The stairs descended into darkness, they were oddly forbidding; Owen didn't want to go down them, especially with Sara, so he pressed the lift button. The doors opened, they stepped inside.

The sign in the lift indicated that they were on the sixth floor; there were buttons for five others below. But they were surely on the first floor—having climbed those stairs—and needed to go back down one storey to reach the ground. Perhaps the lift was second-hand when it was installed here. Owen pressed G, the lift came to life and descended down through 5, 4, 3. They could hear music being played. Down through 2, 1, before coming to rest at the ground floor. The lift doors opened onto a similar landing to the one above, although this time the stairs went up rather than down. There was a single door here too, but on the other side of the landing. Owen opened it and he and Sara stepped into a large concert hall. There was a stage to their right. The auditorium was cleared of seating and two men were shining the wooden floor, lazily swishing polishing machines

185

from side to side.

They returned to the lift and went back up a floor. As they stepped out the music they'd heard was suddenly loud. Owen pushed the door off this landing surreptitiously open: this was less a rehearsal room than a studio, with all kinds of recording equipment, and a band of four young men was playing raucous thumping rock music.

The dark stairways. They took the lift. On another floor they stepped out and the only light was from the lift. When the lift doors closed behind them Owen and Sara were plunged into pitch blackness. Owen groped for the lift button, praying that no one else had summoned it, he pressed it and the doors opened once more, spreading light.

Always the stairway, descending into black nothingness, and each time Owen took the lift. He discovered later on that the building was on a hill, with the cafe at the top. On the fourth floor they stepped out, opened the one door off the landing and found themselves in a shopping arcade. They walked along, past small shops, turned a corner and found themselves looking through the large windows of the cafe, in the middle of which Mel sat reading a paper, sipping her coffee, Josh asleep in her lap. They reached the door to the cafe and Sara ran towards her mother.

Owen has spent so much time forcing himself not to think of Sara; almost as much energy as he's spent trying not to forget her. What a disorientating experience in the cafe that had been, unsettling, surreal, but fun. When they returned to Mel she was unworried, unaware of their adventure. They hadn't actually been gone

186

long at all.

* * *

Holly is almost the same age now as Sara was. Tears slide down Owen's cheeks. For a moment he misses Mel as much as Sara.

The silence of the church is desecrated by a loud booming sound. Reverberating. Even before he has identified what it is Owen knows the children have caused it. It is so close, within the church. Then he understands it was a bell ringing, and he is up, out of the pew and running towards the back of the church. He yells, 'Josh!' Past the organ there is a door, into a tiny chamber, and another door, into the tower. There the children stand, transfixed by their transgression.

'It were Josh,' says Holly.

A rope hanging beside him swings slightly.

'I didn't know,' he says.

'Come on,' Owen tells them. 'Need to go. Right now.' He turns to lead the way back out of the tower and stops: above the door, between the lintel and an arch above it are weird carved animals, upside down. One is a deer, a stag with antlers. Behind it is a net. Perhaps one of the other animals is a dog, a hunting hound. At the crown of the arch is a bearded figurehead. Owen stares at it for a moment. Like the animals, the head is crudely carved: this really must be old. Is it meant, he wonders, to be simply a grotesque figure, or Christ, reaper of souls?

'Come on, Dad,' Josh says.

Owen stirs. 'Yes.' They run through the church. The dog is waiting for them. They resume the

187

path. Owen is sure every inhabitant of the village is watching them, these desecraters of their holy place. Holly is tired, slow, and once more he lifts her up and carries her.

*　　　*　　　*

'Did you know when dinosaurs roamed the earth?' Josh asks, but doesn't wait for an answer. 'Over a hundred million years ago,' he informs his travelling companions.

Owen has the sense that Holly is asleep on his shoulders. Her weight shifts floppily with each step he takes. 'Did you learn that on TV?' he asks.

'No,' Josh answers, apparently affronted.

'You read a book?'

'No.' The same aggrieved tone. It's as if Owen is accusing him of something underhand.

'How do you know about them, then?' Owen asks in a way he hopes is earnest enquiry, and does not sound as if he's challenging the accuracy of what his son declared.

Josh shrugs. 'I just do,' he says.

*　　　*　　　*

They walk along a dismantled railway line. It runs straight through the rural landscape. There is nothing to indicate its former use. Now a farm track, as evidenced by tractor tyre marks, it has deep grass verges and a ribbon of sparser grass running down the middle. Along the two tyre tracks, black earth has pushed up between and over the railway pebbles. Along each side grow trees and shrubs, obscuring concrete posts and

188

rusted wire. Only the strange directness of the track betrays its provenance. Josh cannot believe it's not a Roman road. When Owen explains that trains once chugged to and fro across the countryside, and to cut costs a third of the track around Britain was ripped up just as he, Owen, was born, Josh refuses to accept it: his father is kidding him. So much traffic, so many cars, he argues, who would have stopped trains? There's no convincing him. They walk on in silence. The path is clear, direct, and pulls them forward. Behind them, it leads back to where they've come from.

*   *   *

Although Owen feels a muscular pain in his right shin, and his left knee aches, he is able to absent both them and the weight of his daughter from his mind. His awareness of his body, and of their immediate surroundings, drifts. He is tired. But he has spent much time in these last years in such a state, has sought it. Unawareness. Stupor. It comes naturally now. Owen half ambles, half trudges along, Josh behind him, through the late afternoon, not quite knowing whether he is awake or asleep. Time passes, distance is covered.

*   *   *

'I'm hungry,' Holly says. She has woken up. They're walking on a path that runs right at the edge of a wood. Owen knows they can do nothing if they don't eat. The children will quickly falter without fuel. They must find food if the plan is to have any chance of success. The dog darts off into

189

undergrowth and a few seconds later comes the throttled cry of a male pheasant, flying into the air between the branches of trees. They walk past piles of logs. Recently cut, the aromatic scent of pine resin floats on the early-evening air.

Owen looks around. A number of trees are conifers but deciduous ones. Larch. He walks to the nearest one. 'Pull the needles off,' he says to Holly above him. Dropping their bags behind him, securing her shin with his hook, Owen reaches up with his left hand and plucks handfuls of the needles himself. He puts two or three of them in his mouth, and chews. They are tender and not too tangy, he hopes, for a child's palate.

Owen kneels on the ground and bends forward for Holly to step off his shoulders. From this position he sees yellow flowers and crawls forward: he plucks dandelion leaves and chews them. 'Delicious,' he proclaims. The children kneel down too and copy his foraging. 'Only the leaves. But these, see,' he says, picking now a primrose flower, 'you can eat. But first do this.'

Josh and Holly watch their father put the tube of the flower in his mouth and suck. Owen feels the nectar come through, the sweet liquid falls on his tongue. They do the same. Then he takes a small handful of the flowers and stuffs them in his mouth, pretending to be mad with greed as he does so. This is no long-term solution, but perhaps it will tide them over until tomorrow.

'How do you know about these plants?' Josh asks once they resume, with larch needles in their pockets to chew on while walking.

Owen shrugs. 'I just do,' he says with a conspiratorial wink, which Josh acknowledges with a smile of his own, knowing he's being teased.

*   *   *

Owen doesn't realise, or notice, that dusk is falling until the path they're on enters a wood and, leading downhill, cuts deep into black earth. Dark trees loom high above, arching towards each other in the air above this track. If their leaves were in full bloom this would be an even more gloomy tunnel than it is. There are long, thick creepers growing and hanging from the trees, some dangle in the path like church bell ropes.

After one or two hundred yards the path opens out, the slope levels off, the way a little lighter, but the ancient right of way gave in its gloom a warning, that night is falling. There is a mild, lemony smell in the air that must come from some daffodils they pass. There are no houses around as far as can be seen.

They head towards the setting sun. The dog trots in front and leads the way, jaunty, but then loses confidence and drops to the back and follows them. Or maybe it's endlessly rounding them up. They need, Owen figures, to skirt every town, village, isolated farm: anyone could betray them. So he looks as far ahead as possible, sighting the route they shall take across this field, through that gate, avoiding as far as possible dropping down into valleys, so as not to come smack up against a settlement and be forced to make a wide diversion.

The dog chases the scent of animals off to one side, disappears, reappears in front of them. She has attached herself to them. Her body slithers, serpentine, as if moving not through air but

191

through water.

*   *   *

At dusk they walk in the mysterious light after the sun has gone down and everything—trees, grass, hedgerows, Josh's face—is illuminated, though by no direct source. Owen has been alert not just for sights but for sounds too, of a tractor, of voices, in their way. He is tired but figures he can relax now, people are ceasing their labours and heading indoors. Lights come on.

Holly has been on his back for hours. He can feel her head on his shoulder. Josh marches beside him. The boy seems to trust him. They climb a gentle slope. Each time they approach the top they find it is further on, another field, one more rise. Eventually, gasping, Owen stands on a hill. Holly, lifted and dropped by the bellows of her father's lungs, wakes up, and he swings her round him and slides her to the ground. Leans from the waist, hand on hip, breathing hard.

They can see into the distance north and south, at each horizon there's a creamy glow from the earth, enlarging the darkening sky above as they watch. Stourbridge and Kidderminster, Owen reckons, or rather hopes. He could be wrong. Worcester? Nearer, down in the valley below them, the lights of cars on twisting country lanes are like torches searching for something. For them, of course. They must keep off the roads. Night settles, the distinction between earth and sky is lost to their sight. The cars could be helicopters. Or submarines. No more than a hundred metres away a car wanders along a lane as if lost; the sound of its engine seems to come from a different direction. In far-off villages orange lights hang in clusters, electric fruit in the darkness.

'I'm tired,' Josh admits. Owen can hear in his son's tone of voice that he'd rather not have had to say it. A shy, proud boy.

'We'll walk a little further,' Owen says. 'Till we find a place to shelter.'

'How?' Josh asks. 'Can't hardly see things.'

'Moon'll come up soon, see. Don't worry.'

Owen lifts Holly, eases her back around him, and sets off.

*　　　*　　　*

'What's that?' Josh asks. Owen turns to find his son gazing to their right, up around the escarpment they'd come down from. 'Up there,' Josh says, and without waiting for a reply he scrambles up the bank.

It's hard to identify the place he's aiming for: what seem to be rectangular shapes in brown rock. Owen and Holly watch him ascend, going on all fours where the slope is steep. The dog goes with him, tail wagging, guardian and adventurer both. When Josh reaches the strange shapes he disappears into them. In the moonlight what has happened does not make sense, it's indecipherable. Josh has passed through something; or something has absorbed him, swallowed him.

Owen is on the verge of scrambling up there himself when they hear Josh call, 'Dad! Holly!' They can't see him.

'Come on,' Owen says, taking Holly's hand.

193

There's no doubt about it: these are rooms, carved in the rock. There are doorways and window spaces that must have had wooden frames. Stone houses, once inhabited, there's no other explanation. Dry leaves have blown in and provide a mattress. This is where they will spend the night.

Having made places to sleep, Josh insists they climb up to the top of the rock above the hollowed dwellings. They lie on a wide bare platform of stone and look up at the night sky. There are no clouds. It's warm: heat should be escaping from the earth on so clear a night, surely, but the temperature is rising, that's certain. The dog lies beside Holly. They gaze upward. Stars glitter in astonishing abundance in the infinite black above.

Owen recalls their one foreign, package holiday, on a Greek island. The stars were like this. Josh was still in nappies, Sara four. White skin, brown hair. After a fortnight on the beach their skin was brown, hair bleached, transformed into photographic negatives of themselves. Mel too, altered by the sun she otherwise distrusted, this one time allowing its dominion over her. Swimming, children, sunbathing. Mel's skin first tanned and then was burnished. It shone. Touching her transmuted flesh was somehow more thrilling than if it were a different person, he thought, then. Back in England, weeks of rain, within a month Mel's body was once more white.

Not since that holiday has Owen seen stars like these. In his ignorance he identifies only the Plough, the Milky Way, amongst hundreds, thousands, visible to the naked eye, receding into the deep black immensity of space.

'Feel like I'm looking down on the stars,' Josh says.

'Yes,' Holly concurs. 'Me too.'

'Dad.' Josh chuckles. 'Help. I'm going to fall off the ground.'

'You hang on, boy,' Owen says. 'Don't let go.' He imagines them dropping, one after another, like parachutists, free-falling up into the night sky, holding hands as they plummet, the three of them, on, into the stratosphere, out of the earth's orbit, freezing fast, painlessly, falling into space.

*   *   *

There's still, Owen reckons, fifty or more crooked miles to the border. Can I order, cajole, carry my children undetected, find food along the way? I must honour the plan that came to me in my moment of awakening. We shall go to the hill in the west.

*   *   *

Inside the stone room Holly lies asleep on the leaves. The dog twitches beside her. Josh started talking a minute or two ago, and hasn't yet stopped. He's giving his father a report on his football team, recounting in pedantic detail special moments from recent matches. The boy explains certain laws of the game his father might be unfamiliar with. He begins rabbiting on about girls at school who sometimes try to play football with the boys at break. He speaks of girls with an eleven-year-old's disdain.

'No fun at all?' Owen whispers.

'You get to skill them up,' Josh sighs. 'It's pips.' He continues, in a whisper, with a tired intensity, almost raving. He lies, while Owen sits beside him, leaning against the wall of stone. He can see out.

'I'm glad we called Mum,' Josh says. 'Even if we didn't speak to her.'

'No.'

'She'll know we're all right.'

Owen wonders whether his marriage to Mel was withering before the accident, something he has not allowed himself ever to contemplate before. 'You know,' Owen says, 'we make mistakes. Sometimes some things go wrong, see, and we don't realise it's in our power to make them right.'

He pauses then, and his son looks up at him, but Owen wishes to speak of things that have not to his knowledge been spoken of before. The words will not come, though he thought they did exist, for they'd begun to assume shape in the roof of his mind and the bottom of his throat. But they decline to emerge. He wanted to speak to his son of his own and his family's weaknesses, tripping down the generations. The words will not come.

'Dad,' Josh asks. 'Are you Welsh?'

'A bit.' Owen has forgotten how much. 'My father was half Welsh. My mother was a quarter. So I'm, what? Three eighths?'

There's a child's calculating pause. Owen hears Josh yawn. 'That means I'm three sixteenths.' Disappointment enters the boy's voice. 'That's not much.'

'It's enough for anyone.'

'How long has Wales been a country?' Josh asks.

196

'Well,' Owen says, racking his brains. 'I don't know about long, long ago, but after the Romans left Britain, the Welsh princes just fought amongst themselves, like, for centuries, until King Gruffydd defeated the English king Harold, in 1039. Which I have to admit I only know because the battle took place just outside Welshpool. And then Gruffydd formed the first independent kingdom of Wales.'

'We did the Normans last term,' Josh says, and yawns again. 'William the Conqueror beat King Harold. Miss Selby didn't say he'd already lost to a Welsh king.'

Owen wonders for the first time in his life whether these English king Harolds were one and the same man. He wonders whether he could work it out from the dates. Before he can say anything he realises that Josh's breathing beside him has changed: the boy is sleeping. Owen lies down, rolls onto his side with a rustling of dry leaves, and waits for sleep himself. There is no pain in his phantom hand, but he doesn't notice.

THOUGH I WALK THROUGH THE VALLEY OF THE SHADOW OF DEATH, I WILL FEAR NO EVIL

The sweet and musty smell of leaves, turning beneath to compost. Some of them work their way inside clothes: sticky, itchy skin. Owen wakes with both his children pressed against him. He remembers waking in the night, cold, realising they were shivering, and hugging them to him like animals in a lair. When he uncurls himself his limbs are stiff.

*   *   *

'What are we going to eat?' Josh wonders.
  'Is there nothing left?'
  'No.'
  'Then we'll search, won't we?' Owen says. He knows he'll have to go to a shop, buy food, but it's the last thing he wants to do. 'We'll forage.'
  His eyes become accustomed to the dim light. On the other side of the stone roof above them a bird croaks. Holly laughs, so does Josh, Owen tries to. His head throbs, his throat is desperate for water.

*   *   *

On all fours, like an animal, he licks dew from the grass. He stands, damp blooms on the knees of his black trousers. His children watch. They do not copy.

The sky is blue and the sun warms the earth. A thick ribbon of mist winds through the valley below, shrouding from view and at the same time identifying a river beneath it. They begin walking. In a sheltered dip they come across an apple tree festooned with yellow fruit. Securing a branch with his hook, Owen plucks one and bites into it. It is sweet. He fills the rucksack with apples, not sure whether they are last year's crop still hanging on the tree or this year's come early, and he and the children munch as they walk along.

'This is like the story,' Owen says, 'of the man who sets out in search of the perfect place to live, he searches all around the world, see, but can't find it anywhere. Nowhere's perfect. The longer he spends travelling, the more he misses home. Eventually he returns, like, and wonders why he ever left. For home, after all, was heaven on earth.'

Josh smiles at his father. He shakes his head. 'No, Dad,' he says. 'This is like the story of Adam and Eve, eating an apple in the Garden of Eden.'

'I am Eve,' says Holly. 'We did do it in school. They was really hungry but they ate a poisoned apple.'

'No,' says Josh, 'the snake made them eat it.'

'Why?' Holly demands. 'I bet a snake don't even *like* apples.'

'He wanted them to leave.'

'Who is the snake?' Holly asks. 'Daddy?'

'Yeh,' Josh says, with a gritty chuckle, leaning against his father's side.

*   *   *

They walk on for an hour, two hours, effortlessly

avoiding human contact. Owen checks his compass. The route west takes them across grazing fields and through parkland. Owen realises that Josh is watching him closely. He shows the boy how to line the needle up to north, how the needle obeys the earth's magnetic field. 'Keep it,' he says. 'You can be in charge of direction, see.' Josh's eyes widen, as his hands grasp the device.

'Which way then?' Owen asks him.

Eyebrows furrowed, Josh rotates the object in his hand. It seems difficult for him to believe that something without a battery or electronic screen can be trusted. He looks up, and nods forward. 'That way,' he says.

*   *   *

They see sheep lying under the parasol of an old oak tree's wide low branches, in a way that is pleasing to the eye. There is no need of shelter yet from the sun. It's as if posing for the visual effect offered to such passers-by as these gives the animals purpose. The dog shows no interest, but sticks close to the trio. It occurs to Owen for the first time that the dog may yet protect them.

They see pigs in fields with no grass, only flint and mud drying in the pale sun, and huts like army encampments, as if the pigs might be infantry in the re-enactment of some remote war of attrition.

They pass between monumental steel pylons, a cat's cradle of power lines that throb and buzz high above them. Two pieces of material—one a shirt perhaps, white, the other dark and shapeless— have blown here and each snagged themselves somehow on the same power line some yards apart. It's as if the wind has consciousness and, seeing how the electric cables are strung like washing lines across the wide fields, has used the items of fabric to make the analogy explicit.

The day is warming up. They cross a field of brown cows grazing. Each beast faces east, it looks like it's obeying at this moment of the day some solemn, ancient call to prayer.

They follow a path through deciduous trees. It is hot and sticky, flies buzz and bother them, this unsettled April. 'The British Isles have no climate, like, only weather,' Owen quotes from somewhere. The children peel off layers of clothing. Some items Owen accepts, winding them around himself like a cricket umpire, others he persuades them to wrap around their own waists. In the heights of tall ash trees starlings bicker in different languages, like the sound of an orchestra tuning up. Some leave, disgruntled, while others arrive, on their sharp triangular wings. A squirrel dashes across the path up ahead, an undulation of fir, running away from its own tail, and from the dog, which chases it, in vain, unable to follow the squirrel's sudden change of direction from horizontal to vertical.

The wood is composed of a variety of trees. Oak, ash, rowan, maple, many in full leaf already. A stand of beeches, a silver birch grove, but mostly mixed up by everchanging degrees, so that the undergrowth alters too. Bracken gives way to grass; scrub is followed by stony ground in which tiny flowers—red, blue, purple—cover the ground. In dips and shallows water collects in boggy areas, reedy clumps. Frogspawn in puddles. They pass shadows in which spiders' webs laid across heather

201

have been made visible, their entire nocturnal intricacy, by the morning dew, a forensic feat of nature.

*   *   *

They hear the sound of an engine, hesitate, turn their heads, their ears, trying to locate the direction from which it comes. Josh tilts his head back. Owen and Holly follow his lead. Of course.

'Quick,' Owen says. 'Under the trees.'

From the shadows, through branches, they see the helicopter flutter like a dragonfly high overhead. 'Stand still,' Owen says. The dog sits by their feet. Surely it cannot be looking for them? There is safety in the wood. If only the trees would continue, across all the hills and valleys, into Wales.

When it's been quiet for a minute or two Owen says, 'Okay. Let's go.'

'Wait,' Josh says. He's still listening.

'What is it?' Owen whispers.

Josh frowns. 'I don't know. Something. Someone.' He shrugs. They step back out onto the path.

'We are Robin Hood's gang,' Holly says. 'Me and Josh.'

'What about me?' Owen asks. His daughter looks at him as they walk, comparing him perhaps to images she's acquired of the outlaws.

Holly shakes her head. 'You are too old,' she says, with neither sympathy nor cruelty, nodding towards some aspect of his physiognomy. Receding hairline? Wrinkles? 'You know,' she says.

'Why are we hiding?' Josh asks.

202

'They're after us, aren't they?' Owen says. 'Bound to be.'

*   *   *

Every now and then, when the compass shows them veering north or south, they cut through the trees until they find a westward path. They drink and fill water bottles from a fast-running stream of cold clear water.

Eating an apple, Holly shrieks. Owen looks at her, sees a trickle of blood from her lips. She grins. Holds out her hand, the front tooth, tiny in her palm. She feels around the gum with her tongue, the taste of blood, the odd shape of the absence in her mouth. Owen takes the tooth, wraps it in a piece of tissue paper, puts it in the chest pocket of his jacket.

*   *   *

The morning grows ever warmer. The smell of spearmint. Then wild garlic. Horses' hoof marks in the mud. Blue sky above. Birds fly out of the trees. Little clouds of midges. Owen stops. 'Can you hear that?' he asks. The children stand and look at him. Distant, high-pitched, sonorous. 'A woman's voice.' Fragile, not a song as such, more a melodic wail. 'Up ahead,' Owen says. 'This way.' He walks on, towards, not away, from contact, recognising how illogical this is, but her voice pulls him. The children follow warily, the dog between them.

The voice sounds experimental, the singer trying different notes, for varying degrees of duration. A note ends with a dying fall, or abruptly, or seems to

203

hang in the air after its utterance has ceased. A vocal exercise? It's hardly singing at all, or rather it's new, the woman is seeking, discovering, novel sounds the human voice can make. There is silence, then another note is sung, ethereal, ghostly in the wood. At moments Owen thinks it is not a woman but a child, the pure treble of a boy chorister, doodling in the air.

They walk until they are upon it, in a great scoop out of the hillside. Upon the singer, surely she is here, in this quarry, where trees grow sparsely. There is an undergrowth of shrub and bramble. Her voice sounds close at hand yet still somehow distant. They stand and look around, peer into the brush.

'Car,' says Josh.

'Tractor,' Holly says.

And now Owen sees all around them, hidden in long grass, rusting machinery. Vehicles, refrigerators, bicycles. Each of them peels off and investigates this rustic junkyard. An overgrown exhibition of farm machinery, plough, hoe, harrow, each with its attachment to the back of a tractor. Harvesters, trailers. Warming in the sun, sheets of metal bend and sigh, making these sounds like the voice of a woman singing.

An open-top Morris Minor sits on its wheel hubs, tyres taken or perished into the earth. Nettles grow up out of its interior as if cultivated there like bean sprouts. Josh sits behind the steering wheel of a Rover, turning it this way and that, leaning into the bend as he does so, making the sound of a racing car. The upholstery still gives off a pungent smell, of damp, of hot, old plastic.

Owen hears a squeaking noise behind him,

turns. Holly has found a wheelbarrow and is tottering towards him. Inside sits the dog, obedient to Holly's demands but tense, ready to leap if the barrow tilts to one side. Holly grins. Owen discovers a bottle full of old engine oil and lubricates the barrow's wheel. Its tyre is solid rubber.

*   *   *

Josh stands, looking back the way they came.

'Come along,' Owen says. 'What is it?'

'There's someone following us.'

Owen stops. 'You sure?' Alert. 'I don't see anything.'

Josh frowns, shakes his head. 'Someone. Dunno.' He turns and trots to catch up with his father.

*   *   *

The wheelbarrow handles present no problem to his hook. How much faster they move now, Owen pushing the wheelbarrow, Holly in a nest of outer garments, leaning against his rucksack, facing forward. 'I'm *not* an African princess,' she said just now, and he had to use all his powers of persuasion to stop her climbing out. They pass into conifers, through an aromatic frontier of pine, sweet, resinous, and on into a dark and dank plantation. There is just room to walk one behind the other— Josh leading, Owen pushing Holly in the barrow, the dog at their back—between straight rows of identical trees, on a floor of pine needles. Nothing else grows. An earthy, thick odour. They shiver here, goose pimples on their bare arms. The lower branches have no green needles, up as high as Owen's head, as if each tree, growing straight as a rocket for the sun, is leaving itself behind.

They emerge from the cool perpendicular architecture of the fir plantations back into a still warmer forenoon. A tiny creature flees from wheel and tread. A vole? A shrew? There are berries in a patch of heather. Bilberries. They stop to eat, crouch and pluck and cram them in their mouths. Sweet. Three months early. Stained fingers, lips.

Young ash trees, trunks smooth and slender, spry young trees amongst relatives of varying age, on some the bark dry and cracked along varicose ridges, on others it is gnarled, thrombotic.

*   *   *

They come into a sudden glade, a magic garden of dark green, short-cropped grass. Rabbit droppings betray the gardeners. The dog goes crazy, zigzagging after scented trails. Holly climbs out of the wheelbarrow, steps onto this perfect lawn the size of a large room, amazing here in the depths of this arboreal wilderness.

The dark shape on the ground on the far side of the clearing is a log, maybe. Or the stump of a tree. A mound of earth. A sound makes Owen stop and look up: a pigeon has taken off from a high branch, wings clapping, as if applauding its own successful attempt at flight.

Josh has walked on, towards the mound of soil, or dead wood, or whatever it is. 'Daddy,' he says without turning around, continuing forward across the short grass, though more slowly now. 'Daddy.'

The dog, Owen realises, is not here. Chasing rabbits. He wishes it was. Holly holds his hand. They walk across the clearing and stand beside Josh, looking down on the man's body, which lies on its side, curled up, facing away from them.

Owen is glad they cannot see the face, tilted to the ground. Grey hair. Filthy black coat, cracked shoes. A heavily built man. A heavy body. It looks like it might sink into the ground, sink into its own self-creating grave. The corpse gives off an odour. Of unwashed clothes, stale sweat. Ammonia, tobacco. Bitter, not the sweet stench of decomposition he would have expected. Confused, Owen concentrates on the bulk of the torso. Even as he notices a slight rising and falling, Josh says, 'He's alive,' and walks around to look at the man's face. In doing so he blocks the sun, and perhaps this is enough to wake the man, for he rolls over onto his back and with his eyes closed he yawns and stretches his arms out wide. Owen and Holly on one side and Josh on the other skitter backwards out of reach.

A large head. Bulbous, knobbly nose. Skin dirty, florid here and there, livid patches across his cheeks yet an odd yellow paleness too. A man with a fluctuating heart. With his bloated torso he looks like he is beached upon the grass. Perhaps he simply cannot get up off the ground of his own free will, that is why he is here. Yawning again, he lifts a grimy hand and wipes it down over his face, slowly, from forehead to chin, squeezing his neck, then taking a deep breath and sighing as if to say to himself, Here we go again.

'Hello,' Owen says.

The man opens his eyes. They are blue, paler

than the sky. He turns his massive head to look at Owen and Holly, then at Josh, a silhouette against the sun. His eyes are wide open, terrified, then he squeezes them shut and widens his mouth as if about to cry but actually it's so he can make the enormous effort of turning over and pushing himself up off the grass.

They watch, fascinated, the man's slow-motion maneouvre of himself. He raises up his bulk by degrees, pausing between each precise exertion, rationing his energy. He kneels. He tucks one fat leg up. Kicks and pushes up, finally, in the climactic, most strenuous push like a weightlifter, staggering a little before finding his feet and balance.

The man gulps exhausted breaths, wipes his moist brow. Owen watches. He has his arm across Holly's chest as his grandfather used to do to him, though not to stop her. To shield her.

'Hello,' Owen says again, that the man might turn to him, which he does.

'Help me,' the man says. 'I'm lost. Been wandering this wood don't know how long.'

There's something about the man, Owen senses, that is not dangerous, exactly, but not trustworthy, either. A confidence trickster. 'We've a compass, like,' Owen tells him. 'We're heading west.'

'Been going round in circles. Days. Weeks.'

'What do you eat?' Josh asks, from behind him.

The man does not turn. He bows his head. Then raises it slowly. He looks both ashamed and pleased with himself, licks his lips. Unable to hide his natural greed. He stares disconcertingly at Holly, then at Owen, then back to the ground. 'Food?' he says. 'What is not food? A man'll eat

208

anything. Find the food in the ground. Not a lot'll poison you before your body purges it.'

The man takes deep breaths through his nose. Owen visualises him scrabbling through black damp soil, shovelling it into his mouth, for some root or fungus buried there.

'Come with us,' Owen says.

The man steals a glance over his shoulder at Josh, looks back at Owen. 'I will.'

*   *   *

It's hard to believe anyone could walk so slowly. They have to keep stopping to let the man catch up, and when he does he stops too, leans against a tree, takes deep slow breaths. The dog drops back to walk behind the man, trying to quicken his pace. He is oblivious. The black coat in the heat of the day, his exertion, cause him to perspire freely. Owen offers him a drink and the man empties a plastic bottle in one long greedy swallow.

The woods cannot go on forever. 'Time for you to walk a while,' Owen tells his daughter, lifting the handles of the wheelbarrow so that she can slide out. The man staggers slowly up behind them. 'In here,' Owen says.

The man needs no second invitation. He stands between the handlebars and lowers himself backwards into the barrow, Owen on one side, Josh on the other, steadying the weight. It's the only way to carry him, his bulk above the wheel, knees drawn up, feet inside the barrow. It means the man is facing Owen and soon engages him in conversation.

'Good of you,' he says. 'Take me only as far as a

209

town.'

The man is so much heavier than Holly.

'A village,' the man says. 'Vulnerable out in the open.'

'What to?' Owen asks.

'I'd go round in circles again.'

The wood doesn't come to an end, exactly, there's no perimeter fence, but it thins out, there are clearings, and then they are on grazing land but clotted about with sparse clumps of small trees.

Josh says, 'Look,' and they stop and watch a fox walk across the pasture no more than forty yards away. The fox stops, looks back at them watching him or her, turns and continues brisk but unflustered away.

Owen sees a white shape on the grass. After settling the barrow he kneels on one knee, slides his hook under the hood, grasps the stalk and twists until it snaps. He turns the mushroom over, drops it into the palm of his hand. Pale pink gills, the colour of wet plaster; he raises it to his nose, inhales the smell of earth made flesh.

The children do not like the taste of the raw mushrooms and refuse them, despite their hunger. To save time Owen picks some for the man, who watches with rapt gluttonous attention from the barrow. As Owen pushes him along the man shovels the mushrooms into his mouth, munches them perfunctorily, swallows.

*   *   *

They walk through rolling country. The ground is hard, the wheelbarrow jiggles along. Even with the fat man's weight the barrow is wondrously

210

efficient. Owen sweats, though the toil is not too arduous. He keeps up a steady speed. Josh walks in front, their scout, their tracker. He squints up at the sun, looks down at the compass in his hand, alters direction. Holly sometimes drops off the pace and has to trot to catch up, the dog accompanying her.

An undulating landscape of empty fields. Owen assumes that, in common with his grandfather, each farm tenant or labourer knows every hidden dip and sudden gradient of that crust of the earth which he tends, as he drives his tractor across a field hoeing, rolling, spreading muck or seed or fertiliser. No tractor can be seen or even heard today. Silence, except for isolated cries of buzzards. Owen glances up, watches them ride thermals in the sky above. Their presence, strangely, accentuates the absence of other living things.

*   *   *

Farmhouses set back from the road, situated at the end of drives, have their entrances sealed by cast-iron gates. The man does not trust even one of these self-protected farms, and when no one answers the bells or buttons they press he refuses to be left at one.

It is a long time since Owen last came out of the city. These gates are protecting the wealthy, from what, or whom? Are the poor already marauding around the countryside? Until they met the man they'd seen hardly anyone today or the day before, and Owen had this sense that they were walking along unseen: slipping through a gap between yesterday and tomorrow, catching glimpses of both.

Now, walking at this funereal pace, once again they float between atomised, self-isolated homesteads. From one to the right a dog barks at their passing. The sound seems magnified, as if the dog is barking against metal doors. Their own companion ignores this fellow canine, pads silently beside them. When things fall apart, Owen wonders, will their wealth save them? The guard dog's barks fades into the distance.

*   *   *

Owen's hook is designed to mimic a hand's dexterity, not to bear weight. The right handle of the wheelbarrow drags on the straps of the hook on Owen's right arm. He feels the harness across his shoulders, the pull on his spine, the imbalance between what his body is being required to do there and the way his good arm is taking the weight on the left side, through wrist, and biceps.

*   *   *

They see sheep grazing on a wide hill, a vast flock spread across the green hillside in abundance.

'I can hear them,' Holly calls forward.

Shaking his head, Josh dismisses her claim. 'No, you can't.'

'I could eat some lamb,' the fat man says, his voice so thick with greed Owen can imagine him eating one raw in his hands.

The hill of sheep is like a landscape painting on a huge canvas, so many sheep so motionless, except that as they get nearer Owen becomes aware of a restlessness in the painting. No single sheep is motionless for long but moves imperceptibly forward in the direction in which it happens to be facing, to bend and take another mouthful of grass then raise its head and munch for a minute before edging slightly forward once more.

They are walking towards the slope. Owen hears the sound too, and Josh must have, because he curses his sister under his breath and she says, 'I *did* hear it.'

It is a pleading. Not one or ten but hundreds, maybe thousands of ewes and lambs bleating. It is a weird cacophony, dissonant and harsh upon the ears, yet in this multitude there seems to be some underlying musical tone trying to rise through the din. Plaintive lament for their sorry lot, these ungrateful animals living as wild as any husbanded beast may be permitted to, but it seems to Owen it is the sound of angels, choirs of angelic ruffed and white-wool surpliced animals singing into the valley, a comic anthem of misery and hope.

Owen understands in this moment why his grandfather hated music. The incessant bleating through each and every one of his days. What he craved was silence.

*   *   *

When Mel was breastfeeding her son, Owen remembers, she complained of sore nipples. She brought Josh home from a visit to the health visitor and announced that she was suffering from mastitis. Owen's first reaction was one of

213

bewilderment. The word opened a trapdoor and he was lowered into that summer of his childhood: the smell of lanolin in sheep's wool; of chemically enticing organophosphates in the swilling dip through which they pushed five hundred ewes; the pungent tobacco, kept moist in the tin with a scrap of fruit peel, with which Owen was allowed to roll his grandfather's thick cigarettes. How, in Birmingham's urban sprawl, he wondered, could Mel have caught an infection from a sheep?

*   *   *

'Some of the sheep is asleep,' Josh says, keen to assert the acuity of his eyesight, at least.

Now Owen can see that some lie on their backs or on their sides, not sleeping, and others stand beside them, bleating like mourners. But others graze, pulling teethfuls of grass, moving some inches, working their way around the fresh carcasses of their brethren, some hearts still beating, and the grieving beasts.

Owen stops. The children pause too. As he watches, he sees some amongst the great flock that covers the hillside totter, stumble, and fall in ripples of wool.

'Come on,' Owen says. 'Let's keep moving.'

*   *   *

Owen recalls that first summer on the hill, how much time he spent alone. He'd forgotten, really. An only child, living with his grandparents, the things he didn't do with his grandfather: a bow he made with a switch of hazel, arrows with pigeon

214

feathers in the shaft. They were toys, not tools, and he hid them in the place he played, a copse below the farm, on the side of the hill above The Graig. There he was a Welsh warrior prince, on a raiding party along the English border, or hiding out from soldiers hunting him. A wooden sword, a spear whistling through the branches. In his fantasies he conjured companions, other boys who joined him in his games. With gestures, whistles, he told his comrades to separate, fan out, surround their enemies. Bird calls that his grandfather taught him, Owen in turn taught his imaginary men.

The loneliness of that summer.

*   *   *

He's always been a loner. Has found it hard to make friends, to connect with other people. He never really had much to say. Seeing other men in a pub, chatting, he could not imagine what they talked about. Garrulous men. Gasbags.

He was simply shy, that was all it amounted to. Words felt unnatural in his mouth. Owen was only comfortable in the company of people he was already attached to: his grandparents, his mother, his children. And Mel. Desire had propelled him over his own barricades. Mel. Where is she now? She must be frantic with worry, despite—because of—their telephone message. They should call again. He does not want to hurt her. He never has done.

*   *   *

They walk along a lane for a while. Passing a field,

215

they smell horses before they see them, a pair, the sweet tangy scent they give off. Each pony is clad in a grubby kind of old blanket. They look uncared for, vagrant. 'Like horsey tramps,' Josh says, chuckling to himself.

*   *   *

Many fields are uncultivated, ungrazed. How quickly they are lost, it seems to Owen. Grass grows wild and tough, thistles thrust up from the ground like soldiers, deployed across a slope. Trees, shrubs, weeds self-seed. Scavengers circle overhead. Birds of prey watch for movement in the long grass. At lambing time on Owen's grandfather's hill crows not only stole the placenta, as if it had been delivered to them, but were drawn to and would pluck a newborn lamb's eyes.

A field in which, perhaps, carrots or potatoes recently grew, is covered over. Man withdraws, the chaotic greed of nature reclaims the earth.

*   *   *

The fat man in the wheelbarrow looks suddenly at Owen, as if he'd forgotten where he was, and says, 'Don't think I'm not grateful. I am. I always will be.'

Owen tries to smile, but he knows it emerges as a grimace. His neck and shoulders in real pain now. He's not sure he can carry on doing this for much longer. 'Where are you from?' he asks the man, attempting to distract himself.

The man stares at Owen for a while before answering. 'The earth begat me.' The gluttonous

216

man laughs, a greedy chortle. 'And all of us,' he adds.

No more is said. Owen does not wish to expend effort on words, especially if they make no sense.

The fat man gazes at everything and nothing they pass by, like some bored maharajah. Owen realises that Holly is growing tired behind him, and he decides that he has been a slave for long enough. He lowers the handlebars of the barrow, till the legs sit on the ground.

'We rest,' he says. 'Then we reconsider.'

Owen knows he must find substantial food for the children soon. A pair of brown deer break from a stand of silver birches, bound across the grass some way ahead of them; they look delighted with themselves. The dog ignores them, but dashes off into a copse to their right. Ahead of it a blur of movement, another animal it will not catch. The dog, Owen suddenly realises, is flushing game out all the time.

*   *   *

Amongst some trees Holly kneels beside the dog, holding it round its neck. Owen, Josh and the man stand across the clearing, some yards apart. Each holds a wooden club of sorts. Owen whistles. Holly lets the dog go, it comes across the clearing, nose to the ground, there's movement in the undergrowth, leaves, branches, being brushed aside, Owen runs forward, it happens so fast, the bird rising, slowly at first and for a moment there's hope, but then its wings have room to flap, noisily, desperately, the pheasant rises, it's quickly out of reach. Owen puts his hand over his shoulder and hurls the stick. It misses the bird, spins in a desultory arc across the clearing, lands near Holly, missing her by no more than a few feet. That would be really clever.

He finds a different spot, they prepare a repeat performance. Owen knows the fat man is slow and useless, Josh too small and weak. If the dog brings out anything it has to come to him. It's ridiculous. He'll give it one more go.

This time the dog is desperate to go, quivering beside the girl. Owen whistles and it shoots forward. Out of the long grass between them one, two, three rabbits bolt crazily. Two veer off to Josh's side but one comes straight towards Owen. He raises his stick. As the rabbit passes he brings the stick down hard across its back, catching it just short of its hindlegs. It twists over, rolls, gets to its feet, before it can take off again he clubs it across its neck, once, and knows he has killed.

In the next ten minutes, Owen kills two more.

*   *   *

Josh and Holly gather dry grass, twigs, branches. The man searches for metal, refusing to go far. Owen takes the knife from his rucksack, sharpens it on the stone, lays it on the ground. He lifts the skin of the back of the first rabbit, pinches it in his hook, picks up the knife and cuts into the skin. He puts his fingers into the cut and tears the skin apart down the back and then away off each side of the rabbit. It slides easily away from the flesh, to the neck and the four paws. Owen cuts off the head and the feet. He slits the rabbit down the front of the ribs and pulls out the innards, then cuts off the

218

legs, and cuts the meaty little body in two.

The man comes back and stands, watching Owen repeat the preparation with the second rabbit.

'What've you got?' Owen asks. He stops and looks up. The man has a short length of wire mesh, with small round holes of a size that might allow a golf ball through. 'Looks perfect,' Owen says. 'Fold it over a time or two.' He yells to the children, 'We're going to have ourselves a barbecue.'

The fat man watches Owen deal with the rabbits. 'One sharp knife,' he says. Owen says nothing. The handle is made of black wood. The blade has been utilised and sharpened so often that it's been reduced from an inch and a half at the handle chamfering down to a long thin blade. It's clear to the man, watching Owen skin the rabbits, how sharp the thin blade still is. 'Odd knife,' he says.

It looks like a butcher's knife that the butcher can't bear to let go of. 'Inheritance, like,' Owen says. He wipes the blade on grass and returns it to its leather scabbard. 'Tidy tool,' he says. 'Use in it yet.'

They build a fire. Dry grass crackles, the kindling catches, flames work at the thick dead branches. While the fire burns Owen drives four sticks into the ground and lays the grill of wire mesh across them. When the flames have died down he sets the six portions of meat on the wire. At one side he lays the skin of a rabbit with all the entrails in it. The fur on the skin burns off with a sharp odour.

They sit and watch the meat cook as if it's some kind of oracle, auguries revealed by barbecue, their hunger a kind of fascination. Owen, the children, the man salivating noisily, sucking the saliva in his mouth, swallowing it. The dog waits spellbound. The meat is lean, muscular; sporadic drops of fat fall, spit in the fire. Owen unsheathes the knife to turn the little steaks, each time wipes and returns the blade to its home. As if he doesn't trust himself, or the knife, if he were to leave its razor's edge uncovered.

*   *   *

The meat is unbelievably delicious. The men sigh and groan. The children hum as they eat, Holly squeals, once. Only the dog swallows the hearts and livers as she would any other food, gulping them down in seconds, then crunching and chewing the uncooked legs.

*   *   *

They sit in long dry grass at the edge of a field. The hedge nearby is ramshackle and full of overgrown brambles. Amongst them large ripe blackberries grow. There they are, months too early, ripened in this warm April day. Owen plucks one and tastes it, expecting its appearance to be a deception and to find it hard, dry, sour. But it is sweet and juicy. He makes a cradle out of his jacket. The other three lie in the grass while he picks, and periodically takes a palmful of them over.

*   *   *

Though it's only midway through the afternoon the

children, having eaten, lie back and fall asleep. Flies, insects, a drowsy buzz and murmur like a summer noon.

'Need to move on when they wake,' Owen tells the man. He feels drowsy himself, can sense his body diverting its interior attention to the food in his gut, to its digestion. He should let it go about its work, so that he might have energy later on. The organic mechanism in operation beautifully intelligent.

'I'm ready,' the man says.

'We have a long way to go.'

'I'll come with you,' the man insists. 'I have money. Silver. I'll buy you food when we find it.'

'Don't need money,' Owen says. 'You're a burden, see. I'm sorry to say. Slow us down.'

'How much?' the man asks, pulling a grubby purse from his chest pocket. 'Fifty? A hundred?'

Owen looks away, trying not to laugh.

'You can't say I didn't offer,' the man says, petulance in his voice. 'If you leave me, I'll be lost.'

'You'll survive.'

The man looks aggrieved, though not as innocent as he would like. 'This is wild country.'

Gazing towards the ground, Owen shakes his head. 'I'm sorry,' he says. 'You've been fed. Be grateful.' He feels so sleepy. 'We're in a hurry, see. We have to be somewhere.'

Owen sits beside the fat man. On Owen's other side, Josh and Holly doze. The dog snoozes beyond the girl. Owen lies back. Fruit seeds between the teeth. Purple tongues, purple fingers. The final berry is so ripe it melts in Owen's mouth. He dreams that he is wandering through an orchard. Wasps gorge on fallen fruit. Plums.

221

Apples. He has to watch where he treads. Someone is with him, he isn't sure who, she asks him what his favourite smell is. 'Autumn,' Owen replies. 'Rotting fruit and woodsmoke.'

He wakes, wondering whether or not what his dream self said was true. Are they his favourite smells? Mel, he realises, was with him in the imaginary orchard.

Owen sits up. Josh and Holly are still sleeping, the dog beside the girl. The man is snoring. Owen leans over and shakes him awake. When the man opens his eyes, Owen says, 'Come on. I'm going to give you a lift.'

*   *   *

It is downhill all the way, first across a field then down a track, Owen trundles the fat man in the wheelbarrow, the man jiggled along, but he doesn't complain.

A piece of music comes to Owen's mind, it has a chugging, driving beat which helps distract him from the pain in his shoulders and even adds a little confident velocity to his carriage. After a while a voice emerges in the sound and he recognises 'Silver Machine', by Hawkwind. It was on the jukebox in the pub where he and Mel met, but a memory comes from years before: his parents were drinking and dancing in their front room. When the Hawkwind track played they mouthed the words and gyrated ever faster, kind of together and separate both. It was late at night and Owen watched from the door as his mother reeled to the sofa and his father fell to the floor, laughing. Trying to get up, he couldn't, it was hard to tell

222

what was stopping him, the laughter or the drunkenness.

His father, Owen reflected, was rarely cruel, only useless; unable to stay the course.

The track joined a lane which led to a village. A few yards short of the first dwelling Owen set the wheelbarrow down. Breathing hard, he said, 'There you go,' and turned and began striding back the way he'd come, the man's shouts—'Will you not help me out of this? I'm stuck!'—fading behind him.

*   *   *

Holly is still asleep. Josh is gone. Owen looks around, yells, 'Josh! Where are you?'

Owen dashes in one direction, shouts his son's name, runs in another, casting about him, looking into the distance. He cups his hands to his mouth to amplify his voice, forgetting for a second that he lacks one hand, and lets his hook fall. 'Josh!' Owen shouts. 'Come here. I'm back!'

Holly clutches her father's arm. She is sobbing with anxiety. 'What happened?' she asks. 'Daddy?'

He pulls her to him. 'You stay here,' Owen says. 'You stay with the dog, you understand?' Owen looks at the mongrel, standing quietly by. 'Stupid bloody dog!' he curses. 'Why didn't you bark?'

Owen runs around the side of the slope they're on, and looks to the north. There is no sign of his son in the empty landscape. He sprints back, past Holly, who sits on the ground hugging the dog, and looks south. What is Josh playing at? Surely he wouldn't have left his sister? Owen keeps going until he has found vantage points from which to see a portion of the landscape in every direction, and he cannot see his son. He yells into the wilderness. Eventually he stumbles back to where he left Holly. He has lost Josh. The emptiness inside him throbs with fear. He is worse than nothing: he does more damage than if he had not existed.

Holly is holding something towards him. A note. 'It was in my pocket,' she says. Owen takes it from her with shaking fingers. 'Josh did put it there.' The note reads, *Don't worry, Dad. See you on the hill. Trust me. Josh.*

*   *   *

Owen feels Holly's hand take his. They turn and walk towards the west. The dog trots on ahead, at the prow of their diminishing entourage.

They walk on in the afternoon. The day is still lovely, the sky an unblemished blue, but there is something else now, not yet apparent, but approaching.

Owen thinks about the note. He realises he must have told Josh of the plan, of the hill, and where it is. The boy has the compass. As he walks it comes to him that he can trust his son. Eleven years old, Josh is the same age Owen was that first summer.

Owen remembers how last night, waking in the freezing dark in the stone room, he embraced his trembling boy. He felt, through the boy's T-shirt, his skinny ribs, his puny frame, programmed to grow into the body of a man. Owen inhaled the scent of his sleeping son. He could not absorb Josh into him, that is what he would have liked to be able to do. Owen had put his hand on the side of

Josh's face, cupping his cheek. There was so much more of Mel than of himself in Josh's face, that could not be denied. He'd kissed his son's head. After some time the boy stopped shivering; soon Owen went back to sleep.

Now he walks with his daughter. There is a taste in the air in the late afternoon, a flavour. Not damp exactly, though no longer the dry dustiness of the heat of the day. A change in the weather. It feels as if something's looming in the atmosphere around them, hiding, waiting to break.

HEAR MY PRAYER, O LORD, AND WITH THINE EARS CONSIDER MY CALLING; HOLD NOT THY PEACE AT MY TEARS

The caravan stands on its own in a remote field. Could it be usable? Owen approaches. Although one could just about believe that it was once white it is now mottled green with moss and mould; it looks as if it has spent some portion of its existence underwater. Dusk. All is quiet. The dog makes a circuit around the caravan. Holly goes on tiptoes, jumps up, attempting to see inside. Owen tries the door: as it opens it feels like he's breaking a seal. He fancies there is an audible hiss, as if the caravan has been vacuum packed. Inside, all is in order. Opposite the door, a bench. To the left, in the front third of the caravan, a bench along each wall and a table in between. Owen lifts the long mattress which is also a lid on the bench ahead, and there below is bedding. Everything is miraculously dry. The faint musty smell is less of damp than of long neglect.

At the back of the caravan is the kitchen. Tiny stainless-steel draining board and Formica surface. Owen opens cupboards: below are plates, pans. Above, jars of Camp coffee, sugar, Marmite, tins of beans, fruit, evaporated milk. Corned beef, spam. There's a drawer of utensils and cutlery, and candles. The can opener is of a kind Owen remembers, possessing a sharp point with which he punctures a tin of tuna; he clamps his hook around the tin and levers the opener around the top with a series of jerky manoeuvres. A tin of sardines has its

226

own key attached to its side: he slides the key's aperture over a tab of metal, and unpeels the lid.

Dessert is tinned pears and evaporated milk. Holly eats little. The dog gorges on a plate of bully beef. Every now and then the caravan shifts in the evening breeze. Holly lies down on the bed, sighs, and is asleep. The dog curls up at the foot of the bed, on the floor of the caravan. Owen understands that the dog will not let him or anyone else hurt her.

*   *   *

Owen goes back outside and finds a blue Calor gas bottle beside the towbar, and a connector hanging on a piece of rubber tubing. Clouds are gathering, the wind is picking up. Owen attaches the connector to the top of the gas bottle. The connector's needle opens the valve in the top of the gas bottle with a sigh. Inside, he turns on one of the oven rings, holds his lighter. At first only air comes through the pipes, which blows out the lighter's flame. He keeps clicking it back alight, until suddenly gas comes through and ignites: the invisible assumes shape in four curving arcs of blue and purple flame. Soon Owen drinks his first coffee in days, made from liquid from the jar. It's disgusting. He suspects there's no caffeine in it at all, opens the top half of the caravan door and hurls the liquid out of the cup, into the dark. He leans against the bottom half of the door. He would love a drink. He would devour alcohol, the craving is in his mouth and throat, it's in his brain. His body would eagerly absorb a glassful, a bottle. He's aware of the slight twitching in his fingers—

227

merely thinking about booze makes them tremble just a little more. But then he realises that he has no phantom limb pain, and that he had none the night before. Surely, he decides, he has no need of alcohol.

Behind him, he'd moved the table and shifted the benches and cushions, slotting this piece here, resting that one there, to make a double bed. There were white sheets, blue woollen blankets, pillows and pillow cases, upon which Holly now sleeps, fitfully.

The grey sky is shot through with flecks of yellow and gold, suggesting beyond the clouds a shimmering perfect world, if only one could get there. Then the grey clouds close over every last tiny opening, and all is dark. Buffeted by the wind, the caravan trembles. The wind smells of rain.

*   *   *

The town, Welshpool, was founded beside the River Severn. Owen's mother threw a picnic together, sandwiches and crisps, Kit Kat and Coca-Cola. They didn't go far, out past the railway station, through the industrial area and along Leighton Road. When they reached the river they turned right and followed it on its west bank, Owen wary of farmers who might yell them off their land, his mother unworried. The kind of woman men forgave.

The river snaked through the valley, nosing its way between stone and sand in the soft earth of the fields. Owen floated downstream. His mother curled up, dozing on a rug. Owen was a star in the water, lying on his back in the sun, carried by the slow river. The log must have been travelling that little bit faster. The boy was unafraid of watersnakes, or pike, but the log was a torpedo he'd not considered. It struck his head with a dull kiss.

The boy lost consciousness. He knew this when he came to, however many moments later, still lying on his back, having floated unaware, dead to the world. There was pain at his left temple. Understanding what had happened, what had almost happened, a chilly nausea swam through the boy, and he floundered. He scrambled to the bank, and stumbled alongside the river back to the picnic spot, nearer than he'd expected. He felt sick though he'd swallowed no more than a mouthful of water, and trembled with fright and relief. He lay shivering a long while, wrapped in a towel in his mother's arms, before he could tell her what had happened.

*   *   *

Owen is woken by his daughter moaning beside him. He gets up and lights a candle, leaves it burning on the sideboard at the far end of the little caravan. Holly is feverish, her forehead on fire. Her ear hurts. He gives her two spoonfuls of the Calpol in his rucksack. He strokes her arm, pats her. She sobs until the medicine takes effect, then sinks into sleep.

Four hours later he wakes again. Holly is tossing about the bed. A spasm of movement, then she's still for ten or twenty seconds. Suddenly her legs jerk, her body twists, then she's still again. It's as if her restlessness is choreographed; performed, not by her but upon her, her body the medium in which another force operates. She wakes, in pain. Owen gives her more Calpol. Holly speaks in a voice thick and syrupy as the medicine.

'Does Mummy know I am sick?'

'Not yet.'

'Will you tell her?'

His eyes ache with tiredness, but it's no trouble to stay awake. 'We'll tell her. We'll send her a message.'

Holly's breathing is congested beside him. 'Have *you* had a sore ear, Daddy?'

The caravan shivers in the wind, too exposed alone here in this field. 'Earache is horrible, isn't it?' Owen murmurs. He fears tomorrow. Will they have to find a doctor? He thinks he can hear rain fall, whispering, out in the darkness; then he hears it above him, pattering on the roof like a thousand fingers.

'Can you die or anything?' Holly asks.

'No,' her father whispers, stroking her forehead.

'Good,' the girl breathes. 'Good.' Her voice is already falling away, and in a moment her breathing becomes regular, less sinusy, once more asleep. Owen closes his eyes. The rain is drumming upon the roof of the caravan.

*   *   *

Morning. Holly sleeps. Owen lets the dog out, steps outside after her. The rain falls soft but distinctly. He thinks he can sense each tiny drop upon his face, each momentary, pleasant sensation. He wonders how much rain fell during the night. The ground in the field feels spongy

230

beneath his feet. Returning to the caravan, raindrops cling to its tarnished plastic surface like beads of perspiration.

As he straps on the hook, Owen registers that it feels increasingly uncomfortable, unwelcome. There used to be an old man in Welshpool Owen would see around, his jacket sleeve pinned to the shoulder, the sleeve like a sling of air.

Holly is awake, and hungry. Owen concocts a breakfast of tinned mandarins followed by a tin of baked beans and sausages, sweetcorn and mushy peas, with a cup of hot Marmite. He describes it as holiday food. To his somewhat surprised relief she eats everything, delightedly.

'How's your ear?' he asks.

Holly frowns as she chews a mouthful of sweetcorn. 'What ear?' Then she remembers, shaking her head at her silliness. 'Oh, yes.' The night just passed already history. 'Fine,' she says, and giggles. As if he might not believe her, she says, 'I'm all right, Daddy.' He knows she's not: her eyes are wide, she looks a little startled by her own high spirits. A brittleness.

*   *   *

Owen folds up the bedding, returns the disconfigured furniture to its original layout but leaves a mess in the kitchen. He puts half a dozen fresh tins in his rucksack and they set off from the caravan, westward.

They cross a field, go through a gateway, across another field. No animals graze the rich green grass. Small, soft raindrops alight upon their clothing. Like kisses, Holly says. Sinister ones, they

231

accumulate, slowly soaking fabric. Owen is glad when they are able to get under some cover, out of the open.

First they climb a steeply wooded spur of what looks like a range of hills. The summit is a plateau of bare moorland, where they would be exposed, both to view and to the elements: sheets of rain drift back and forth across the moor. So they skirt around the top. Stopping for a drink, they look down on squares of yellow. Owen stares until they suddenly make sense. Daffodil fields. Black soil.

Rain falls with a steadily increasing intensity. Reaching the western side of the range they begin to descend through trees, slipping and squelching in leaf-covered mud. Water oozes and gurgles at their feet, around the trunks of alder trees, the roots of brambles. As they descend, the trickles become rivulets, with a sound of small coins tumbling. Rain falls through the trees, plopping on dead brown leaves. Here and there water collects, damned by an upturn of earth; there are ferns and sedges, and the water swells and eddies.

'My feet's wet,' Holly says. Owen can see her jeans stained up to her knees. Her hair is wet from the rain. He wonders how waterproof her jacket is. They are descending the wooded hill between runlets of water which alter course and veer loudly one towards another, joining forces or even speeding straight across each other and carrying on their separate journeys. Water bubbles up as well, out of the mountain as if it's regurgitating water it swallowed higher up. Owen and Holly slosh and slide, part of a great surge downhill. Rippling currents of water converge, in bubbling congregations, gathering into a stream that has cut into clay. The deluge of water, its gurgling rush, makes Owen feel hectic, hurried. He grabs Holly's hand and they run slithering down the hill.

The stream shoots over a bank of clay and unites with another coursing across the wood at a diagonal. There is no sound now other than this hurtling roar of water. It feels to Owen as if they are cut off from outside, from beyond the few yards around them, by the noise.

The ground flattens out. They carry on running, beside a thick turbid stream, a deep storm drain into which water gushes and cascades. The brook makes less noise now. Owen realises the dog has been barking with excitement, it jumps around them, he couldn't hear it. He and Holly are both soaked through. She is falling ill beside him. His irresponsibility is shocking, even to himself.

*   *   *

Flooded fields reflect the thick, slow clouds. The rain falls intermittently. Holly sits on Owen's shoulders. He suspects she is shivering. 'My ear hurts, Daddy,' she says.

They come to the river towards which all the water is heading. It is in spate, inundated, almost overflowing, the great watersheds of the Welsh hills pumping into it. Grey water churns south with an unanswerable power. Owen turns right and follows the river upstream. Holly says, 'Look, Daddy,' and he can feel she's pointing north-east. He sees half a dozen swans, floating on bright green water. His course takes him between the river and the swans. At a certain point he realises that their field is not flooded. They are grazing on the grass. Seagulls are the only birds in the air.

*   *   *

They come to a road, and a bridge across the river, which surges below them. A little way further on they come to a T-junction. Owen remembers that the village referred to on the signpost as being two miles away to the right is large enough to have a bed and breakfast, probably. Or a pub with a room to stay. He has to risk contact now. Somewhere for Holly to get warm, dry her clothes. They are less than a day's walk from their destination.

*   *   *

They walk through a housing estate, identical brick houses, slate rooves. Aerials on the top of every house. Satellite dishes. Buddleia grow out of chimney stacks, their drooping stalks, the colour of their flowers—yellow, blue, purple—against the drab bricks and grey slates. A small, rural version of the estate Mel lived on when they met. He remembers the first time he walked her home. She spoke so readily to him, words tumbled out. He listened, calculated, summoned courage. At her door he kissed her on the lips. Her mouth was warm.

Some houses are boarded up with plates of gunmetal grey, perforated steel. Others have no doors or window frames, they look toothless, their black interiors open to the wind and rain. Cows graze on the front gardens, wander across the road, pausing to drop their pats of soft dung.

There is no pub or shop or B & B. Some

234

cottages appear inhabited. Owen senses that their passage is watched by unseen eyes, but he could be wrong.

On a hill outside the village stands a cluster of masts, enormous white dishes, one huge globe. Some kind of listening station; plaintive instruments, receivers pointing, Owen imagines, at the ether, hoping for a signal from beyond. A message from the deities of space, presiding a little out of reach, unknowable but imaginable, hiding as gods will do, awaiting us in the fields of infinity.

It is raining once more. They walk through the valley and Owen knows that if it were clear he would be able to see in the distance the hills amongst which is the one they're headed for. But the rain is colder than this morning, and seems to be falling less as drops now than as pins, painful, penetrative. He lifts Holly down off his shoulders. She's trembling, barely conscious. Her teeth are chattering and strange noises issue from her mouth in her delirium, syllables without sense, like someone blessed with a holy spirit, babbling in tongues. Owen takes off his jacket and wraps her on his back, puts the hood on his head so that the jacket drapes over her, and resumes walking.

The dog has lost its appetite for dashing here and there, content to traipse along behind them. Bedraggled, her hair plastered to her lean frame, she looks half the size she did. Owen thinks he could carry Holly forever. She's surely lighter than a soldier's backpack. If she were lame he would be her means of ambulation. As she grew heavier so he would grow stronger; would acquire the nobility of a horse.

They must make a detour, he realises, to the

small market town two or three miles south-west of here. The rain falls like a cloudburst, a monsoon, with a great roar that must be the accumulation of each one of millions of drops hitting the ground but feels like the sound of the rain itself falling through air. They must stick to the lane now, with visibility reduced to feet, inches, in front of them, a darkness of water. Where the lane is flat it becomes a long puddle; on each incline or declivity of tarmac water courses, made dramatic by gravity. A rider on a horse approaches: a torch attached to saddle or bridle illuminates a beamful of plummeting needles of rain, as if to reveal them rather than clarify the way forward for the rider. Owen backs onto the sodden verge and hides in the hedgerow. What would he look like if the rider could see him? A hunchbacked tramp and his dog. An idiotic rambler. The horse does not stop but trots on past.

*   *   *

Owen knows he needs all his strength and determination to push on, to carry his daughter through this torrential, punishing downpour to safety. Then a song comes to mind, and within a moment he is singing it inside his head. An American folk song.

> Lay down, my girl
> Lay down with me.
> Let us lie on the ground
> Long grass all around.
> We'll hide there, we'll play,
> In the night

236

And the day.

He thinks there may have been another verse before that one, but it doesn't matter. He is lost in the song, as he imagines that he sings it. Oblivious to the rain.

> Lay down, my lady,
> Lay down with me.
> Let us lie on the ground
> Our children around.
> They'll hide and play
> Into the night
> And the day.

Owen hears it in a voice in his head that is an imitation of the voice of the singer, one of the last songs the man recorded. This man made each line last longer than one expected, strumming on his guitar then going on little unpredictable runs of plucked notes, then strumming again. The man's voice in Owen's head is hollowed, his body and all it has lived through resonate in every word, the voice of an old country singer, a dying man.

> Lay down, my love,
> Lay down with me.
> Let us lie in the ground
> Black earth all around.
> We'll hide and we'll play
> Through the night
> And the day.

The rain batters the earth. Tumultuous, the river behind them will burst its banks; there will be

237

chaos and destruction. The animal kingdom huddle in their burrows, fold their wings, curl up and hope the deluge will spare them. Owen trudges into the town. No one is outside on the main street but lamps are on in small shops. He enters one and asks the way to a doctor. Someone gives him directions to the health clinic, some streets away. Someone else says they just saw Dr Green go into his house around the corner.

Owen knocks on the door of a large house. A woman opens it. 'Dr Green?' Owen asks. The woman looks horrified at this lunatic. She directs him two doors away.

A man opens the door.

'Dr Green?'

'Yes.' The man frowns. 'The clinic's on Market Lane, just along—' he begins, but Owen interrupts.

'My daughter,' he says, turning around, taking his right arm from beneath her buttocks and unhooking the hood of his jacket off his head. The jacket falls to the floor. 'Please,' he says.

'Come in,' says the doctor, stepping backwards and to one side. Owen enters the hall. The dog stays in the porch as the doctor closes the front door and then, as Owen relinquishes his good hand from holding Holly, the doctor takes the unconscious child and carries her into a sitting room.

Owen heels off his shoes, peels off his sodden socks. At least the water has washed off the mud. Barefoot, Owen follows the doctor, who has laid Holly on a sofa. He calls a woman's name, 'Anna,' over his shoulder, as he removes Holly's sopping clothes. A woman appears in the doorway. 'Towels,' he says.

Owen stands, watching, grey water dripping and seeping from him, his clothes, onto the doctor's carpet. He thinks that he ought to be the one to take off his daughter's clothes; he's not even assisting the doctor. Anna returns with an armful of towels. Holly is semi-awake, half helping her damp shirt peel off her. Her pale body shivers, her face is red, she is trying to talk. Sounds come out of her mouth but they are barely words, certainly not sentences. She moans or gasps disconnected syllables, delirious.

Anna leaves the room with a sodden pile of clothes. She is in her late forties, early fifties, elegant, trim. She strides between furniture, round the corner, with a striking purposeful efficiency, as if she might be blind, the exact placing of each footstep practised a thousand times. A moment later she returns with a child's pyjamas and helps her husband dress Holly. The blue pyjamas, made of thick cotton, are a year or two too large. The doctor takes Holly's temperature with an old mercury thermometer he shakes and checks before placing in her armpit. Anna brings a duvet, which she drapes over the child. Owen stands, dripping, useless, like a foreigner in a strange country where he doesn't speak the language, where he understands nothing, but waits, hoping that things will be explained to him, in sign language, with gesture and demonstration; that things will be made clear, that he will be given a role to play. He is almost invisible now.

'How is she?' he asks quietly.

Anna, who is sitting at the end of the sofa and gently rubbing Holly's blonde hair with a red towel, looks up in surprise, as if she'd forgotten

239

Owen was there. Dr Green says, without turning round, 'Fever. I'll give her something to bring it down.' He's peering into Holly's ears with his thin torch, and murmurs in agreement with himself, confirming something he'd suspected. 'Open your mouth,' he says, and although Owen is certain that his daughter is asleep, her lips obediently part. 'Wider,' the doctor says, and he peers down her throat. Then he undoes the buttons of the pyjamas they'd only just put on and listens to the organic mechanisms inside her through his stethoscope. This practice has all his life struck Owen as some kind of superstition. 'We look for omens,' a medic had once told him. 'What things will become.'

*　　　　*　　　　*

Dr Green carries Holly upstairs. They put her in a single bed in a small spare room. Anna fetches some of her husband's clothes—pink socks, thick fawn corduroy trousers, boxer shorts, a blue pastel shirt and pink V-necked sweater—and persuades Owen to give her his and to take a hot shower. He does so quickly and returns to Holly's bedside. He strokes her arm. Dr Green puts his head around the door. 'Don't worry. She'll sleep through. She's going to be fine. Supper will be ready in a moment.'

'Thank you.'

'You can sleep next door, in our son's room. He's not here in term time.'

*　　　　*　　　　*

The doctor's clothes are only a little too big for

Owen, space allowed for the loosening waist, but their shoulders are of equal breadth, their height and length of limb much the same. Owen pads down thickly carpeted stairs. There are paintings, some of them centuries old. The furniture is antique. The old house has odd shelves, niches, in which rest interesting artefacts, heirlooms, mementos of travel. Statuettes. Seashells, pebbles.

Downstairs in the sitting room a wood fire blazes in the grate. Walls are thick with books. Chairs look deep and welcoming. There is a damp patch on the carpet in the middle of the room. Owen is aware he has never been in a house like this, all these objects of personal value. He studies framed photographs on the mantelpiece: they have one son; two daughters, one has graduated from university, the other is still at school. There is a photograph of the younger girl in school uniform, aged fourteen or fifteen, pretty, brown-eyed, intelligent. She looks like a younger version of her mother, Anna; and like a teenage version of Owen's daughter Sara.

*   *   *

'Edward, give Owen a glass of wine, won't you,' Anna asks her husband. The three of them eat a lasagne and salad at a table in the kitchen. Their daughter, they say, is staying at a friend's house tonight. This information causes Owen a momentary stab of sadness he can't explain. Time is all tangled up.

'This is so good,' Owen says. Every mouthful of pasta, meat, béchamel sauce, crisp topping, every crunch of salad, taste better than he ever knew.

They do not ask him any questions. He keeps expecting them to, and wonders why they don't. In time he understands they aren't going to. He feels an urge to tell them, to confess. What might he expect? Understanding, forgiveness? Hardly. Absolution?

'This rain,' he says.

'Used to it now,' Edward says. 'Round here.'

'Caught out in it, see,' Owen begins. But they show no curiosity, do not prompt him to continue. Anna gives her husband the news of some acquaintance she heard from at work today. It seems she is a teacher. Edward says he hopes their daughter and her friend will not be consorting with certain individuals this evening. Something comes back to Owen: he thinks that walking through the town earlier he saw no cars.

They have red Leicester cheese, biscuits and fruit for dessert. Neither Edward nor Anna ask about Holly. Owen remembers, with a jolt, the dog: she'll be trembling in the porch for sure, already loyal as a lifetime companion. 'It's all right,' Edward assures him. He gestures over his shoulder, back towards the depths of the house. 'She's in the drying room. I found an old tin of dog food. Ours died six months ago.' He smiles. 'It's good to have a dog in the house again, isn't it, Anna?' His wife harrumphs, and he chuckles, evoking some unserious marital discord.

* * *

'The gentlemen will retire to the drawing room.' Edward smiles. 'Bring your glass.' He carries the second wine bottle, Owen follows into an unheated

242

conservatory. Edward lights candles on a small table. The rain stopped some time ago. Ice is forming on the glass roof and windows. They sit in wooden garden chairs, Edward produces a tin of tobacco from his pocket. 'Anna banishes me here,' he says. 'Better than outside, I suppose.' Having taken a plug and a paper he slides the tin towards Owen. 'Help yourself. It's not exactly Virginia, I'm afraid.'

Owen is aware of Edward watching him roll a cigarette. He asks, not about the lost hand, but about the tips of the fingers of his left hand.

'I had a job when I left school, involved working with battery acid, see,' Owen explains. 'Didn't bother with protective gloves, did I? Being reckless, like you are.' He studies his one hand. 'When it's cold the tips of the fingers crack open.'

The two men drink the white wine, smoke their hand-rolled cigarettes. The dog slopes into the conservatory and lies beside Owen's chair.

'You know,' Edward says, 'you were only able to walk in the way you did because of this deluge.'

'How do you mean?' Owen asks him.

'You slipped past our lookouts. Every town is protected now. Wilderness in between.'

'What is it you have here?' Owen says. 'If you don't mind me asking, like. Is this how things are?'

'We support ourselves,' Edward tells him. 'A certain amount of trade, of course, with market towns like ours, each specialising in a particular industry. Medicine comes from Yorkshire. Most of our clothes from a town in Somerset, though there are two tailors here, and people make their own. It's been much easier since the train lines were opened up.'

243

Owen sips the English wine. 'Education?' he asks.

'Information shared on the Internet. No one stops the brightest leaving. Some do. Many stay.'

'Food?'

'Everyone works on the land, at least a little. In the allotments. At harvest.'

Owen tries to imagine the town around them; he saw nothing in the rain earlier. 'What does this town specialise in, then?'

'Furniture. Ours is a town of carpenters and cabinetmakers.'

Owen sucks the wet stub of his cigarette. 'A bed of roses, is it?'

Edward shakes his head. 'It's not a good place to contract a serious illness.' The doctor takes a slug of wine, savours it around his mouth, swallows. 'The surgery we offer, or gain easy access to, is not sophisticated. Prolongation of life is not a priority. Preventative health is.' He begins to roll another cigarette. 'This will not be a great place to grow old.' He looks at Owen and shrugs. 'People need to be useful. We can only sustain a certain number. If we accept someone from outside, he or she has to be young.' He licks the cigarette paper and rolls it tight. 'There's no other way. Some say it's brutal. They're right. It is.' He lights the cigarette, then as he exhales holds it up in the air in one hand, wine glass in the other. 'The tobacco's pretty awful, the wine's improving. Civilisation,' he says, smiling.

Owen raises his glass. The two men salute each other.

Edward gestures back over his shoulder, begins to say something but stops, deciding words are not needed, or insufficient, and merely nods at his

244

companion.

Owen smokes what he knows will be his third and final cigarette. The bottle of wine is empty. The doctor, he senses, will declare at any moment that it's time for him to hit the hay or travel to the Land of Nod or sleep the sleep of the just.

'Suppose I don't want to leave her?' Owen says.

He wonders whether Edward, gazing at the floor, is going to look him in the eye. 'I doubt whether you have much choice,' he says. Then he lifts his gaze to meet Owen's. 'She's ill.' Edward stubs out his cigarette in the heavy glass ashtray. 'She needs time to recover.'

*   *   *

When he wakes, in the single bed in a child's small room, Owen thinks for a moment that it is Christmas Day. Something has been placed at the end of the bed during the night. He moves his feet and it rustles like the stocking that had once been there, when he was six or maybe seven, with small objects wrapped in newspaper. One single Christmas morning. A retractable pencil. A satsuma. A tube of fumey chemical goo with which you could blow a huge ball. A plastic knight on horseback. His father gone but his mother had put them there while he slept.

Owen sits up and leans forward. Anna has folded his washed and dried clothes, and put them in a large paper bag. He lies back. Something has come to him from the night, whether from a dream or the processing of the unconscious he's not quite sure. That there is something familiar about Anna. Certain gestures last night—how she held her right

245

hand near her face when she spoke, and the way she stood leaning against the counter in the kitchen—these things remind him of his grandmother. They suggest a different background to her husband's: that he was born into this life, this class, while she has risen into it.

Not only his grandmother. They were gestures Sara already showed signs of having inherited.

* * *

Owen gets dressed. He goes through to Holly. Children look exhausted when they're asleep. The smell of yeast and rising dough. He goes downstairs. Coffee. Warm rolls. Home-made blackberry and apple jam. There are jars of different sizes on shelves along one wall of the kitchen. Jams, jellies, chutneys. Fruit in syrup.

'Help yourself,' Anna tells him. 'I'll give you a tray to take up to your girl. She'll be hungry when she wakes.'

'She's sleeping now.'

'She'll wake ravenous, believe me.'

'The coffee's good,' Owen says.

'We're getting there.' Anna pours cornflakes into a bowl. Puts honey in one dish, raspberry jam in another, on a wooden tray. 'Edward said to say goodbye. He had to go.'

Owen nods. He eats toast. He feels looked after by this maternal woman, though she can hardly be more than ten years older than him. Anna sits down. She cups her mug of coffee as if to warm her hands. 'Her mother,' she says. 'Is she not with you?'

Owen swallows the rest of his own mug. He

246

shakes his head. Gazes at the surface of the wooden table. 'No,' he says. 'She's not with us.'

Anna says nothing but waits, offers a silence that Owen may fill with further words if he so wishes. A generous, expectant silence. He looks up, and into Anna's brown eyes. It is as if Sara is looking at him, as if his daughter had not stopped at all, her destiny curtailed, but quite the opposite: she has grown and overtaken him.

'She'll find us, for sure,' he stammers. 'Don't worry.'

*　　*　　*

Owen takes the tray upstairs. He finds Holly in the slow process of waking. Josh always woke with his eyes wide open, alert, inquisitive, and jumped out of bed. Holly prefers to luxuriate in her unstretched limbs, under the warm covers.

'Breakfast is served,' Owen says. He opens the curtains. Holly goes to the bathroom. Within moments of her return excitement—staring wide-eyed at what's on offer on the tray across her lap—has given way to a regal demeanour.

'Yes, I think I do like strawberry jam better.' Holly rapidly accustoms herself to having breakfast in bed, makes it look like an everyday occurrence.

Owen sits on the bed. Watching one's child eat is almost metaphysical in the pleasure it gives, appreciating the nourishment he or she gains. The beauty of the brutish process.

'Did you look under your pillow?' Owen asks.

Holly scrunches up her face at her father, then feels behind her. Her expression changes when she discovers something there, and brings it out,

247

grinning. A pound coin Owen remembered to put there last night. The tooth fairy.

Anna was right: Holly eats everything. Her father removes the tray, she leans back against the pillows, replete, in need of further rest. Owen feels his daughter's forehead: her fever is gone. He strokes her arm. Holly pushes her pyjama sleeve up to her shoulder so that he can reach further. Soon her eyelids become droopy. Owen realises he has no idea what will happen next, there is no plan. This is a moment that could not be improved upon. Perhaps this is how things will stay, somehow, forever.

Holly opens her eyes and looks at him and says, 'You have to go, Daddy.' It's as if she's just remembered something she was supposed to tell him. 'You don't have much time.'

He leans down and they hug. He feels her hand pat his back. Owen raises himself back up, Holly closes her eyes, and he resumes stroking her arm until she falls asleep.

O SPARE ME A LITTLE, THAT I MAY RECOVER MY STRENGTH; BEFORE I GO HENCE, AND BE NO MORE SEEN

Owen walks out of the town. Over these past days he has made his way west; now he heads north. It's no more than five miles away—as he climbs the rise into the Camlad valley he can see it—the middle one of three hills there on the far side of the valley.

His breath condenses before him. This weather is still insane. The sky is a dark, deep grey, almost black, a single enormous cloud heavy with water or ice. He pauses for a moment to listen, realising as he does so it is silence that has prompted him. There is no sound of either birdsong or running water, the accompaniment to his and the children's odyssey. A stillness that is more like autumn than spring, as if the earth is holding its breath, this great organism anaesthetising itself against the approach of winter.

Each and every one of us, Owen thinks, must undergo our own apocalypse. Is that why we are ready for the world's?

A haunting sound, the hoot of a wood pigeon, reaches Owen. He's not sure for a moment whether it is from the wood up to his left or from his memory. Another sound, mechanical this time: a quad bike, from higher up there, somewhere along the Kerry Ridgeway. The whine of its engine might have been designed expressly to irritate such men as his grandfather. Owen walks on, but a little later is stilled by the shrill cry, almost like a seagull,

249

of a buzzard. He looks up: the brown bird soars in wide, ascending circles on its broad rounded wings until, at a certain magical moment, as if conjured out of the grey sky, it disappears from sight.

*   *   *

Owen recalls his grandfather staring up into a blue sky. Owen gazed up too. 'Can't be,' the old man muttered. A buzzard soared, seeming not to need ever to flap its wings. It looked as if it must be able to see a route ahead for itself on the currents and thermals and gusts, the shifting complexity of wind made visible in its sight.

'What can't?'

'Do believe it is,' Owen's grandfather decided. 'Look at the long tail. Honey buzzard. Never heard of one this far north.'

The boy asked the reason for the bird's name. 'Feeds on bees and wasps' nests,' his grandfather said.

'Does it feed on honey?' Owen asked.

As if a piece of food had gone down the wrong way the old man retched into laughter, chuckling to himself at the boy's stupidity. He coughed up phlegm that he spat out before saying, 'Insects, of course.'

They were leaning against the gate to the field above the cottage, Owen standing on the second rung. His grandfather composed himself from his rare outburst of pleasure, sighing and shaking his head. Owen wondered if he would always be stupid. He wondered whether he should stop asking questions, saying things, exposing his ignorance, or rather accept that his role in life might be to give other people amusement by the depth of his imbecility. He thought he could detect a degree of contemptuous affection in his grandfather's voice. Except that, braving a glance up at his grandfather beside him, Owen saw that his mood had shifted: he was considering something that made him not only solemn but angry. Owen assumed that what annoyed his grandfather was his own issue's idiocy. Of how it reflected back at him.

But then it struck Owen—this thought in his mind as if it had materialised there out of some powerful elsewhere, a subversive invasion—that his grandfather was wondering whether actually such birds *did* eat honey. And realising that he didn't know. That he had laughed at his grandson, yet perhaps he was the ignorant one, and the boy's enquiry was curious, intelligent.

*   *   *

It is only after he's climbed a stile and is crossing an empty field down towards the river that Owen realises with a surge of panic that he's left his hook behind in Edward and Anna's house. He'd forgotten to strap it on, though it is something he's done every morning for the last six years. The occupational therapist, he remembers, Andrea, told him that after the first week he'd never forget it again. Well, seems she was wrong. The omission as absurd as forgetting to put on your trousers. The sleeve of his jacket flaps loose from the stump, just below his elbow. Had he left it behind for Holly? A hideous memento. Perhaps it is something else, another part of him, of which he

251

must be divested.

Owen decides that probably he is glad to be without the hook, but he wonders whether he'll be able to accomplish one-handed what he still has to do. There is only himself left. The blade, in his jacket pocket, is sharp.

What makes Owen stop and turn to look behind him, he doesn't know. There, twenty metres away, is the dog. Realising that he has stopped, she pauses. She glances at him with her grey eyes. There is fleeting eye contact before she gazes off to the side.

'What are you doing here?' Owen demands. 'You stupid dog. Why aren't you with Holly? Or with Edward and Anna? They'd be glad of you.'

She won't look at him. His grandfather told him how you could tell from a collie's eyes whether or not they'd make a sheepdog. Dogs with light eyes were often the sort who would get mesmerised by a sheep: would lie down and refuse to get up and on with the job, whatever the shepherd said. Stuck, he called it. Dark-eyed dogs on the other hand could be too meek, the kind to turn away from confrontation with a ram or cussed ewe.

'Go back!' Owen commands. 'Shoo!' Adopting the guttural tone he remembers. 'Get on, get on, scat!' Advancing towards her. Shyly she rises and retreats. But when he turns and resumes walking away, the dog, after some seconds, once more follows.

*   *   *

You've not grown up, she said. We've grown apart. I want different things than I did. You've not

252

moved. Stuck in a rut. Pulled me down. I have new friends. I'm ashamed to be with you, to be seen with you, in your grubby clothes, your out-of-date haircut, the hand-made tattoos on the fingers of your one hand. Look at you. Think you're still nineteen? I'll show you. Yes. Wait.

She went next door, scrabbled around in a shoebox, came back with their oldest photo, their first together.

Look, she said, pointing at the snap a pal had taken of the two of them, sitting at a white plastic table outside the Red Lion. They leaned together and grinned at the camera, desiring to imprint upon the celluloid a statement in chemical colour: we have found each other.

You're the same as in that picture, see? Mel said. The same, just older. But me. She shook her head. I'm a different person, I'm not the same person.

It was true, there was no denying it: the photo offered irrefutable proof.

Can't stand it no more, don't you see? She said, despairing. She began to cry. Been trying for years. So fucking stubborn. Can't take it no more.

Mel was right, Owen understood that. He'd imagined that it didn't matter, that they'd support each other through continuity or change, but what he hadn't appreciated was that if you changed, then your perspective altered too. That things looked different from where Mel had moved to. He'd not considered that.

*   *   *

The temperature has dropped. The sky darkens. It

253

is as if the slate-grey cloud above is the belly of something far greater, a looming threatening presence. What happens next takes Owen some seconds to assimilate. The sense of dread of the sky, and look, here, something is falling. But what is falling does not seem to be harmful. Nothing injurious would fall so slowly, in this mesmerising slow motion, nor in such gentle profusion. No single one of these countless falling objects—if that is not too strong a word, an exaggeration, for such insubstantial entities, they are more like notions than things—no single one could be assured of hurting what it alighted upon, for one could step out of its way. Only, it is true, into the path of more of them, but there is no pain to their contact.

Owen's mind leaps towards comprehension. It is spring. A breeze has whipped up ahead, above, blustered through an orchard, blown here this shower of apple blossom.

The white petals land on grass, Owen's clothes, his skin. They dissolve. How extraordinary. No sooner has the blossom fallen than the earth absorbs it, spring turning to summer in a moment of burning cold.

Owen's mind trips once more: not petals but snowflakes melting on his skin. On the ground they are beginning to settle already, a pale wash on the green grass, becoming gradually thicker. He walks into the gentle storm.

*   *   *

If she changed, it wasn't her fault. She'd not done it on purpose, to confuse or to hurt him. If it hadn't been for what happened to Sara.

You. You were driving the car.

Mel's voice became someone else's, her face metamorphosed, the very odour of her body changed. Two people in love becoming strangers to each other. She had borne his children. He could not be responsible for Mel's feelings or opinion, but his own, now and forever, he would take hold of.

*   *   *

The world is white, but is a blur, for the snow is falling thickly, an abundance, a multitude of large flakes. Owen can feel them on his hair, a cap of ice crystals forming itself upon his head. The air is still, there's no wind to swirl the snow around: it's not a blizzard but a benign cascade. It comes back to Owen from a school lesson how at a certain temperature water vapour in the atmosphere high above him has frozen into these crystals, to drift down to the earth. Physics of such hypnotic beauty seems outrageous, really.

He is thirsty. Having no water, his rucksack another thing he realises he left behind, Owen stands with his face upturned, mouth open. Snowflakes melt on his tongue. He feels them land on his closed eyelids, their weight accumulates like coins.

There is no sound. It is as if the very silence of the falling snow has not merely dampened sound but neutralised the auditory realm. Owen reaches the road that runs along the other side of the valley and turns left along it. A car overtakes him, headlights on, being driven extremely slowly, as if the driver wishes to study the snowflakes as they fall in the twin beams of yellowish light. Owen cannot make out occupants, only the outline of the vehicle drifting past him, its engine no more than a murmur.

The signpost to Hurdley is white. The mind supposes that the snow has covered up only the black lettering. Owen knows his way from here, and heads up the lane before climbing a stile to cross the ascending slope of a field. He marches with his head down across a lush carpet of snow. It settles dry on the ground, his feet are not wet or cold inside his shoes, which crunch and squeak on the impacting snow. Each step indents itself. Owen stops and turns around and for a minute or two watches the footsteps being filled up, obliterated. The dog is only four or five metres behind him now, the dark patches of her coat covered in white, as if she has suddenly aged.

Owen walks on. There comes into the mesmerising silence a sound: intermittent, every two or three or four seconds, something that is difficult to identify. It could be a series of identical objects, machines, passing by with metronomic regularity. They seem to be up ahead, but then Owen realises he's passing them, off to his left; or else they have veered off course. Surely he is walking in a straight line. The sound recedes, but before it has entirely disappeared behind him it reappears in front. He is in a scene from a film, with stereo sound fading out on one side, in on the other.

As he comes closer than he was before to the source of the sound it occurs to Owen that the whooshing is like the wings of a great white owl,

256

flying in front of or around him. Actually, high above him now. He trips on something, staggers almost headlong into a wide metal post. A tower. Too thick to put his arms around. Looking up, the tower disappears into the blurring snow, but Owen knows now what these are. Windmills. Wind turbines. He stumbles away, disorientated.

They weren't there before, of course. But he was trying to skirt the first hill, not climb it, and they must be situated on the hummocky plateau across its top. He must have ascended without realising.

The snow falls, ever more heavily. Owen's skull is a compass, his mind the needle thrown out of alignment, no longer able to tell whether he is walking north or south, east or west. Uphill or downhill. In a straight or crooked line or round in figures of eight, in curlicues of confusion. In random, circuitous scrawls across the arctic surface of the earth. He is lost. The snow has obscured the world around him and Owen is lost inside himself.

It is a matter of chance that he notices what happens next. He does not see clearly but registers, it feels like he guesses, the white shape that overtakes him. The dog looks like a white husky. She trots along without looking back. He follows.

*   *   *

When Holly was a baby, Owen was unable to bathe her one-handed. You didn't want to get your hook wet, not if you could help it, so he'd take it off. He just had to have someone there to help. Mel refused. 'I'll do it myself,' she said. 'No need for you to.' He knew that she couldn't bear his stump and the tiny baby in conjunction. So he got Josh to

257

help him. The three of them in the bath, father and son with the baby in between them. Floating in warm water. The boy took on the responsibility: his hands around his baby sister, in case his father let slip his grip on her soapy skin.

The second time, Mel came back earlier than he'd expected. Into the bathroom. Her fury, making out she'd walked in on an imminent disaster. Leaned in and scooped Holly up as if saving her. It was the last time he tried it.

*　　　*　　　*

Owen stops. The dog continues ahead of him. He watches her disappear, dissolve into the slowly falling cascade of snow. After a few moments she reappears. It's her black snout he sees first. She returns to him, and turns round once more, waiting to lead him on. Owen starts walking, and so does she in front of him.

What is it, he wonders, that hovers just outside our senses, beyond our understanding? We are given glimpses. In the silvery darkness a badger lumbers through the trees. You are kissed on the lips by a woman, she is opening herself to you. A child grasps your finger as she totters forward. Some vast reality of which we perceive a tiny part. It evades the vigilant eye, our yearning.

In some way, Owen suspects, his thirst was not just a retreat from pain but a response to the pull that has always been there—was there in childhood—into a dopey oblivion, an unknowing rapture.

*　　　*　　　*

When the snow stops falling it's almost as inexplicable, as magical, as when it started. The sky lightens, from dark to light grey, from grey to white, from white to blue, with every moment the world around them becoming ever more visible. Hills, fields, hedges, copses of trees. Apart from the four, five, windmills up on the hill behind them, the landscape is familiar, little changed since his childhood. They are climbing the hill on a path cut into the rocky face, during the days when miners dug their tunnels here, for lead and barites.

The sun comes out and in a moment the air is warm. The snow melts almost before Owen's eyes, from the tops of hills, nearest to the sun, downwards, the landscape elegantly divesting itself of its cloak of snow. The grass is bright and greener than it was before, as if minerals in the snow have vivified it. No. Owen's eyesight has been cleansed. And the oxygen demanded by his lungs for climbing is in his brain, refreshing his perception, seeing the grass as it really is.

The stone path ends at a flat area shaped like a shoe, its front end against the hill, like a footstep, as if it was made by a giant's toecap as he strode over this island. There is a single metal pole sticking out of the ground beside a slight groove in the ground that runs straight out to the edge of the terrace. Owen surmises there was once a rail to carry small trucks for the miners.

Above the terrace the climb is steeper. The dog pads beside him, her tongue lolling. Already the grass from here on up has been dried by the sun. It could be summer. The ground is hard, the grass rough. Sheep pellets are scattered. Sweat

259

lubricates Owen's skin. He takes off his jacket, wraps the arms around his waist; a clumsy, awkward operation that takes longer than it would if he had his hook. He looks around. The rolling patchwork of fields in the valleys to the west and the south, back across to the hills up around the Kerry Ridgeway. It's not a mountain he's climbing, it's only a hill, it must be less than five hundred metres high, but every now and then Owen stops, not just to get his breath back but to take in the view below and around him, which has both broadened and shifted in perspective.

The air in his head. He understands how much he loves this landscape—those episodes of boyhood and youth—the experience of it was mapped upon his mind, an interior topography which he has ignored ever since. A life wasted in the buildings, the paved streets of a city; some of it at least in its gardens. How he wanted to bring the children here.

He resumes climbing the west face of the hill. The wind makes his eyes water. Tears dry on his cheeks.

*   *   *

Flies bother the dog, and Owen too. There is a sound, a bird's call, a grating *chack-chack*. Owen looks around. He sees wheatear, with their white rumps, bowing and bobbing off the ground, making brief bouncing flights as they chase after flies.

They cross an old path or foundation of a wall, the remains of an Iron Age hill fort like a chain looped over the shoulders of the summit of the hill. From here the ascent flattens into a small landscape of undulations and slopes. Off to the southern side of this habitat is a steep rise to the peak.

It is upon coming up into this area that Owen sees them. Mel is standing with her back to him, gazing north. Holly is wandering off to the left, peering over the lip of this plateau, calling in a voice that starts high on the first syllable, and drops on the second. 'Ro-sie. Ro-sie.'

Josh does not seem to be here. But then Owen glimpses his sandy-coloured hair up at the top, and presently more of his son emerges as he comes across and runs down towards the others. 'A falcon,' he cries. 'Mum. Mum. Look.' She turns as he approaches. 'Peregrine falcon.' He reaches her and promptly turns around. They both scan the sky and Josh points. 'There!'

Owen shifts his gaze to the bird, a female, almost as large as a buzzard, with its long pointed wings, its short tail. Its wings beat fast then it glides a short way, before beating its wings again. As if acknowledging its audience below, it lets out its falcon call, *kek-kek-kek-kek*.

'She's got a nest in the cliff,' Owen hears Josh tell his mother. He turns his gaze back to them. Mel has her arm round Josh's shoulder. Holly walks over to join them. Perhaps this Rosie was an imaginary friend.

*   *   *

The three of them stand together. The shifting corners of their triangle brought to one point. They face away from Owen. It's Mel's turn to point now, and though he cannot see it from where he

261

stands below them, Owen knows she is pointing across to the old barn or perhaps the ruins of the barn in which they'd celebrated their wedding. It is she who has brought them here.

Owen knows they cannot see him. He takes a few heavy steps in their direction but the gaze of each one of them has passed across the place where he stands. If he were visible they would have responded to him.

What feels more strange, for some reason, is that they are talking to each other but he can no longer hear what they're saying. Perhaps it is because they issue their words into the air away from him. A breeze takes the breath from their mouths and disperses it into blustering wind. Instead he hears the plaintive squeaky cries of a meadow pipit, and turns to his left to spot it and watch. It flies up from the grass, dips and veers, and goes back to the ground again. It sings a tinkling trill in flight, starting as it leaves the ground and reaching the end just as it lands, each time.

Something is happening to Owen's hearing. He cannot hear the meadow pipit when he looks at it. He returns his gaze to Mel and the children and then he hears the bird. As if a person's auditory ability was purely mechanical, microphones are facing the wrong way or something; some dial is in need of adjustment.

He can hear other things far away, he reckons. The whine of a chainsaw. The tolling of a church bell.

*   *   *

262

Mel has an arm across each of her children's shoulders. Then Holly turns inward, towards her mother's body, and slips backwards out of the embrace. She looks towards Owen and breaks into a smile. 'Rosie,' she says, bending forward. 'Rosie.' The brown mongrel dog walks fast towards her with a sort of shy shuffle, wagging its tail. She kneels down, and when the dog reaches her she hugs it, talking quietly.

Once again Owen cannot hear, though this time he cannot hear anything else either. Nothing at all. His ears are filled up with silence. He cannot hear them, they cannot see him, he is observation, he is mind.

*   *   *

Mel kneels on the ground in a spot where a rock and a hillock shelter her. She has opened a cardboard box, and opens a transparent plastic bag within the box, unfurling the bag over the outside. She lifts the box, tilts it and pours a grainy grey-white powder onto the grass. She stops, moves the box to one side, and pours again, making a second pile. The children watch, scrutinising the accuracy, the fairness, of the operation. As the box empties, Mel pours with increasing care to make each pile the same size.

When the box is empty Mel pulls apart the flaps that make up the bottom, and folds its sides together so that it is flat. She puts the cardboard into a bag that was lying in the grass, and pulls out a sheet of paper.

*   *   *

263

How is it possible to love a woman, to make children together, and let her fall out of love with you? To fall out of love with her? It is possible, it happened. It seems like insanity now.

*   *   *

Owen would give anything to watch his children. Just a little longer. He has nothing to give. They will live their lives unseen by him.

Will he see Sara now? He does not believe so. Of course not. But he is such a stupid man, he has been so ignorant, he knows nothing, nothing at all.

*   *   *

Mel is reading from the sheet of paper words Owen cannot hear. First Josh, then Holly, pick up a handful of the powder. Josh says something to his sister as he turns his back towards the wind, and she copies him. Josh hurls the handful of ash up high into the air. It swirls away from him.

Holly watches and seems to change her mind. She bends and throws hers on the ground like a farmer scattering seed.

*   *   *

Owen is mind, dissolving, like snowflakes, like alcohol in the flesh of a broken man, like ash on the wind, like breath to the sky. The cells of consciousness are relinquished into blue.

*   *   *

For all flesh is as grass. Mel reads slowly, deliberately, in a voice not used to reading. *And all the glory of man as the flower of grass. The grass withereth, and the flower thereof fadeth away.*

But the word of the Lord endureth for ever.

*   *   *

Yellow gorse, green grass, the smell of sheep on a Welsh hill. Josh swerves and veers down the hillside, his arms outstretched, calling like a lapwing. Holly and the dog chase each other. Mel follows them down, towards the car. No one sees them.

ACKNOWLEDGEMENTS

Many thanks to Anne Marie van Es, Carl Cato and Anne Zigmond in the Prosthetics Department, Nuffield Orthopaedic Centre, Oxford; to ferreter Ann Truman; to Andy Garden of the Institute of Traffic Accident Investigators.

Particularly helpful books were *Phantoms in the Brain* by V.S. Ramachandran & Sandra Blakeslee, and *Badgers* by Michael Clark; and case studies from online publication *The Emperor's New Clothes: Divorce Process & Consequence* by The Cheltenham Group.

The author is grateful to the Royal Literary Fund for a Fellowship at Oxford Brookes University that supported the writing of this book. He also benefitted from a stay at Mount Pleasant Retreat for Artists, Writers and Musicians in Surrey.

Heartfelt thanks to Haydn Middleton and Rebecca Gowers; to Craig Weston, Henry Shukman and Richard Parry; to Hania Porucznik; to Jason Arthur.